CHAPTERS

1. IT'S A GIRL…AGAIN
2. SCHOOL BREAK + HEART BREAK
3. ONE IN A MILLION
4. POLICE WITHOUT BRIEFS
5. ALL CHANGE
6. THE LAW
7. RUBBER-DUBBER-DUB
8. UNDERSTANDING
9. OUT ON MY OWN
10. UNIVERSITY OF PAIN
11. STINGING IN THE RAIN
12. MAN IN THE BOX
13. PUPPET ON A STRING
14. HIT BURNT HAIR
15. BOIL IN THE BAG
16. DARK SARCASM IN THE CLASSROOM
17. NO SUGAR CAIN
18. JAMMED ROLY POLY
19. THE RELENTLESS TIME
20. CRAP PARTY
21. CATALOGUE OF ERRORS
22. ALL CHANGE

23. NOT EVERYTHING IS FUNNY
24. POP GOES THE…?
25. ONLY IN MY WORLD
26. FIGHTS OF FANCY
27. DIEING TO MEET YOU
28. THE END IS NIGH
29. OUT OF THE DARKNESS
30. NEVER UNDER ESTIMATE OUR PUBLIC SERVICES
31. LET THEM BEAT CAKE
32. THE END

ANNECDOTES

1. INVITATION TO A PARTY
2. EEERRRMMM SORRY
3. HALLALUYAH
4. KISSAGRAMS
5. GRRRRRRR
6. PARTY
7. SHOES
8. DIY
9. FISH
10. MINES A PINT
11. FART STORY

IN MEMORIAL
THE LOSS OVER AND OVER AGAIN
THE DEAD
SHORT STORY; THE PEOPLE
WHO?
WRITTEN FOR NEILL
AN EXPLANATION
MY EULOGY
MY GOODBYE

The start of something big

Some of the names have been changed to protect the not so innocent and the very guilty and, in some instances, where I have forgotten the exact happenings with a particular client, I have improvised. You must forgive me if I have filled in those gaps with possibly slightly inaccurate details. All of the instances written about are completely true, though in some cases I have merged experiences to protect those actually involved. It is a Mistresses duty never to expose her client's identities and if a reader suddenly realises that I am writing about them, they may be assured that only I and them know who, what, where and when and that these are confidences that will never be broken.

1. IT'S A GIRL...AGAIN!

I wouldn't say that I just fell into my line of work, I've always felt that it was looking for me, but I did go around the houses and do several other jobs, before I found my calling.

I'm a Londoner. Born in Central London at Hyde Park Corner in St Georges Hospital, the breach half of identical twins. I have been told so often that I should write all of this down, but in honesty I am unsure where to start and definitely unsure where to finish?

I am not suggesting for a moment that I have in mind a trilogy or some other great tome, merely that my life has taken so many twists and turns in the last sixty-four years, that just as I think that I have finally gained some type of normality, everything changes!

Suffice to say that I was born, one of twins at St Georges Hospital, Hyde Park Corner, London on the sixth of September, nineteen fifty-five.

My twin poked her head out first and promptly proceeded to howl and yell loudly, (a recurrent feature of her life). I appeared about twenty minutes later and despite being turned twice, greeted the world arse first (a recurrent feature of MY life). We had two older siblings, a silver cross double-ended pram supplied by the young Doctors who delivered us, a set of two parents and we grew up at the top of seventy-four steps in a building overlooking Chelsea Square. It was exactly seventy-four steps and it became my habit to count each and every one either climbing up or heading down.

To our left there was Chelsea fire station and then the nursing home where all the student nurses lived whilst studying at the Brompton and Royal Marsden Hospitals. At the end a pub.

To our right was a very old, walled Jewish cemetery taking up the rest of the street, opposite another pub. Both sides of our building as I grew in height and curiosity; were of enormous interest to me.

On the left the Fire Station was strictly 'out of bounds'. It housed several families but of the utmost interest at the top, was an old lookout over London. To gain access to this tower, one had to climb a rusty old straight ladder on the roof, which we had been assured would either snap whilst ascending it, thereby bringing about our untimely end or that the force of the wind would lift us off, sweeping us over the buildings, only to be splattered onto the ground below in the Jewish cemetery. I confess I was never sure if it were the idea of my death that upset my mother or the thought that I would be 'naturally' buried in a cemetery of the wrong denomination?

The view, providing one remembered and thereby avoided the hole in the floor, was fantastic. My imagination soared like a bird over the rooftops, taking me to another world amongst the buildings where all sorts of adventures could happen.

The nursing home was an imposing, red brick, Victorian building which strangely only came to life after all the lights went off. Within five minutes of darkness various semaphore signals bounced from torch beams at the darkened windows and the amount of varied hoots, whistles and other bird sounds, could easily, if one ignored the shadows lurking under the trees, transport you to some far away jungle, definitely not in Chelsea. When I was little this hive of activity was merely interesting. As my age and understanding increased I had visions of all these people bumping about in darkened corridors, relying on the smell and touch of their partners to affirm that they had reached the right room? And what if two were to wear the same perfume? Worse, what if the live-in matron got up to use the loo and also wore the same perfume?

The pub.... Simply avoided and not spoken about in polite company. We were a very teetotal family.

On the other side was the cemetery, a different world entirely. Surrounded by a huge wall, overgrown with many graves collapsed and broken, squiggles on the headstones which I was convinced were hieroglyphics', this was a world in the heart of central London that was an oasis of wildlife. When I wasn't trying to terrify my twin by staring out of the window and telling her that the bodies were climbing up the wall to our bedroom, I watched foxes laze in the sun or play. Badgers bustle about like fat ladies in tight clothing; Owls swoop down to the ground hunting when not sitting on the roof of the Marsden silhouetted against the sky. I longed to be able to enter this secret garden and at various times nearly broke my neck trying to scale the wall or spending hours trying to unobtrusively wiggle a piece of wire around in the rusty old padlock in the inane belief that one day it would just fall open.

It is with the utmost sadness that I never got to enter this hallowed ground. As things happen; rather strangely my eldest sister married a man who actually paid to clean and tidy the old cemetery up and re-open it for various Jewish ceremonies, but by that time my sister was trying to pretend that I didn't exist and to me the nature of the place was destroyed, if you'll forgive the pun?

That left the pubs, need I say more? Actually, maybe I should

I will explain a little about this pub business:

The building in which I grew up had an open door to the street, a passageway leading to stone steps that after two flights changed into stairways made of wood. At the bottom of the steps to the right was a cupboard that held the dustbins. As an aside, this cupboard became the 'temporarily broken down' lift to my eldest sister's friends and boyfriends. It was well known by the rest of the family that she had delusions of grandeur and blamed mother and father for failing to be rich, but where the rest of the structure of this lift was hiding, was anyone's guess? Her 'friends' never questioned the lift or that it was always out of order, which means they were all either very kind or very stupid?

The design meant that our building had a door, always open, day or night and unfortunately drunks from either of the pubs, both right and left, used to use it as a toilet on their way home. My poor mum would carry hot soapy water, scrubbing brush, etc. Down the seventy-four steps and get down on hands and knees and scrub as if her life depended on it, to get rid of the smell of urine. Over time it would become unbearable and my mum who had never even stepped inside a public house, (her parents took The Pledge and if you don't know what that means, look it up) would write long letters asking the publicans to inform their customers, not to piss in our hallway. This never had the slightest effect, so my mother would take a torch, chair, huge bucket of water and her knitting and would wait on the first landing for the noises associated with a drunk pissing. Without prior warning she would leap out of the chair and throw the whole bucket of water over the offending drunk. The ensuing kafuffle had to be witnessed to gain full enjoyment and was much praised by the other residents. My dad, who often had to work well into the night was less than enthusiastic, but that was because she had once fallen asleep whilst on her vigil and his entering the building woke her with a jolt. Half asleep she soaked my dad with the whole bucket of water……needless to say, he really wasn't a fan?

My eldest sister was ten years senior and the other only four years. Our dad was a chauffeur for an Entertainment Agent until the silly man he worked for, married a young wife and afraid that his money would run out, locked himself in the library and blew his brains out. I think more by opportunity than a genuine interest daddy became an Undertaker after that. Mum was a trained tailor having left school at 14 and gone to trade school. Before the war she worked for the fashion house LA chasse with Hardy Amiss and at Norman Hartnell's studio, but by the time we came along she was earning money by doing alterations and repairs at home.

Both my parents came from very working-class backgrounds, their own parents being in service. Both of my granddads were chauffeurs, my grandmother on my dad's side worked her way up the servant ladder to become a housekeeper, who I personally believed must have murdered any competition to get where she did, and my mum's mum was a Ladies maid. In those days the Ladies Maid actually made the powders and cosmetics that her Mistress wore. It was a skilled position and the duties involved were of a much more personal nature than the average maid. It was her duty to make repairs, clean and iron clothing, set them out and then help the Mistress dress. She would be expected to do hair and to attach whichever form of garnish was required, take out furs, remove moth balls and air outside where necessary. It was a position both aspired to and the cause of jealousy, but it was something in the world of the servant that a woman could be proud of. Depending on the generosity of the 'Lady' of the house, depended on the perks the ladies' maid received, and what she could use for her family. Old Winter dresses with full skirts made warm coats for children at school and the skills of the woman came into their own as she re-used wool, bonnets, underwear etc. This gave women like my Grandmother a special meaning when using the phrase, 'Grand Mother' as she had all of airs and graces of her 'betters'.

From a very early age my sisters and I grew up tainted with the affliction of 'knowing one's place', a hangover from the strict hierarchy of those upstairs and downstairs years. I don't believe in that sort of class distinction, never did, but strangely my knowledge of it stood me in good stead when it came to my chosen profession. In my world I was definitely upstairs' and my customers? Well definitely on the lower rungs, preferably with the tip of my polished boot squashing their cheek with the glint of a sharp, stiletto heel hovering above the eye which wasn't being pressed firmly into the carpet!

Growing up I would guess, for the times, was fairly normal. I was lucky enough to be in the catchment area of a very good school and my mother made sure that we could all read and write before we started primary.

Very little money, strict but fair discipline. The usual amounts of tears and cuddles, sibling rivalry, stealing each other's clothes and in my case two of my sisters having sex with two of my partners.... All the usual family things.

As stated I was a twin. There was one thing probably different in my life from the majority of others at that time, other than just being a twin and that was rebelling quite firmly to being one half of the same person. The outside world thought that identical twins were two halves which together made for a 'whole'. Unfortunately, so did my twin, but being half a person was not an option for me. I can't remember when I first objected to us being dressed the same or when I started sideling away when my sister was hogging all of the attention, but it wasn't appreciated generally and my twin turned into a bloody limpet! I hated it. Not her, but the more she clung to me the harder I fought to separate myself. Nobody understood and my family was as exasperated with the things I did to give myself my independence, as was my twin sister. I remember at this time a pattern formed and it stayed well into adult life, probably only diminishing at the death of both of my parents. As one year rolled into another there was this unspoken division between the 'good twin' and the 'bad twin' and it doesn't take the reader much cerebral energy to work out which one was which?

This unspoken labelling that I suppose my actions had created, worked in two ways. On the plus side it meant that I wasn't always subjected to long speeches about my selfishness, or aggressive questioning about where I was going, with whom and why couldn't I take my twin? On the downside my twin was believed no matter how absurd her claims were. She was clingy, apparently adored me, needed my presence and her intentions were as white as the driven snow. She was also a consummate liar and a master manipulator.

As an example of this:

During my twenties I rather stupidly married a man who was an alcoholic and of course this didn't go down terribly well with my teetotal family. For reasons I cannot remember, my sister appeared on my doorstep in a terrible state and begged me to go and do her evening job, as she needed the money but was too upset to go. Like an idiot I swallowed all this and started going out every Wednesday evening to do her rotten tele-marketing job until one evening I got the strangest feeling and instead of going on, something made me get to the tube station and turn back to go home. I can't explain it but I had that sick, butterfly feeling in my stomach. I lived in a basement flat and could see into the rooms from certain angles without being seen by those in residence. I saw, what honestly, I knew I was going to see, which was my husband and my sister having sex. Despite being hurt and angry I left quietly and sat in a pub until it was the normal time to return home. I kept this secret. I didn't go back to her job and have no idea what lies I told her to get me out of it, but I kept quiet about what I had witnessed. Sometime later, when that marriage inevitably went to the wall, despite my grief, I was summoned by my parents to their home and was a bit surprised to find my twin also in the room, snivelling into a piece of toilet paper.

With my mother looking flushed and upset, hovering around my sister and my twin very determined not to catch my eye, my father announced that it was because my twin had no desire for me to be hurt further that he would not be calling the police. It was against his better judgement but my twin was adamant that no authorities be brought in because of the pain and shame, it would cause me? I just about managed to stay quiet, despite my gut telling me that something was coming that I wasn't going to be best pleased about. To this day I remember this moment with pain and pride. I wasn't going to be dragged into yet another of my sister's dramas. My dad fixed me with his gravest stare and I could see his body quiver slightly with the controlled anger.

'Your Husband' he spat at me, 'raped your sister'

The sudden silence dropped into the void with an almost perceptible groan. I looked down at my feet and calmly put my jacket back on and picked my handbag up. I fixed my father with an inscrutable sneer and said:

'I know. Every Wednesday' And with that I left the house and returned home. I've no idea what was said after that and my heart was broken. I had too much to do picking up the pieces of my life to become embroiled in yet another of my sister's 'damage limitations' to herself. It was never spoken of again. so, I have no idea who and what was believed. There are so many things left unsaid and things that should have been talked about, but it's all too long ago and most of the participants are dead!

Prior to this 'revelation', my ex had also tried to hurt me by slinging his affair at me during an argument. I had taken the wind out of his sails by informing him that I knew, but he had obviously contacted my sister to warn her. She always found a scapegoat and always made sure that it was paraded in front of anyone who may think badly of her. We both suffer from mental problems, sadly in this instance being a twin to a nut case isn't something I can shrug off. It took years to be diagnosed with bipolar disorder and even more years learning to understand and control it with CBT and the correct medication, but my twin? I personally believe that she suffers from an undefined personality disorder, the basis of which is a maladaptive character and thinking pattern. On top of this she has, Narcissism, Hypochondria and a complete lack of empathy. She is incapable of laughing at herself and suffers from a 'pseudo victim' mentality. This is only my opinion, and I could cite hundreds of examples if I had to, however that would become a book all on its own. Several volumes probably and despite living with all the horrible things she's done to me; it still manages to churn me up inside and that isn't the direction that I wanted to take you in. Members of my family have a strange way of re-writing history and then clinging to a memory as if it were true. I think we are all guilty of this to a degree, but my father and siblings took it to new heights. If a certain situation was put to them, I am sure that the two versions would differ in practically every way possible. My eldest sister has the strangest recollection when it comes to a car accident that nearly wiped her off the planet. A boyfriend to rushed me to the Hospital because I was told she may not survive. I organised to stay at the hospital, and did. Despite both parents and at least one of my sisters agreeing to my version of events, as far as she is concerned, I never went near her? It just didn't happen?

I think before I completely move on, I should make an admission. The flat that we lived in had at one time been two separate dwellings, so the toilet was outside of the front door down a few steps because it had been shared. This meant that with no lock on the street door to the building and no lights on the staircase, there was a certain vulnerability when having to use the toilet once the sun had gone down. Sometimes I waited until my twin had to go to the loo and would then slither down the few steps and slowly, but deliberately would turn the handle as if trying to secretly enter. I would then creep back upstairs, and nonchalantly join the rest of the family. Sometimes I hid behind the front door so that as she panicked and fled up the steps, I would jump out at her causing her to nearly pass away from the fear and shock! Other times I would just linger and secretly wait to see how long it was before she panicked and hollered the whole building down. Cruel? Yes, but just a tiny thing compared to the cruelty and lies that over the years she put me through. I still have problems hiding a smirk just thinking about it.

2. SCHOOL BREAK AND HEARTBREAK

Secondary school was a bit of a blur, mainly because the memories I do have confirm my notion that it was shit. We arrived at this huge building in Putney and from the moment a sound came out of our mouths, the 'posh' way we spoke placed us firmly in the position of being targets of ridicule, bullying and physical attack. To give you a rough idea, we had our hair set on fire on a bus, (weirdly nobody on the bus took the slightest notice. Not even the conductor?) Our packed lunches taken, (usually strewn all over the playground. Rarely eaten, but my mum was an awful cook and just as bad at making sandwiches) drawing pins placed on our chairs, pins in our coat pockets, and in our shoes during gym. We were slapped, poked, punched and I saw the bottom of so many toilets whilst I was held down and the horrible thing was being flushed, that I could probably tell you the maker of any toilet just by staring at the bend at the bottom of the bowl. Not the greatest party trick, but still…

My twin made my life at this time, so much more difficult than it had to be. She was a total physical coward but had been born with an infuriating arrogance that meant she couldn't keep her mouth shut, when something offended her. I was continually being, 'called out' for a fight because she had placed me firmly in the firing line. Despite myself, my upbringing required that I support my sister no matter what and looking back, short of turning into one of her tormentors, I had no choice but to become her champion. She would insult, or annoy girls without a thought and would then panic and try to find me so she could hide behind my skirts. There were times that I would see her hurtling towards me and would take off and try to hide from her because I knew that I was the one who was going to get hurt and if she was running it would be a fair guess that the 'offended' would be right behind her.

It was at this point that decided that I either cut my own throat or I learned how to 'bluff'. Learning how to fight was not an option. I dropped my posh accent and started to be as verbally aggressive as our nemesis. I was loud, stepped into people's personal space during an altercation, got in their face and my mantra was, 'bring it on'. The first time I tried it I blew the whole thing by squeaking in a trembling voice, 'I won't hit you'. The result was a punch round the ear that had me off my feet and half in and half out of being lodged under the desk and chair, which put me in the perfect space for a good kicking. The next time it happened the look in the eyes of my foe soon made me realise that if I was going to get battered, it was as well to get in a few blows first. I hardly laid a hand on her but my mouth played a good fight and as soon as I saw that flicker of doubt cross her face, I had her back up against the wall, shouting in her face and taunting her to risk hitting me? The magic worked.

Very soon I was playing in the super league. I had status, people wanted to give me their sandwiches (a real bonus) and I was left alone without ever having to raise my fists. I had a sharp tongue, a dry wit, a bit of mystery (I was still a loner) and my sister basked in my glory. It was a lesson worth learning even though the adults in my life now labelled me a trouble maker. To retain one's position I was occasionally confrontational with teachers and parents alike. I was developing my personality and my progression was a perfectly normal part of growing up. As I said, school was shit and I was very happy to wave goodbye to it with only six O levels. Most of my memories are better off forgotten, but there was the odd moment that can still make me smile. These were the days of the little victories, like being allowed to remove myself from 'prayers' because I was an Atheist and could explain what that meant. Spending gym lessons in the library instead of freezing my bits off outside when I was unable to take part, and hurtling along corridors beating an outraged tutor to the Headmistresses door. Strangely the Headmistress who ended up being made a 'Dame', quite liked me, but I did spend a great deal of my lessons in her office. I remember her once stopping me in the corridor with a genuine look of concern about my health, because I hadn't been sent to her office for over a week and she supposed I must have been off sick. On the subject of not taking part in sports, with hindsight it was strange that nobody seemed to notice that I had a permanent period from 1967 to 1971? If anyone had actually thought about it, they would have realised that the extent I was apparently bleeding, i.e. weekly, I should have bled out!!

To get another earlier statement out of the way, as I was growing up another of my sisters moved in on a man I had loved. The 'first' love of my life, always special, and though my gut told me what was happening when I told my mother, she believed that I had to be mistaken. My mum had a strong sense of what was right and wrong and she ignored my Fathers influence. This was partly because he wasn't around that much when we were growing up, but also that his standards of behaviour when it came to honesty were not as pure as her own. She believed that the personality was formed by the people who were always around you and that their influence on the way 'you turned out', was the stronger. In those times there really wasn't any understanding of genetics and inherited traits from both parents. Most people believed that whoever was the main carer in their education of life, influenced the physical and emotional make-up of the child.

When mum had an embolism in her carotid artery none of us children were asked our opinions. My instinct was that my dad, who had spent his whole life after the war being 'looked after' by mummy, was almost stupidly possessive of her. He wasn't interested in what was best for her, just what was best for him. After the surgery there was noticeable changes to her personality and because I loved her, I agreed for my parents to come and live in the same town as me. I did not expect my sisters to become involved in the daily drudgery of cooking and cleaning for them both, but as mummy disappeared into the fog of dementia, I had expected my sisters to visit on a fairly regular basis. I was wrong. As there was more pooh, more aggression, more hallucinations and more, 'just getting into bed when your mum phones in tears because she cannot remember who and where she is, but somehow she managed to remember you'… I was left to deal with it on my own. In those moments you get dressed again and go around to their flat as your dad sleeps through it all and clean her up because there's faeces everywhere and put her back to bed and hold her hand till she sleeps. When she finally drops into a regular sleeping type rhythm you carefully disentangle your hand from hers and leave quietly so that you can go home and get some shut-eye. You creep into your home and quietly slide under the duvet to get some sleep and then the phone goes again and your partner has to bully you awake because you are so tired, and you can't believe it has started all over again.

She lived for seven years, disappearing into a world where she didn't speak, move, a tube attached to give her food and never meeting your eyes. I'll never know how much she understood before she became the shell I was caring for. There was a period before she had completely lost her marbles, that she had begged me to release her from her pain, and I did try. For the last year of her life she went into a specialist home, but I still saw her every day. I never realised that it wasn't that easy to give her a way out and despite trying various things, she didn't succumb. I remember being so incensed when she got pneumonia and my father had her placed on antibiotics. It was the selfishness and cruelty that I couldn't understand. After she died, I was expected to take on the responsibility of my dad, but my heart wasn't in it and I organised for him to go and live in the same area on the South Coast as one of my sisters. She had always been daddy's favourite and she was willing to take it on, if that is the correct way of saying it, because even at 90 something he was still with it, totally independent, wasn't in a wheelchair or anything, so the odds were that he was going to go on a bit.

When I got the call to say he had been taken into Hospital with an aneurism my partner got home from work and without question got me to his bedside the same evening. When I walked in the first question was, 'what had I done to my hair?' and the second was, 'where was my eldest sister, why wasn't I her?'

I slept on the floor of his room for seven days and I was the only one of his children who held his hand as he left this world and slipped into the next. Two of my sisters saw him once for an hour mid-week and the other who was actually in the Hospital herself, despite me sending a message to say things were imminent, couldn't get to his room before he died because she was speaking to her boyfriend? My parents were working class, which seems to have been a huge disappointment when it came to their wills and the small amount of money we all received. I may have mentioned that my eldest sister is a millionaire, so she had purchased the flat my parents lived in, collecting the rent and service charge? And when it came to the amount of roughly £2000, that we all received after probate, she rushed to get her hands on it as quickly as any of us??

I was actually probably closer to mummy and her way of thinking than any of her children, but I appeared to the world, and her, much stronger than my 'sisters' and emotionally a bit 'hard'. I remember my sister coming into my bedroom and sitting on the side of my bed when mummy had asked her about my accusation that she was dallying with my boyfriend. She gently dismissed my fears and asked how I could possibly believe that she could do such a thing to me? She welled up at the pain of my accusation and told me how much she loved me. A week later she abandoned her husband and ran away with him, the first man who in my eyes was 'the one'…….

Hmm 'told you so' comes to mind. Wounds like that never really heal and I still have daydreams of finding her in the shower and doing a 'psycho'!!!

3. ONE IN A MILLION

I was determined that who I was and who I became would be completely individual to me. I didn't copy fashion; I created my own style using original 40's clothing with my own designs and innovations which my mum made with enthusiasm. I didn't follow mainstream bands or have posters on my bedroom walls. I dropped out of college in the first year, dyed my hair a vivid red with Henna and married a homosexual man by the age of seventeen. I do sometimes wonder if subconsciously I chose this man on the basis that I didn't have any brothers and he definitely wasn't going to be seduced by any of my sisters?

The union was not a happy one and was all too brief. I loved him and threw myself headlong into the relationship. For some reason when I caught him in bed with a young man my heart broke and my world shattered. Did I mention that I can be a bit slow, a bit dumb?

Making matters worse, our dramatic ending became the talk of the department store where we both worked and the humiliation of being the butt of peoples whispering and jokes was too much to bear. I lost my marriage, my job and my sanity. This would be the first real appearance of instability in my mental make-up, but I like everybody else, put this down to the trauma of the break-up. When I was released from Hospital, I felt completely adrift. It was a sad part of my life, maybe I had thought that I could change him? Needless to say, I was divorced at nineteen and was possibly the first woman to get my own divorce in this country. I couldn't afford solicitors and I wanted to change my marital status, so I bought the papers (several sets if I'm honest), paid my seven pounds fifty and eventually purchased my own freedom. A chapter of my life was over with and it was time to pick myself up and move on. I joined the merchant Navy and literally ran away to sea where the inevitable happened. I was emotionally very vulnerable and ultimately ended up having a torrid affair with the first Officer, which within a very short time, became a topic that would be gossiped about in the passenger-ship world. In this instance he was the one who fell hook, line and sinker and although people go through life and attempt to ignore when they have broken someone's heart, I still feel guilty about this episode and how I ran away rather than face the man who's heart I broke. Sadly, over two years after I had run back to England and had had no contact with this man, he appeared on my mum and dad's doorstep. Thankfully my father was working and wasn't at home when he arrived. There must have been a white charger tied up downstairs at mum and dad's, but I didn't re-appear to feed it.

As it happened, I was in a really unhappy marriage. I can honestly say that my husband was one of the kindest, most thoughtful men I have ever known and initially was a good provider, but he was a medically recognised alcoholic and had been battling this fight since he was 13. This was the age he lost his father who died of sclerosis of the liver, as a complication of alcoholism. His mother alternated between being drunk and taking 'The Pledge' as did one of his sisters, whilst another sister completely abstained from alcohol but only because she had drunk so heavily that she had seriously damaged her organs and another sip of drink would probably have shuffled her off. She was waiting for a liver and kidney transplant when I was with her brother, but I did find out years later that it all took too long and she ended up hitting the bottle and dying within seven days.

My First Officer tried everything to win me back, and my mum was so taken with him, she actually said that if she had been younger, she would have run off with him herself! He was a Greek national whose father had died and had left his only son with the responsibility of looking after his mother. This is a very Greek thing and taken very seriously. Old people aren't moved out of the communities they have lived in and often were born in. The family take the responsibility of looking after the person, and in large families either take it in turns to live with them or move the elder around and have them live in their own houses with them. Old people are employed to watch over young children, small animals and the making of things like bread and play a much larger role in the household. When they become too old to do any of these types of duties then the coin is flipped, and often it is the grandchildren still at home, who provide the care and comfort for the aged person. Old people are to be listened to, revered and bent over backwards for, which is great if they are benign and sweet and friendly; but a nightmare if they are actually like a big, black tarantula that leaps out of the darkness to strike, roles you up in venom and then leaves you hanging, picking at you every now and then? When a son, brought up in the traditional Greek way has a mother famous for being viciously insane he does the only thing he can do…run away to sea and try and find a wife!

I was taken to meet her and had actually learned quite a lot of the Greek language so that I was capable of being polite to her in her own language. When we met, I bent over backwards to be respectful, but she greeted me, a short, fat bundle of black with a sneer and her hands on her hips; and insisted on babbling aggressively at her son in Greek. I had been led to believe that I would be staying at the family home that he had purchased for her, which actually had four bedrooms and three with en-suite and I actually felt sorry for him when he had to explain that I would be staying at the local hotel on my own whilst he stayed in the house with his mother. In those first few seconds, despite his marriage proposal, I knew that it would never work. Unless the woman dropped dead from the shock of discovering that I had accepted his proposal, which out of spite was unlikely, I knew with the utmost certainty that I would murder her at the first opportunity.

He was a good man and I never meant to hurt him, but try to remember those alarm bells that at times I ignored? Well this time I had the sense to hear them loud and clear and walked away. I sincerely hope he did find someone who he fell in love with, who loved him back? But I'll never know.

As I said, I did many things before I became a Dominatrix but my instinct is that the various jobs and my experiences are probably not something you would be interested in. I'll give you a very fast run-down and then get into the interesting bit. I've been a salesperson, make-up artist, beautician, receptionist, switchboard operator, telesales (a REALLY low point in my life) graded lenses in a lens factory (a point in my life that was SO low that I chose to walk out and ultimately ended up spending some nights living in Hastings caves and washing in the sea in the mornings. Cold and horrid but much better than being treated like a non-person in that particular factory). I was a supermarket checkout person, merchant seaman, various minor managerial positions in various lines of work, barmaid, entrepreneur, employment agency dogs body and tea boy and then in another incarnation, the manager of the same. There have been many different hats on my head, some of them extremely ill-fitting!

I actually enjoyed being a barmaid and always remember working at a great pub with a really diverse customer base. We had a regular who was always waiting for the doors to open at eleven. A nice old boy who was probably as old as the pub, but always managed to have a laugh and a wink with the younger crowd as well as his fellow drinkers. It was a Lunchtime and he had taken his usual pint to his usual table and was surrounded by his usual friends. It was quite a slow morning and I noticed that our friend had hardly touched his pint and had a bit of a slumped demeanour. His friends were talking with the usual lack of interest, peppered with moments of unbridled hilarity of a shared joke. It was one of these moments that attracted my attention because one of his mates playfully dug him in the ribs and instead of him reacting his head dropped perceptively onto his chest and he wobbled a little before resting in an even more pronounced slump. I watched fascinated when one of his comrades rose to get another drink. He offered his mate another half, just shrugged when he was ignored, purchased a communal packet of crisps and went back to his seat and his conversation. As the morning wore on, I was a little busier but as closing time approached, I realised that most of the other gentlemen had left and only his closest mate was still sitting there. I was about to approach them when this gentleman got up, handed me his empty glass and motioned towards his friend.

'Bill seems a little quiet today', he said, 'don't wake him up too sharply', he grinned. With that he shouted his goodbyes and left the pub.

I knew that the man was dead. I had kept my fingers crossed throughout the session in the hope that nobody else had noticed because dead people are not conducive to a quiet drink, or noisy drinks for that matter. Unless of course you want a very.... Very quiet drink, then it may work? As the time had worn on, he had become noticeably paler, more sort of slumped and obviously was not his usual 'slightly' animated self. I had spent the whole session dreading someone getting boisterous (well, just being alive really) and either tapping him or God forbid, slapping him on the back. In my mind's eye I had seen him slowly topple forward, banging his head on the table, spilling his mate's pints and then slowly sliding under the table in an undignified slump.

I took over the responsibility (I thought my Governor was, going to be next on the list when I pointed out the corpse) and everything was tickety-boo by the time we opened for the evening shift. As always, as the evening wore on Bill's comrades gradually wandered into the pub and I decided to take it upon myself to gently inform his friends what had happened. There was a moment of complete silence as they all, in unison, stared at their pints and then the odd tut or sad shake of the head from various recipients to my news. I was about to leave them to it, but as I started to go back to the bar, I just caught the ensuing conversation before I left.

'Well I must admit he was quiet today, wasn't he Frank? Never even laughed at my jokes'

Reply: 'That's not because he was dead Alan, he never laughed at your jokes'….

4. POLICE WITHOUT BRIEFS

After traveling for a while and wandering from one job to another I settled in a British Seaside town. I became friends, through my husband at the time, with a very beautiful girl who seemed to be under the impression that I was a complete idiot. I confess that this was a perception that she wasn't the first to harbour, nor under any circumstances was she the last. I must have just looked stupid, probably still do?

Without a shadow of a doubt I knew she was a prostitute and weirdly if you stripped her of make-up and put her in a nuns' habit, there was just something about her that you would still know that whatever was claimed, that she was still perceived as a prostitute. I certainly did but played along with the illusion of her spoken career so that I would not offend her. In time, when she obviously felt more sure of me, she announced it one day in a whisper whilst we were sitting in a wine bar. I really didn't know what she expected of me but saw that she was completely thrown, when I stated simply that I knew. It was almost comical and I quickly changed the subject when she asked me how? Funnily enough, some years down the line she actually said what I had always thought,

'It doesn't matter what I do or what I wear, I still look like a brass!'.

And she was right.

She ran her business from a flat (purchased without a mortgage) in Brighton and had a 'maid' with her whenever she was on the premises and was working. The word 'maid' in this instance is just a word for someone who takes phone calls and gives a waiting punter a cup of tea, unlike a maid in my later line of work. For me and my ilk, a maid is a gentleman who wears a black dress, a perfectly starched apron, black stockings and a little white cap whilst on my premises and is there at my beck and call. Maids in my establishment did all the cleaning, ironing, washing, shopping, dog walking and were there to pander to my slightest whim. In the world of the professional prostitute the maid is either paid a set rate or a portion of the profits, depending on the number of customers. In my world the maid paid me for the privilege of serving me and I expected a very high standard of work. Those who thought they could obtain a beating by producing shoddy work just found themselves beating a path towards the front door! Sorry, being beaten as they approached my front door, but a beating that was not to their liking. My maids had to produce an extremely high standard of work and only when I was happy with the result, could they have a beating of the type they liked. Maids were actually a group that were higher in the pain category, so once the session was drawing to a close the beating would be within the bounds of severe!

To change direction for a moment so that the reader has a better understanding, I shall digress. Being a Dominatrix, a 'professional' Dominatrix, means being very astute. We have to learn to read body language and between the lines of the spoken word. When 'interviewing' a new customer, the questions about their preferences: bondage, stripes (left when using a cane) fantasy, corporal punishment, maiding, verbal abuse; and then the upper levels which include needles, torture, erotic asphyxiation, caging, etc. are the various levels of work a mistress can be trained in. Many ladies on the fringe of this line of work would dabble on the periphery of S & M, but it would be just a 'dabble' and by no means interfered with the staples of their work. As with anything, it has its place, but the real aficionado understands all of the nuances and secrets of the underbelly of the craft. The whole point of the meeting is that the Master or Mistress is in charge, which would fail miserably if everyone had to be asked, 'What would you like?' It would ruin the mystique that a Mistress somehow reads the mind of the individual, because he or she is so worthless that they are transparent.

In a later chapter, I will try to give you a more accurate picture of what my job meant to me and to the customer and hopefully answer any questions that might be hovering around your brain. But as is so often the case, I will just paint a picture and then you decide what it is that you can see?

So:

I was between contracts for daytime work. At this point I was a freelance business advisor. I would find a space. Do the homework and set up a business for the client. My contract could last up to a year and a half, whilst I showed the client how to run the business, wages, tax, accounts, personnel etc., before handing the business over to the client and moving on to something new. I was running a 'kissogram and entertainment agency' at the weekends but kicking my heels during the day. My friend's maid was off on holiday and I offered to step in and answer the phone for her. I think most people have a curiosity about the truth of the business of being a prostitute and vice has an enduring allure for everyone, even the 'tutters'.

Shortly before this my friend had had to visit the local police station for an interview concerning a vicious rapist who the police believed was also using prostitutes. There is an element who believe that prostitutes have an inside eye which hopefully gives then an instinct into the punters character and to a degree they're often right. I once had a DI say to me that it was the girls with heavy drug habits who invariably were the ones who come up dead. The desperation and fear of 'come down' means that either the instinct is blurred or ignored, but that any experienced 'brass' would get a feeling. Experienced or not, they just choose not to acknowledge it because the desperation at finding their next hit, out-weighs their inner voice. There is an element of truth in this statement, but it is not altogether correct. Some prostitutes have the same sort of 'smarts' as the Dominatrix, but I personally don't think it can be learned. I do think there is an element of learning involved, but I think that humans used to live on their wits and senses like all animals and that when faced with other living creatures there was an element of telepathy used. This sixth sense was the same as sight, smell etc. but as language developed, humans lost the ability of the 'silent conversation' and the warnings that are screamed at us, without a word being spoken. I believe that some of us have a residue of this 'sense' still within our make-up. When people use phrases such as,

'Go with your gut' or 'Trust your instinct' they are recognising that there is something in our make-up that we should use to help us find our way in life. Maybe that makes us less developed on the scale of evolution. But do we lose more than we have gained?

When training dogs, my mantra was, 'think like a dog' and those that got their heads around this simple observation, usually trained their dogs in half the time as those who couldn't understand what I meant.

I also have a theory that those of us who still have a trickle of this sense, even if they are unaware of it, tend to lead more precarious lifestyles than those without it. The risk takers and of course prostitution and to a lesser degree running a dungeon, would come under that umbrella.

In Brighton the police force had a far more enlightened view of prostitution and active brothels than many of their counterparts elsewhere in the country. Their policy was to try to work with the women 'on the game' either working individually or in the brothels, to prevent the other forms of crime that attaches itself to 'working girls'. Brighton in this respect, is an area, which is almost as busy as London. As long as a woman/women kept a relatively low profile, stayed off the streets, kept an orderly 'house' and refrained from dabbling in other forms of vice, the police gave the same measure of protection to those on the periphery of society as they would to the more regular 'joe'. Concerning prostitutes, it was policy that they would treat them the same as any other woman/man reporting a crime of assault, theft or anything else illegal. They refrained from 'raids', 'stings' and other forms of harassment and tried to foster a mutually beneficial arrangement with this band of 'workers'. Having said this, prostitutes have an inbred suspicion of the police and history shows that this was often with good reason, so when the police wanted help from my friend, she asked me to accompany her wearing a smart suit and carrying a briefcase. She approached the desk and gave her name and after waiting only a few minutes a plain clothed policeman came and collected us. Nothing was openly said, but my friend asked that I be allowed to go into the interview room with her to give the impression that she had legal representation with her. At the time I thought it was a bit silly, because if I was some sort of lawyer, surely I would have given my name and produced a pen and legal pad once in the interview room. As it was, I just sat beside her saying nothing. The police were unlikely to believe or care whether she had brought a 'brief' with her, to an 'off the record' interview, but actually a few years down the line, one of my own customers (a police inspector) made me realise that actually, she had been very astute. I didn't remember him but he had obviously recognised me.

When I was standing in front of him in my dungeon on his first visit to me, naked, wearing a collar and lead, he suddenly asked,

'Didn't you used to be a solicitor?'

5. ALL CHANGE

My curiosity had been peaked and my friend was more than grateful for my help. Generally, it was a laugh. My friend had a wicked sense of humour and a very colourful turn of phrase. She was happy to explain the various services offered and what those entailed. She was scrupulously clean, and we spent the first hour at the flat cleaning and dusting and then clean towels were inspected, condoms replenished, 'outfits 'checked, bathrobes and flannels placed in a position to encourage the customer to shower (something, sadly the average punter in her line of work ignored) and all crockery bleached (she hated tea stains). Her shower was almost permanently on as she showered between clients unless her punter paid extra to have her 'un-washed', and on busy days she would shower and then oil herself at the end of the day so that her skin didn't dry out. If I could pick up a little job being the maid, like this now, I'd be more than happy. The money was good, the company fun, a lot of the customers actually became friends with me and I didn't have to do what for me was the distasteful bit!

The flat had a lounge, two shower rooms, and toilets, a dressing room, a kitchen and three bedrooms. One of these rooms was always locked.

It was whilst working as the maid that a lady turned up to see my friend. She was with a client so this woman explained to me that she rented the flat when my friend didn't work (she only worked three days a week and I knew that somebody also used the premises and that it was her room which we didn't clean or go into). I confess, my youth and stupidity made me rather shallow and as I sat opposite this lady, I was wondering who would want to have sex with a woman of her age (late sixties) and whether she was actually kept busy? Once I saw the amount of cash this older woman handed over because I watched her count money out and pass it over to my friend. I was impressed.

This was my first meeting with a mistress in the S&M scene who was paid for her services. I hadn't 'got it' yet; but as time went on and I saw more of her, she relaxed in my company and more and more little snippets were coming out that had me a bit confused, but also very interested. At this time, I turned away a contract as I was mulling over the idea of writing a book about the business of prostitution. Obviously, this has been done before but I was looking for a different angle. My friend had introduced me to a few other ladies and I discovered that some of the stories associated with their line of work were hilarious. I had dabbled in writing before and had had a few things published as well as penning a regular cartoon for, of all things, Amateur Photographer and I quite fancied the idea of becoming a proper author.

Meeting 'Sheila' (the name I have decided to give her) more regularly and often when my friend was 'busy', meant that in time the subjects we talked about were much more varied and in some cases obviously more personal. When she first told me she was the wife of a serving police officer (due within months to be retired) I thought she was pulling my leg, but on pressing her gently, I discovered that what she said was completely truthful and it was this conversation that unlocked the other door in the flat, quite literally.

I carefully asked how her husband (my friend who owned the flat was single) felt about her having sex with strangers? To which she spurted a whole mouth of tea over me and laughed so much that my friend poked her head around the door and asked us to please keep the noise down as the laughter was putting her punter off!!

"The only man I have EVER had sex with is my husband of 40 odd years" and as she said this I noticed for the first time a really steely gaze. There was no way you would question this woman at that moment and if you had…then you had to be some sort of masochist, and it clicked.

This was the moment that a door opened for me in my psyche and literally, into the world of the Dominatrix.

The door which had always been locked in my friend's flat was now opened wide for me and I was given a virtual history of each implement and its usage. Over time I became a 'novice' to this lady, who painstakingly showed me how, why and where all of the implements could be used. I wasn't just told, I was shown the ways, sometimes with just an ordinary demonstration and at other times invited to watch how the implement could become a far more 'nasty' tool within the confines of S & M, and how far the implement should be used. Her dungeon had a Gothic style of lighting, over a mirror that covered most of the far wall. As I looked around I couldn't help myself. A large smile started to encompass my face and though some of the objects in the room were quite frankly baffling, over time I became fully immersed in the imaginings, the staged theatre and the ability to use those various items to produce that which the customer was seeking.

She was knowledgeable not just on the uses of items, but also their history, especially things used by the Spanish Inquisition. This was a group of very dangerous monks, sanctioned by the Pope of the time, to seek out Heretics, Infidels, Witches and other undesirables that after torturing them into admission, were subsequently burned at the stake. Inquisitors often applied torture devices to the recipient's body and these included heated metal pincers, thumbscrews, boots in which boiling tar could be poured and various items designed to burn, pinch or otherwise mutilate their hands and feet or concentrate their venom on all of their bodily orifices. Although torture was basically forbidden by the church, in 1256 Pope Alexander IV decreed that Inquisitors were in the divine service of the Lord and therefore could clear each other from any wrongdoing that they might have done during torture sessions. I suppose it is the same logic that embraces the confessional. As long as you say sorry and agree to spend some time praying, you're ok, no damage done! The fact that there was a pile of ashes in the town square and a few less people in the village was just a bi-product of being in the service of the Church and the Town was now ridded of any nasty heretics…probably?

It was a terrifying time with cruelty that hadn't been seen in these times until Isis reared its ugly head. The most frightening part was that people used this as a way to settle scores, 'right imagined wrongs' and cruelly get rid of anyone who they didn't like, by pointing the Inquisition in their direction. I remember reading at school of a case where two rival business men pointed fingers at each other. The inquisition questioned both men by way of the 'rack' and something akin to 'waterboarding' and decided that both men were guilty of immorality and sins against God, so they burnt both of them!

Women who had been revered as Mid-wives and healers suddenly became Witches and had to be eradicated at all costs. Hundreds of women were burned at the stake because they refused a suitor, was a boring wife, a so-called bad mother, infertile, or a victim of rape. Anything a man could think of that sounded reasonable was accepted as suspicious and could therefore instigate the intervention of the Inquisition. Owning a cat could be proof of being a witch as cats were often suspected of being a witch's 'familiar' (the devils' creature that the witch had sex with…a cat?). I imagine that during this period in History there were many cats curled up quietly in front of the fireside that suffered a rude awakening, when they were turfed out into the countryside to fend for themselves!

Sheila knew of a carpenter who specialised in such things as wooden pieces of furniture and the standard was amazing. Each piece was fashioned with his own hands, including the design and he would try to keep them as authentic as possible. All the mistress had to do was say what it had to be used for and he would do the rest. His work was strong, serviceable and lovely to look at, if you like that sort of thing I suppose?

She also put me in touch with a blacksmith who was as an amazingly gentle man who produced such things as an 'Iron Maiden' and 'scold's bridles' again, almost exact replicas and some really 'nasty' items which had specific uses or had been adapted slightly to be more serviceable. When I retired, I gave some of my equipment to museums as replicas of the actual devices of the times and they were incredibly grateful. The rest I sold using imaginative wording through 'Exchange and Mart' and was actually very surprised by the amount and the type of people interested in my pieces. If I wasn't careful the supposed buyer would grill me about how and why said objects had come into my possession. The minute the conversation started heading in this direction, I simply terminated the visit and locked them up with no further discussion. They were expensive and had been made with care and I wasn't about to spend time giving demonstrations to those who I knew would never purchase anything. When they all finally sold getting the garage back was a bonus in itself, especially the large pieces, but strangely I was quite sad to see the last piece leave. I was saying goodbye to a huge part of my life. A past which earned me a living and gave me memories which can set me off laughing even now and even when I'm alone. I really enjoyed it and I guess that by writing it down and you reading it, I'm hoping that you'll enjoy it too, even though it's just a small slice of what was my reality. It's a slice that you hopefully find acceptably juicy?

6. THE LAW

I had taken the step into the world of Sado-Masochism and initially I shared a dungeon with Sheila. I wanted to understand the heart of being a Dominatrix so I read everything I could, studied the law on the subject and within a very short time had started to amass my own 'toys'. Women in my position were known as a Dominatrix, Mistress, Mar'm and several other descriptions for the same person. It is a woman who is the epitome of perfection to the 'slave'.

There is nothing she can do or say which can be questioned by a mere man/woman (this is the same for a Master who also sees both males and females). She is to be revered and worshipped no matter what and it is only right that the 'person' in front of her, pays for that privilege. It is also possible for a Mistress to receive gifts, which can take the form of pieces of equipment, clothing, cash, shares, holidays, etc. And depending on the customer's income, he will also be expected to arrange lavish dinners, tickets for the theatre, opera, whatever tickles the mistress fancies. I have a love of Champagne, preferably Bollinger, and I would drink a bottle every evening. All of my clients knew this and as such I expected gifts of champagne, as well as the normal fee. I still love Champagne, but now it never has quite the same flavour as the bottles that I drank in those days and that somebody else had paid for!

I had decided that I was going to be the best that I could be and as such I should look the part. I confess that when I looked in the mirror, I liked the look of the woman staring back at me. Putting on the clothing was like becoming the 'real thing' and it helped to give me confidence. All mistresses want to look sexy, but possibly not in the way you imagine. For instance, I never bared my breasts or would wear something very low cut. I always wore thick black tights and thanks to Marks and Spenser's cotton gussets, (easily cut out without ruining or laddering the tights) I could keep my tights on if it were necessary to pee on my customer.

When I first started out, I was not as confident as I had to appear in the presence of a customer, so along with my clothes I always wore a masquerade mask. It helped to have something to hide behind.

There is a rule that every working Dominatrix whilst working, locks the dungeon door if for any reason she has to leave her client and this is because of the law.

British law is rather strange when it comes to the services of a Dominatrix.

Wikipedia says this:

The relationship between BDSM and the law changes significantly from nation to nation. It is entirely dependent on the legal situation in individual countries whether the practice of BDSM has any criminal relevance or legal consequences. Criminalization of consensually implemented BDSM practices is usually not with explicit reference to BDSM but results from the fact that such behaviour as spanking or cuffing someone could be considered a breach of personal rights, which in principle constitutes a criminal offence.

English law

United Kingdom

British law does not recognize the possibility of consenting to actual bodily harm. Such acts are illegal, even between consenting adults, and these laws are enforced; Brown being the leading case.

[10] R v Brown dismissed the defence of consent, meaning that the men charged with sexual offences could not defend their actions. It has been pointed out that people can consent to activities such as boxing and body piercing, which also result in pain, but apparently cannot consent to BDSM.

[11] This leads to the situation that, while Great Britain and especially London are world centres of the closely related fetish scene, there are only very private events for the BDSM scene which are in no way comparable to the German "Play party" scene.

Operation Spanner was the name of an operation carried out by police in the United Kingdom city of Manchester in 1987, as a result of which a group of homosexual men was convicted of assault occasioning actual bodily harm for their involvement in consensual sadomasochism over a ten-year period. The resulting House of Lords case (R v Brown, colloquially known as "the Spanner case") ruled that consent was not a valid legal defence for wounding and actual bodily harm in the UK, except as a foreseeable incident of a lawful activity in which the person injured was participating, e.g. Surgery. Following Operation Spanner the European Court of Human Rights ruled in January 1999 in Laskey, Jaggard, and Brown v. United Kingdom that no violation of Article 8 occurred because the amount of physical or psychological harm that the law allows between any two people, even consenting adults, is to be determined by the jurisdiction the individuals live in, as it is the State's responsibility to balance the concerns of public health and well-being with the amount of control a State should be allowed to exercise over its citizens. In the Criminal Justice and Immigration Bill 2007, the British Government cited the Spanner case as justification for criminalizing images of consensual acts, as part of its proposed criminalization of possession of "extreme pornography".

[12] Following the Audio-visual Media Services Regulations 2014 the video distribution of some BDSM practices has become illegal.

Thank you, Wikipedia, for consenting to me using this piece in my book. I am exceedingly grateful.

Now I have included this to explain the things, anyone, considering going into such a business, has to know. Yes, you pay your taxes, but what you do is still illegal whether you do it for love or money. The average mistress doesn't have the same amount of foot traffic as a prostitute, so providing she insulates her premises for sound, her business often flies under the radar of most neighbours, therefore they tend not to attract the attention of the local constabulary. However, some Police forces actually target businesses like mine because it is effectively an 'easy' collar. A prostitute will be given a fine for solicitation. Prostitution in itself is not a crime, however, to 'solicit' a person to enter into an act of prostitution, i.e. To offer sex for money, IS a crime. The difficulty for people like myself is that we are not offering sex. A true Dominatrix only offers a range of services that may result in sexual excitement for the patron, but it is far more cerebral than physical. So, the charges we faced was one of GBH or ABH, both of which can carry hefty prison sentences. In some cases, a police 'visit' would result in confiscation of all 'equipment' pending going to trial. The equipment we use from Horsewhips to Stocks and cages is expensive and the more equipment a mistress has the more 'types' of service she can offer. This could last for over a year without going to Court, effectively closing the business down.

With the introduction of the PACE Laws I am unsure whether it would be possible these days, but when I was working, it was.

With that in mind, one was always very wary of the 'casual' visit from a detective constable. Invariably there would be no warning and it would be stressed that this visit wasn't official, but the police are, by their very nature, nosey, so it was important if one had a customer, to lock the door of the dungeon if interrupted during a session. You cannot be arrested for owning an assortment of BDSM equipment, potentially it could be for photographic purposes? But that can change in a heartbeat if nosey detective constable happens to open a door and sees Mr. Smith, shrouded in rubber, apparently hanging from a butcher's hook with weights on his nads!!

As I have said, these 'visits' would be casual and without warning, but having made the introduction they were expected to make an appointment, just like everybody else!

In a later, more experienced lifetime, I was living in Manchester running a 'dressing service' for Transvestites and a dungeon in the basement. Manchester police did not like that at all. They were affronted because I encouraged these 'weirdo's' to dress in women's clothing and sit around being 'ladies'. If they had known a dungeon was also on the premises, I suspect that they would have thrown caution to the wind and charged in, weapons drawn, dogs snapping and snarling at their heels. As it was, some poor bastard would get pushed through my door and have to pretend he was interested in the dressing service. His conversation would be stacked with sexual innuendo in the hope that I would offer a sexual service to him. Instead I smiled sweetly, allowed all of his loaded questions to float over my head and I would lead him like a lamb to the slaughter into the 'back room', to introduce him to the service. This was an elegantly decorated lounge where my 'ladies' sat around drinking tea and admiring their painted nails. Once over the threshold I would introduce him to my clientele, push him forward towards a seat and then abandon him into the company of whoever was in that particular day. Then I would return to the shop and smugly wait until he came rushing out of the door, running across the shop, bellowing a thank you over his shoulder as he hit the pavement at a speed somewhere around 30 miles per hour, with obvious relief.

Another little game I played to infuriate the local constabulary was informing them when I had clocked we were being watched. Two officers in plain clothes would stake out the shop at a 'safe distance'. I would then telephone the police station and, as a good citizen, report two suspicious men sitting in a car near my shop. Almost as soon as I had replaced the receiver, the two officers would glumly move off!

In fairness it wasn't just the police who were confused by the service I offered, so I will quickly explain. I would charge £70.00 for a shower and clothing which included silicone boobs and hip pads. Underwear of any description had to be clean and supplied by the customer but in the event of arriving without, we sold in the shop underwear sets, hosiery, wigs and clothing. Once dressed the £70.00 also included make-up and hire of a wig. False nails were extra, as was any change of clothing, wig or shoes. We offered appointments with a dressmaker for bespoke clothing and also a fee for offering to store suitcases of lady's clothes for those afraid to have them at home. We also offered a laundry service and ironing which had to be paid for, free tea, coffee and biscuits and various 'evenings' of entertainment. A bit like the W.I, we had book clubs, recipe b's, sewing clubs, all incredibly boring but how us ladies supposedly fill up our vacuous lives, in the eyes of the average transvestite in those days. All of which brought in more money

Talking about confusion, one particular day is embedded in my memory. It was a fairly steady day. I had an insurance salesman, a gentleman who worked for a well-known drains company who sported a Hitler style moustache (and insisted during make-up that mascara was applied to it) a fairly well known wrestler, a lovely retired gentleman of 80 odd and a 6ft 2" builder's labourer, plus a maid doing the teas and coffee's in full Victorian, starched uniform. I was in the shop and a gentleman entered and hovered around the clothes rails, looking very nervous. This is not unusual, as many men do not 'come out' as a person who dresses in the clothing of the opposite sex. Most Transvestites are not gay, they only enjoy dressing up and are not looking for any type of sexual contact with persons of the same gender.

I let him hover a little longer and then managed to catch his eye and ask if I could be of assistance. His demeanour was such that I thought he might be more comfortable if he chatted with a 'tranny' rather than a woman, so before he managed to splutter much out, I gently guided him into the lounge and asked 'Patty' (our tranny with the Hitler moustache) to make him feel welcome and explain the service I offered. With that I left the room to summon the maid to offer tea. It was a matter of minutes before our visitor came back into the shop and headed straight for me. Before I had a chance to open my mouth he leaned towards me in a conspiratorial fashion and said,

"Sorry dear, I thought this was a new brothel' and with that he left.

The thought of that poor gentleman looking around at my 'girls' thinking that this is what I was 'offering' as a sexual encounter blindsided me. Thinking about it, I guess it would have been worse if he had asked me,

"How much for the one with the moustache?"

7. RUBBER DUBBER DUB

It took time to learn the mental side of my work and how to judge how much the customer really wanted to fulfil their fantasies and how much the Dominatrix wanted to push them.

I liked Sheila and I liked the idea of what she did. It offered me a way to earn a decent living, on my terms, self-employed (registered as a Beautician) and it fulfilled the 'actress' in me as well as the aggression that I suppose we all harbour, both male and female, and that we would ordinarily not have an outlet for. The morals of this line of work weren't mine to think about. As far as I was concerned, I was not having that type of close relationship with customers that I deemed as being intimate. Nobody actually touched me, and for me that fulfilled my own criteria of what 'being personal' with me, meant.

When it came to the question of whether my customer was being unfaithful to his loved ones, I don't believe that I had the right to judge other people's relationships and when people have attempted to judge mine, I have not reacted well. I think we all have to do what is comfortable to ourselves and if that involves different people and let's call them 'props', well as long as the person or persons they are with are also comfortable, then it's entirely down to them. On the other side of the coin, you would have to be a hermit from birth not to realise that when it comes to our sexual proclivities, we are just not all wired the same and some of the things we need to 'get us off' just aren't common enough to be brought up in company, even a company of two.

Sex is a very deep-seated need for most of us, so what happens when we find someone and it comes to the bedroom, if we have fetishes 'vanilla' sex no longer seems to satisfy and we're just not always singing from the same page. Relationships are made up of lots of different angles and every individual has to decide what they are prepared to give and what we are prepared to give up. If the thing they initially refrain from, because either with or without the partner, is sexual and is not generally acceptable or workable within the relationship, then as time goes on, despite the relationship being good and workable on other levels, the itch becomes unbearable and the chances are that they are going to try to scratch it, one way or another. I don't feel that that is my business and I can comfortably say that I never felt guilty about my work, regarding my customer's private lives or loved ones. Later I will try to explain what a Dominatrix is and what sets the real Mistress apart from the amateurs who dally on the edges of our world.

I listened to Sheila, her advice, stories, experiences and when I took it upon myself to step into her world as an equal, I had already decided upon my own set of boundaries, my limitations and which services I would offer. I have only ever stuck at a job that I enjoy and am prepared to give 100% This job was not only an interesting way to make a living but I loved it. I had almost stumbled onto a path, that ordinarily I would never have had the opportunity to embrace and I was grateful. I had in my youth wanted to be an actress and I think this fulfilled that ambition in some ways. When 'working' I had various costumes and I rarely purchased items 'off the peg'. Before when I was growing up, I designed a lot of my own outfits and my mum was brilliant at working without a pattern. It allowed my artistic side of clothing to have a free reign. When I made the decision to take this path, I realised that a part of my 'image' was to wear bespoke clothing and I managed to find a very good tailor who specialised in leather. I occasionally wore rubber, but I found it a pain to put on, rather sweaty and difficult to remove. I also had a very bad experience wearing rubber and without a shadow of a doubt, me and rubber didn't really sit. In defence of my stance I will tell you about it. I remember a session where the customer was obviously into rubber. He hadn't said anything, but looking through the items he brought with him, you would have to be a Donkey not to realise that rubber was 'his thing'. He was a good payer and a regular.

In this instance I was working alone; a situation you would only place yourself in if you were completely confident with the customer booked in. Slightly groaning to myself, as it was late into the afternoon, I thought I would give him a treat and so I struggled into a rubber dress, rubber stockings and elbow-length rubber gloves. Because I was on my own, as I struggled and wriggled to get them on, I used such copious amounts of baby powder that by the time I had actually managed to get dressed, I looked like I had been through a snow storm!

I checked my watch and realised that the customer was due within twenty minutes and without thinking about it

I threw myself into the shower, all rubbered up, to remove the powder off the clothes I was wearing. It never crossed my mind what the result of my actions would be. I guess it's not something one would normally think about?

The session started out completely normal. He had paid for two hours and in my head, I knew how to pace it, but after thirty minutes I started to feel a bit constricted.

I didn't react but as the time wore on, I could actually see that the bits of flesh visible, were starting to look a bit swollen and I started to keep one eye on the clock. As a professional I just got on with the job in hand, but with each minute I was starting to feel more and more uncomfortable and I couldn't wait for the time to finish. My discomfort, despite myself, meant I was a tad harsher than I would normally have been but I was getting desperate to finish and thought that if I was nastier than normal, the client might call a halt, which is the prerogative of all customers. Unfortunately, the nastier I was, the more my customer appeared to enjoy himself and ultimately, I worked for the full two hours, feeling more and more as if something were squeezing my chest and more like my circulation was being cut off which meant that there was an embolism heading straight towards my heart!

I literally called a halt at the second that the session was over and bundled the customer into the bathroom to shower and get dressed. Even before he was out, I was having real problems just to get my gloves off. It was as if they were at least three sizes too small and the flesh above the edge of the glove had swollen to five sizes larger than normal. I couldn't even get the tips of some sharp scissors into the tops to cut them off. Despite myself I was starting to panic and then I realised that my customer was standing in the doorway watching my struggle. He looked a little confused and then asked 'the' question,

"you didn't get wet after putting this on, did you?" …..

I don't remember exactly what my reply was, but needless to say I admitted my mistake on the basis that by now I was starting to believe that I may be squashed to death by a pair of rubber stockings, gloves and a rubber dress!

The ensuing hour was like an episode of 'twister' with both of us pulling and tugging with very little gain. No sooner was an edge pried away from its position than it would immediately swell causing suction and the edge would return to its original position with a slap, causing even more discomfort. My customer decided to go to the local shop and purchase some oil, whilst I prayed that he was sincere and would return. I waited for what seemed like an age and was just starting to think, 'Fire brigade?' When to my enormous relief there was a light tap on the door. By now I had the distinct look of one of those balloon animals, the type horrid children's clowns make, so there was no time to be lost.

We decided that the best place for me would be standing in the bath and pouring the cooking oil straight down any and all of the tiny little gaps we could make by both tugging at the neck of the dress. The sensation of cooking oil easing its way into every tuck and fold of my body had to be blanked out. It was revolting and every time I moved it created a terrible glooping noise akin to a wet fart. If I had had doubts before concerning the use of rubber, the experience cemented its fate in my mind's eye and I made a silent promise to myself that the only people who were wearing rubber in my dungeon was the punters!!

I don't really know how long it took and how much rolling, pulling and tugging we had had to do, but just as we achieved the final tug to remove the dress (the stockings had been scraped off me earlier) I slipped on the huge puddle of oil in the bottom of the bath, ending up with me naked, I flat on my back and my legs in the air. On the way down I had cracked the back of my head on the edge of the bath and the expression of concern on 'my gentleman's' face gave me some indication that something, apart from looking like a stranded jelly baby, was wrong. I attempted to rise but by now my customer was practically on top of me, pinning me down and shouting

 "Don't move!"

The blood gushing from my head wound was alarming but I was far more worried that with all of the oil, my punter was going to end up slithering over the edge of the bath onto my chest, thereby suffocating me as I bled to death. It took enormous patience to take back control of the situation, but after endless attempts slipping and sliding about, he finally allowed me to stand carefully with his help and get out of the bathtub. With a pillowcase pressed firmly against my head we wiped off as much oil as we could, I threw on some clothes and was promptly bundled into a car to head for the hospital.

I ended up having thirteen stitches, a blinding headache, bruises over parts of my body that I hadn't thought could bruise and a lifelong loathing of sunflower oil!!

8. UNDERSTANDING

My love of leather was a benefit as I was definitely not going to wear any more rubber and PVC was an absolute no-no. The 'dabblers' wore PVC and no real Mistress would consider using a fabric for herself that looked and felt so cheap (Dominatrix snobbery), but we all had 'those' types of items in our closet so that our 'maids' may occasionally be made to wear them or they could be borrowed by those who I was training to take up my line of work. I never considered my clothing like some sort of uniform because I wore leather all the time, as well as always wearing high stiletto heels. I'd done jobs where I had been on my feet from eight-thirty to five-thirty and I would never have dreamed of wearing 'flats', so I didn't think about it. Having said that, any Dominatrix worth her salt has at least one-foot fetishist on her books, who can be called upon at the end of the day to look after tired and aching feet with their tongues…and pay for it!!!

These days my preferred footwear is a pair of riggers and if not them, my wellington boots, but I retired eighteen years ago and now I could not even imagine trying to catch my sheep wearing thigh length boots!

Looking back, it had been obvious to Sheila that I had a 'real' interest in her way of making a living and after several sessions in the pub after work she told me that she thought that I had all the attributes of a good Dominatrix. Honestly, I was flattered.

The way she 'sold' her way of life was as follows:

Imagine feeling beautiful, special, adored and so exquisite that you are only touched in the places that 'you' allow. The tips of her fingers or toes perhaps? It sounded good to me! As an aside, of all the things I miss since retiring it is the feeling of being lovely. I know it's shallow, but like so many I have battled issues with my self-esteem and thoughts of being ugly and worthless. To have many men, constantly telling me how beautiful and precious I was, really gave me a sunnier disposition towards life.

It was sold to me on the basis that I would be worshipped as a goddess. That I deserved to be rich, listened to and cossetted and any punishment doled out because the slave's work is not to the mistresses' satisfaction, is to be expected and respected. The fantasy should be worn like a cloak that fits perfectly across the shoulders. A persona that never truly leaves the Mistress no matter whether she is working or not. This is what Sheila meant when she spied in me the characteristics that would 'make a good Dominatrix' and once captured, I discovered that I could also meet people who I believed, given the opportunity, would be excellent in my line of work. Once I was 'living' the lifestyle there was another interesting phenomenon that without exception proved itself to be true. A submissive seems to be able to almost smell a Mistress or Master as soon as they enter a room. I don't mean purely in a social situation. I noticed that when I was browsing in a store, there would invariably be someone who started to follow me at a safe distance. At first, I thought that I must look terribly shifty to have store detectives continually following me around in various stores, until one gentleman sidled up and tried to make conversation. I've no memory of what he said, probably just an observation about whatever I was looking at, but he ended the sentence almost in a whisper with the word, Mistress. At that particular moment the penny dropped and I actually felt relieved that I didn't come across as some 'Queen of Shop Lifters' every time I entered a shop. Once I was more experienced, I carried business cards in my pocket and when I was certain, I would discreetly pass one to the body hovering within my periphery. I'm not saying that there weren't times when I actually WAS being shadowed by a store detective, but thankfully it really wasn't that often. Surprisingly I actually gained quite a bit of business through this method of recruitment but as I shopped in an ankle length leather coat, soft leather gloves and stiletto boots I guess I was an advert for those in the know?

Once while shopping in Harrods, as I attempted to pay for a beautiful, napper leather handbag, an extremely well-dressed gentleman intervened as I was about to hand over my debit card. He wasn't English, but spoke English beautifully and I would have guessed that he had probably been educated in this country. Oddly I didn't get the feeling of a submissive, but I happily allowed him to pay the £200 for the bag and thanked him politely. When the transaction was complete, he introduced himself with a slight bow of the head and gently took my hand and touched his lips to my glove in an unusual introduction, being that we were in Harrods? He invited me for lunch in the restaurant and honestly in my head I was just thinking, 'this is getting better and better'.

Once seated and champagne ordered this lovely man (who I am afraid I cannot identify) explained to me his knowledge of the S&M scene and soon revealed that he was not a submissive or a Master. He was just someone who had recognised my calling and decided, as he was on his own, that it may be entertaining to invite me for lunch. Our friendship was sealed within the first hour of his company and I remember his laugh which rippled across a room, without being intrusive. I had always believed that despite his money and influence in certain circumstances, I would never have asked him for anything to do with his niche in life. After many years I did something rather stupid and was arrested and taken to trial. I admitted my guilt and tried to get my head around probably getting a prison sentence. Carol, who was with me at this time, without my knowledge contacted my friend and asked him for help. Whilst I was out on bail, I received a visit from a gentleman who informed me that he would be representing me and also informed me that the date of the hearing had been changed. I admit that I wanted to plead guilty because I was wrong, but I had no idea when I waived my right to a solicitor that if convicted, I could have received a sentence of 'life'!!! I truly hadn't seen that coming and this man who appeared on my doorstep with his card and his help, was like a golden ticket in a raffle. I did go to Court and pleaded guilty, but I received a suspended sentence for a given time and a tongue lashing from the Judge. I had known before I stepped into the witness box what the result would be, but it isn't something you actually believe until it is over. When I became aware of the 'interest' my friend had taken, I tried to apologise for him being made aware of my problem, but he would hear none of it. He promised me that we would never speak of it again and we didn't. When I lost him to cancer, I lost one of the most influential, kind, funny and caring people I had ever known. His funeral was such a 'public affair' that I couldn't risk attending, but I know that he would know I had wanted to and why I couldn't.

Sheila had explained to me in the early days of training, some of the 'mind-set' of the average customer. It wasn't unusual for a gentleman to request his humiliation to be performed in front of an 'extra' woman or man, and pay handsomely for the privilege. Sheila had mooted the idea to me when I was first starting out and I made sure during my working years to have people I could call upon when this service was required. It's actually a real money spinner having the ability to incorporate exhibitionism into the mix, which on the scene, i.e. being with like-minded people, is quite a strong aspect of S & M.

Sub-missive's who would normally never risk being around anyone but their Mistress, will actually get quite turned on by the idea that they are being 'show cased' within an area that they know and understand. It's the comfort factor that they are only being watched in front of another strong woman. Depending on the role that the 'extra' were to play, depended on who I called, but as often as possible I tried to use someone who wanted to pay me for being a watcher or some type of participant. There are a lot of young women who are nervous of entering my world but either enjoy being a voyeur or need the experience of being part of a 'session' without being the one to take responsibility for what is happening. Often it is a way of feeling more experienced before setting up their own premises. The key is to try and find a person who is willing to pay to be included and of course the punter who is willing to pay extra for a 'watcher'. It is always preferential to get two for the price of two, so to speak!

Controlling a session where one has to incorporate both sets of 'wants and needs' and make sure that everybody has a good time and feel that they have got their monies worth, is what the Dominatrix aims for. It actually requires quite a lot of work in the cerebral area for the Mistress, but the successful ones actually enjoy having to think about the session and become really quite inventive in this type of situation. I think a way of telling you that

I was good at my job is the revelation I give you now, that every single customer who visited my dungeon, always came back for at least one other appointment. Obviously if I were 'on the scene' in Spain or Germany as an example, the slaves I met did not specifically pay me, but then I had been brought in by the promotor who paid for the hotel, air fares, taxis, a budget for food and drinks, an extra ticket for a maid or slave. If I was 'putting on a show' I would be paid a bit more, but I had a good reputation for giving a promoter a good deal for what he had paid for. What was amazing was how often I would take an appointment and then when they arrived, I realised we had met before in a club during an S&M bash! (pardon the pun please).

I also always sent out invites, mostly to Germany, when I was planning a school day, but that is a whole other chapter.

9. OUT ON MY OWN

I had 'trained' over a couple of years whilst running another business and learned how to run a dungeon, keep things clean, advertise, avoid the law, learned the body language and how to 'read' a customer and so much more that would fill a book on its own. I never paid Sheila a penny. She taught me everything with love and humour because she believed in me. It was actually the first time in my life that somebody had taken me under their wing and coaxed out of me a person who felt strong and needed. I have no way to completely thank her, though she told me on her death bed that teaching me had been a joy and that she had never laughed so much in her life, I still feel that she was one of the most important people in my lifetime and when I remember, those early days, I think back with fondness and a smile.

My training went well and I picked up things easily. Ducks to water come to mind and I felt I had found my calling. I read anything I could get my paws on, discovered the various underground magazines which advertised services, clubs and parties and purveyors of bespoke equipment as well as general items associated with the trade. Sheila had told me that when I wanted to set up on my own, I had to decide what elements of the BDSM scene I wanted to cater to. Quite early on I decided that I wanted nothing to do with any role swapping, anything that put my safety at risk either physically or health-wise, wasn't even considered.

Coprophilia was an absolute no-no, Erotic Asphyxiation (though in later years I did offer this to certain customers in a very controlled environment), Queening, sex and various other services which even I hadn't heard of!

Inevitably there comes a time when you feel that the time has come to do it for yourself and I started to look at premises that I thought would do.

It was important that you have the space, the bathroom facilities and place yourself in an area with low daytime foot traffic. Unlike 'working girls' you do not have men constantly turning up on your doorstep and the ones who are seen by neighbours are with you for far too long. The average person thinks that 'punters' looking for sex are going to be in and out in a matter of minutes. Actually, I was told once by a 'very experienced' working girl, that she had turned 6 tricks in half an hour. The thought of the conditions in which this would be possible has me baffled but I didn't want to show too much interest, so I let it slide.

It was quite exciting to decorate, equip and set up my own dungeon but it is when you actually work that you find that what you thought was right, just isn't. You make changes and over the years, as you gain more experience, your dungeon will come together and become a part of you. Space is important because whips and canes demand room so that they can be wielded properly and the premises must be easily cleaned. In the latter years, I had a rubber flooring that was cushioned and if I had wanted to, I could have thrown buckets of water over it without any damage.

One assumes that they have become confidant enough on their journey that when they have everything ready. Dungeon ready, phone lines connected, new towels, soap etc. 'It will just 'happen',

But when you get your first glimpse of the customer naked, wearing a heavy dog collar, on hands and knees, wobbling along holding the handle of his leash between his teeth, you think that the silliness of the situation would instantly make you relax. After working for a while that is true, but the first time?

My first ever customer, a bit like your first kiss, is someone who you will never forget. I was seated on my personal throne, a bespoke object equipped to be several different 'tools of the trade' in one. It was made for me by a customer who obviously understood the needs of the

Dominatrix and it had been lovingly crafted and decorated with his own hands.

The customer crawled into position in front of me and knew to acknowledge my presence without speaking. This involved an extremely dramatic bow, placing his forehead on the ground and spreading out his arms as if crucified. Without a word I raised myself and stepped away picking out a vicious little switch from the array of canes, paddles, whips and other dungeon paraphernalia. Stepping lightly back I pressed my stiletto heel onto the back of one of his hands and when he flinched, brought the little switch down hard on his backside three times in quick succession. Curling his leash around my hand I jerked him into an upright position, exposing to my horror, an erection like a Guard on parade.

For a split second I couldn't think of anything that I was supposed to do as I stared, transfixed, like a person who suddenly finds a snake behind their toilet just as they sat down. Under my scrutiny it bobbed slightly and a tiny bit of precum dribbled out of the eye. I suddenly realised that I was expected to do something and without looking at my slave's face I viciously attacked his member with the switch and started to berate him for his lack of respect. He didn't scream, so I just went at it faster and harder. I was transfixed as his dick bobbed this way and that whilst taking on a purple-ish hue. I was determined to 'kill it' and I was suddenly brought back to my reality when I realised that he was begging me to be forgiven. The poor man was looking straight at me and as I looked down again, I realised that his dick had turned into a sort of purple, squashed sausage, definitely devoid of life.

I composed myself and barked, 'assume the position'. I have no idea why I used that phrase and can only assume that at that moment I remembered this particular phrase that was used in some American cop show. It just felt like it fitted and without hesitation he immediately went back down into his crucifixion style bow. At that moment I felt the power he had turned over to me, and as I pressed his head hard against the dungeon floor with the sole of my boot, I felt quite satisfied with my performance. By the end of the session I had had him hanging upside down and being smacked with a paddle, tried out several different bondage moves and then used a few different knots with various ropes. I checked the time and then put on a pair of disposable gloves and tightly wrapped a slim cord round and round his poor tatty dick, leaving only the head free. Once again, his dick rallied but it looked horrible and had become swollen and painful looking. With a quick clip around the ear I strode out of the dungeon and softly closed the door behind me. It is a rule that a Mistress always adheres to and that was to never forget to lock the door when a customer was on the premises in bondage. I sat down in the kitchen and despite myself I started to giggle. His dick bobbing about had reminded me of that fairground stall where you are given a hefty mallet and have to try and bash the worm as it pops up! The bruising of his member guaranteed that he wouldn't be able to have an erection for weeks without passing out!' I chuckled to myself. After a few moments I returned to the dungeon and released my customer from his 'Dick Tie' by suddenly jerking the string and watching his poor knob yanked about by the momentum of the curled rope until it was finally released. The gentleman had arrived earlier with what some might say was a 'very handsome Dick' and left with something that looked like it had been chewed and spat out by my dog. I felt great!

I also discovered that most 'Acolytes' had to pay a Mistress to be trained in the arts of Domination and that unbelievably they were queueing up to be trained. I confess that the way I fell into the business was lucky because like most apprentices the pay was usually poor against a large lump sum paid over to the Mistress for a set number of weeks training and no obvious qualification at the end of it. They were never allowed to bring in their own customers and had to pay extra for the use of some of the equipment. I cannot talk for other ladies in my business, but many had no interest in whether the trainee had the 'gift' or not and was extremely amiss in showing properly how the equipment was used. It isn't rocket science to understand that a dungeon and some of the equipment can be dangerous, even life-threatening, so the importance of understanding how it all works and what it can be used for is very important

A few years on I set up rented premises that had in its history been an undertakers and butchers, which not only gave me space and an impressive array of hooks and a defunct 'human' storage facility but also supported my business for Transvestites, a shower and toilet and kitchen on the ground floor, my dungeon and dressing room on two lower floors where we had installed a wet room and separate toilet, a laundry and a self-contained little flat at the back of the property, with a walled garden. My living quarters were above the property and had three bedrooms which meant that trainees were put up on the premises and did not pay for food, use of the dungeon and all of its equipment (under my supervision), the 'outfits' etc. And I always tried to include a visit to a couple of clubs so that the trainee could see how to involve themselves in the 'scene' once the training was over.

I never saw any of my protégées as threats and although I knew that some would end up on their backs because it was considered easier, some I quite enjoyed catching up with when we met. I know that some Ladies did the same as I and occasionally I would telephone a Dominatrix and ask her to accommodate the slave I was sending her. We did this with regulars, partly to keep them interested but also to 'spread out' the fantasy. With many customers, there were both written and unwritten standards and it was quite interesting to weave a fantasy about a 'secret club' where only strong women could be members and that each lady had her own set of 'subs' who would occasionally be sent out to show one of the other members, how well they had been trained.

10. THE UNIVERSITY OF PAIN

I didn't just drop everything else in my life and head for 'those' shops which sell the sort of things a Mistress would need for her dungeon, all in one go. I was a novice, though Sheila said I was a natural, I recognised when I first started taking an interest that if I was contemplating a change in career, I had a great deal to learn. The implements used, especially those which inflict pain have to be used in a controlled manner. By that I do not mean that the full power of the device is never used, but that the user uses the implement in such a way that it must be in line with the client's needs.

One of the most interesting things I learned was to take control of an implement from the elbow down to the wrist, rather than swinging from the shoulder. This gives the person wielding the cane, paddle or another object, a much better control over the amount of 'pain' it inflicts. I was also shown how to avoid the object springing back so that the Mistress gets a secondary spanking, whilst dishing out her 'subs' punishment. The first time I picked up a 'cat-o-nine-tails', by the time I had mastered it I was black and blue!! If I had ever wondered if I had any inclinations towards accepting pain myself, that particular lesson confirmed for me that I was well and truly on the side of the 'giver'. When I got home and inspected all of the accidental welts and bruises, I decided that those who crave this type of domination, were obviously mad!!

In fairness, I always minimised my own interest concerning those who chose to indulge in the punishment aspect of my work, with a shrug of my shoulders. I never felt the need to explain the inexplicable to those curious about my customers but I suppose that like most people, I have been curious about the why's?

Most Dominatrix over time will have a list of regulars and some of these become almost friends. I say 'almost' because the relationship between a Mistress and her slave can never cross certain boundaries. It is the illusion that the Dominatrix is the 'perfect', untouchable creature that can never be attained, which fosters the Mistress versus slave relationship. In the early days of my own career I was approached by a gentleman who ran a Brothel but had installed a dungeon. He offered the use of the dungeon to me on a rental basis, but when it came to the fine-tuning of the business, he obviously expected me to offer a sexual service as well. When I explained my own services and the reasons for the definitely no sex rule, his jaw dropped. He could not understand that somebody would pay for something without being allowed to touch and/or get their jollies off!

I will state here categorically that a 'good' Dominatrix will never have casual or any other type of sex with a customer. It is that rigid boundary that we would never cross, and that sets us apart from others working within the sex industry.

I have asked customers what and why they become addicted to the various modes of the S & M world and I will share two of those with you now. One customer explained it this way: You have a hole in a tooth and over time the thing becomes infected, and you suffer a raging tooth ache. For some reason you keep placing your tongue into the hole which intensifies pain to a point which is unbearable. You remove your tongue and savour the release from the agony that you have just suffered by putting your tongue in the hole. The sudden relief is intoxicating, so as the normal pain threshold returns you again stick your tongue in the hole. The sexual element brings in another dimension, but for the moment let's just deal with the pain side of things.

Interestingly, many people who I have given this analogy to, 'confess' that this is something that they have a vague understanding of. This doesn't make them into my customers, but a little bit of common ground has been reached. I had an odd habit myself at school. Some of the desks had a shelf under the main desk for your books, which if you had your legs crossed was about shin height. I wasn't the most academic pupil and often got detention for falling asleep in class, which defeated the benefit of sleeping through subjects that I had no interest in. The trouble was that as the teacher droned on, I could feel my eyelids start to droop.

Anyone who has ever been kicked in the shins knows what a sickening pain arises from that type of injury. I learned that by swinging my leg and tapping the wood fairly gently it still produced enough of a bite to keep me awake. The reason I mention this is because if I'm honest I actually grew to not just tolerate the pain, but in a perverse way I had learned to enjoy it.

I mention this to help explain another of my customer's addiction to really severe pain.

I will not name this person, suffice it to say that he was a British hostage captured in an African country whilst working for a British company. The British Government refused, on the surface, to become involved, but as always, the advice was not to pay any type of ransom. This gentleman was one of three taken whilst visiting a factory belonging to the company he worked for. From the moment they were captured and moved to a 'safe' area the torture began. They were accused of spying for the 'other' faction involved in a civil war, the side with whom Britain had a reasonably good relationship. This gentleman remained a hostage for three and a half years. One of his fellow prisoners was released after two years. He was dumped when he became so ill that his jailors were convinced, he would die and therefore he was no longer of any value to them. The people who found him transported him to a hospital where he was lucky enough to be put in touch with the British Consulate. The other two men finally escaped together after three and a half years. Both were at a point where they would have to take a break for freedom or die trying.

My customer told me of the horrendous treatment all three were subjected to. One of the daily rituals was to be taken, naked, out of an underground prison, tied to a pole and whipped and beaten until they lost consciousness. They would then be revived by buckets of water and salt would be rubbed, viciously into the bleeding welts. Although extremely painful this did actually help sterilise the wounds. My customer told me that as they beat them, they would laugh and humiliate them and that they liked nothing better than to see the men with tears running down their faces. My customer knew that he couldn't stop them or fight them, so he decided to 'teach' himself to enjoy it. He told me that during these sessions he would link sexual fantasies to the strikes. He said it wasn't easy, but over time he learned to turn this severe form of torture into something that turned him on and when during one session he spontaneously ejaculated, things started to turn. Initially his jailors were so affronted by what had happened that they brought in ever more nasty and painful types of torture. He laughed, genuine laughter because he knew he was winning. Once it had happened, inevitably it happened again and finally, the beatings stopped because realising that this now gave him pleasure, they were no longer interested in doing it. Obviously having spent so long teaching himself to enjoy this terrible treatment, unlearning the sensations that helped him survive, was almost impossible. I cannot allow you, the reader to confirm this story, but I personally had the means to find out that this story was absolutely true. Behind the scenes the British Government did everything they could to try and obtain the release of these men and when they were finally found alive and repatriated, they were given all of the help that was possible to help them adjust to being free. My customer was a single man when this happened to him and because of his experiences, he believed that it was better if he refrained from intimate situations with women, unless it was to humble himself before a 'Mistress' who would hurt him in the way that he could gain sexual gratification.

The sexual side of BDSM is another aspect of my work which is difficult to explain to the layperson. Many customers contain the final act of relief until their session is over and I was never aware, (deliberately) if they waited until they were home? Some ejaculate spontaneously, in which case they will normally suffer more punishment and will be made to clean up after themselves. Cleanliness has to be a watchword for the Dominatrix because ultimately, she will be around bodily fluids. In my own premises nobody entered the confines of my dungeon unless they had showered and were squeaky clean and I still wore black disposable gloves at all times. Cleanliness was an absolute must and it was the duty of my maids or trainees to handle laundry, dusting, hoovering, washing up, replacing paper towels, etc. I personally handled the steriliser or supervised its use. All rubbish was either shredded or disposed of in a careful manner.

This reminds me of a customer who would regularly arrive sweaty and smelly and would try to duck in and out of the shower without actually getting wet. At the time I was working with another lady and had a live-in 'maid' and when he rang, we would try to think of all sorts of reasons why we could not accommodate him. If he managed to obtain an appointment, it was because we hadn't earned enough money that week. This particular day was extremely hot, which affects business, but when the call came I wasn't actually there to take it so I learned second hand, that 'Mr. Smelly' was on his way. I was horrified, but we had no means of contacting him to cancel so we made a plan. I had literally got to a point where if he never returned, I'd be happy.

When Mr. Smelly arrived I personally chaperoned him into the bathroom, told him to remove all of his clothing and pushed him under the flow of hot water. With that I clicked my fingers and my apprentice appeared with a large bucket of soapy disinfectant and my maid arrived wearing a full-length rubber apron and holding a toilet brush which had an unusually long handle. The scrubbing began! My maid obviously (well to me anyway) was a man and I have noticed over the years that men in a position of power, even if subservient by nature, are far harsher than women in this type of situation. Whilst my trainee held the bucket aloft, 'Lilly' scrubbed viciously every centimetre of Mr. Smelly's flesh, even his face, and head. Finally, when I was convinced Mr. Smelly was clean possibly because he had turned almost purple in colour, I allowed the last of the disinfectant to be thrown over him and then the temperature of the shower was turned to cold. Trying to keep a straight face whilst he whooped and squealed, dancing around like a marionette with Lilly shoving him back under the flow of cold water every time he tried to avoid the spray, was one of my proudest moments. I dared not look at my trainee because I could see her shoulders heaving under the effort not to laugh out loud and even Lilly had a sort of demonic smile. When the ordeal was over Mr. Smelly was handed a role of strong blue paper to dry himself with, which was a bit like trying to dry yourself with sandpaper. Lilly removed his clothing to the washing machine. Mr. Smelly stood in front of me naked and shivering, patting himself down with a few squares of paper until I barked that it was time to get on his knees and follow me into the dungeon. He was just about to go down when he hesitated. 'What?' I growled.

And Mr. Smelly, without a hint of irony asked, 'I don't suppose your maid could clean my car?

Later that evening myself, my trainee and even Lilly drank champagne (my maid was allowed a small glass) and sat and howled with laughter over the day's exploits. When I remember and think back to the look on his bright red, scrubbed face, I can-not help but smile.

11. STINGING IN THE RAIN

When I look back, I cannot help but wonder if those people in my youth would look at me then and recognise the person who I am telling you about. My best friends were nearly always male growing up, but my weird lifestyle as I got older, meant that I left people behind. Oddly as this situation I am about to tell you about went down, a friend of mine called Toby bounced into my thoughts. I had a real crush on him for years if I was honest, but it was one of those things that was never meant to be. I think when Toby wrote to me, (we probably wrote each other every two to three years) there was a sort of quirky feel to his own life and when some of the funny instances happened in my life, I would think that he was probably one of the few people from my past who could look at it and smile.

Something I should mention is that I rarely if ever worked completely alone. No woman in any sort of trade that allows men into their space, behind a closed door, cannot take the risk that all of those men have perfectly harmless intentions. A lot of people think that my customers were weird, perverts, probably very dangerous, but nothing can be further from the truth. Weird, possibly, perverts yes, I suppose so (I would like to thank God for giving us such varied proclivities), but dangerous, not to me?

The men, and occasionally women into BDSM that seek out a Dominatrix are subservient. They place themselves naked and at their most vulnerable in your hands. It isn't the type of thing they're going to mention in the office, so once they entered my domain, nobody would know where they were. If they never came out again what would point the police in my direction? There is a great deal of trust between a Dominatrix and her customers, a trust that neither should break.

I always employed somebody to answer the phone, make appointments, make tea if customers overlapped but mostly to just be there. I also always took one of my dogs. A large, quiet, unfriendly animal who was as tall as a deerhound and sturdy like a greyhound who had been taking steroids that I would sometimes use to intimidate men visiting my premises. He had come into my life in strange circumstances He was a strange deep orange colour but brindled a bit like the markings of a tiger and I had no doubt that he could and would bite and I have the scars to prove it, but he had ultimately decided that I was probably his best bet and guarded me with absolute faithfulness. He was very perceptive and I knew always to trust his instinct when it came to his summation of other people. He had his usual blank stare with huge yellow eyes which were very disconcerting, at anyone who was harmless but irritating to him. The snarl or sneer which he used to prevent other humans from getting in his face and wanting to pet him and then the cold, silent look where every muscle in his body was ready to spring and a low dangerous growl would be emitted almost as if he knew he had to warn, but wasn't going to make it loud enough to signal to them his intensions. When he had an accident and chased a squirrel on to a main road which required surgery, they found four bullets lodged in his chest. He had been lucky that no vital organ had been damaged, but it was obvious that when whatever it was that had happened, he wasn't taken to a vet. Strangely, although he was a grumpy animal and was in the habit of showing his teeth to strangers, he had no problem with the vet at all? He was hard work to train because his instinct was to bite first and then see what the human wanted of him, but once he decided he was mine (although he always made it clear he would have preferred to be a man's dog and that he sort of put up with me) he guarded me with his life. Bruno had one very disconcerting, embarrassing obsession with people who suffered from achondroplasia, which was painful for me because a really nice girl, born with Dwarfism used to walk her spaniel in the park. It was as if he smelt her coming from five miles away and as soon as he knew she had entered the park, his ears would twitch as his head shot up and he was off. Hurtling towards her he would bark loudly and incessantly, running around and round her, jumping up and down so all four paws were off the ground, completely ignoring her dog but refusing to allow her to walk forwards or backwards. Bruno definitely wasn't PC and I was almost humiliated by his rudeness especially when school kids were coming to and from, using the park as a through road because they would laugh. In a way I can see the humour of a big dog scaring a dwarf but we're not allowed to find this sort of thing funny and I'm damn sure she wasn't laughing. I tried everything. I tried walking with her, wrestling him onto the ground so she could pet him (muzzled of course). Her holding him on a lead, which was disastrous because he set off at a run and I could see her tiny legs battling to stay up with him, until he finally pulled her over and she was being dragged along, nose in the grass while I shouted at the top of my voice, "Let him go!"

Ultimately I agreed on set times for me to walk my dogs so that we didn't meet, but then one lunchtime I was sitting outside the park café with a friend called Vikki when a strange yellow bus turned up, opened its doors and a pile people with various handicaps were disgorged right in front of the cafe. Both Vikki and I jumped out of our chairs and started running about like headless chickens looking for Bruno, but it was within seconds, he appeared and let us know exactly where he was, barking and bouncing and circling as if he were trying to round them all up and get them back on the bus. There were people going in all directions, screaming, crying and swearing whilst Vikki and I were desperately trying to grab my dog as he twisted and turned out of our grasp. In desperation I bellowed, "JUST STAND STILL!" and after two or three attempts everyone finally stopped. I grabbed Bruno, stuck him on a lead and marched out of the park with Vikki. I could never cure him of it, till the day he died he still acted like an arse around people who were physically different. Naughty Bruno!!

Although to some, bondage, pain, rubber etc. is extremely odd, most of the time it was same old same old, perhaps with a different kink, for me. I was rarely surprised, having detected the type of service the gentleman was looking for, and perfectly willing to oblige providing the correct fee was offered.

One afternoon I wasn't feeling my best having had a nasty cold and I had said to my maid that I would be grateful if there wasn't too much physical exertion on my part. Heavy paddles and whips can really take it out on you and I was hoping for a nice bondage session where I could tie them up and forget about them. My trainee knocked on the lounge door and had a confused look on her face as did my 'maid' who had sidled up behind her. She explained that she had someone due imminently and no matter what questions she had asked; she could not fathom what it was he wanted. Of course, one has to be careful of Mr Plod arriving and they were always vague, so I said that I would answer the door and told the maid to go to his own quarters and to stay there. I could see him desperately pulling off his apron and uniform as he trotted off. Once out of sight the doorbell rang and after looking through the peep hole decided to just open the door.

The man standing before me practically bounced over the threshold, holding a beat box in one hand and a watering can in the other. My girl was looking to me for some sort of reassurance. I pulled a face and said to her,

"trust me, when and if 'they' ever turn up, they won't be carrying a watering can".

My gentleman was small and very wiry and like my girl I had no idea what sort of service he wanted. He had stood in front of me, head down and muttering, 'yes mistress', to everything I had told him that I would not do, so I decided to tell him to have a shower and I gave him the envelope for payment and closed the bathroom door. When my girl looked at me quizzically, I shrugged and got ready for the dungeon. At the appropriate knock my girl went to get the gentleman and retrieve the envelope.

It was part of her job to give me a signal that told me what had been paid and whether it was for an hour or more. The signal denoted an hour, but for the life of me I had no idea what was meant to be happening during that hour! My customer had changed into a white leotard, white tights, silver ballet pumps, a long blonde wig, thick, black, false eyelashes that seemed to be stuck to his eyebrows, wielding two washing up liquid containers and stingy little pony whip.

At one time in my life, as stated, I had a dressing service for transvestites. They paid for 'dressing' and I did their make-up, however some insisted on doing their own which at times had me either crying with laughter (after they had gone of course) or completely perplexed. I couldn't understand that they could not see, what I could see? I could not believe that when they looked in the mirror, they saw a 'well made up Woman' and I saw someone who had had an octopus let loose on their face with a box of colours!

Well this chap's eyebrows were very definitely wrong, but they had that unique ability, that where ever you looked, you just couldn't help yourself being drawn back to these horrid fluffy things on his face and staring at them with incredulity. I wanted to ask if he realised that the eyelashes were actually meant for the lids of his eyes and that where he had placed them made it look more like a tribute to Groucho Marx, but I didn't say a word. Silently he handed one washing up bottle to me and the whip, then dramatically placed the beat box on the floor and posed dramatically in the centre of the dungeon. Just as the strains of the Nutcrackers Suite started filling the room with music, he hissed, "Squirt me Madam", and then started leaping and prancing, up and down on his toes, dramatic hand and arm gestures and movements that were supposedly ballet. I let out a long sigh and then squirted him smartly with what appeared to be a mixture of washing up liquid and a sickly perfume. Immediately he spun towards my girl who taking my lead, did the same, and both of us kept up the pressure with the soap as well as stinging his buttocks with the pony whip. At intervals he raised the watering can and allowed the same smelly, bubbly water to rain down on him. The suds were now starting to form large slippery puddles on the dungeon floor, but the more we tried to contain him the more he seemed to go into a frenzy with his dance moves. Inevitably after leaping about and attempting what I thought may have been a 'Sissonne' he landed in a puddle and we watched as inevitably he skidded dangerously towards the wall. Unable to remain upright, with a grunt he landed on his hip, tried desperately rolling onto his butt to save himself, slammed his head on the floor and letting out a little involuntary whimper, with a whoosh he disappeared under the bondage bed, leaving his wig like a wet dog in the centre of the floor. Within seconds he reappeared on his hands and knees but the floor was by now so slippery that we just watched as he relentlessly tried to get to his feet, looking more and more bedraggled and now sporting one false eyelash stuck under his chin and the other, half way down his back.

I stood and gingerly stepped across the floor towards the door, giving him a vicious thwack with the pony whip that caused him to grunt and the soggy eyelash to waft up into the air and then settle in a pile of soap suds. I left the room. My girl went and got him a bucket, clean cloths, mop and supervised the clean-up of the dungeon. The man was still in his leotard and on hands and knees when my girl turned to me and with a wink said, "Mistress?"

"Yes" I replied walking towards the entrance. With a nod of her head my eyes scanned the area she was highlighting. The man on hands and knees was having a problem with his leotard which had decided to allow the crutch to squeeze its way right up the crack of his arse and leave his bollocks dangling sadly, all alone with eyelash attached!

"Those suds get everywhere" she said with a laugh. I didn't even try not to laugh, but even I had to wonder where this particular fetish had formed.

if you are too young to know who Groucho Marx is, look him up

12. THE MAN IN THE BOX

It was one of those cold miserable days where all you can think of is sitting in front of a log fire in your pyjamas watching television. I'd arrived at my usual time, with Bruno in tow and a hot bacon and egg sandwich. This is the type of sandwich you like to devour on your own because you know it's going to be messy. I put the kettle on, adjusted the heating and started to read the paper.

At this time, I had a young woman working with me who for personal reasons had left her home town Manchester and was sharing a dungeon and sometimes my home with me. On this particular morning I wasn't expecting to see her until about mid-morning, as she had been out the night before. There was nothing booked in and as I scoffed my sandwich, I was anticipating a fairly easy day.

At about eleven the telephone rang and one of my regular bondage gentlemen booked an appointment. He was a very nice chap who as well as his fee, always brought me flowers, a bottle of champagne or some calf skin gloves. I had these in many styles and colours and wondered if he stitched them himself, as they were so beautifully made. He had been coming to see me since I had worked with Sheila so we were very comfortable with each other and he always treated me with the correct deference.

In my own dungeon I had several objects designed to restrain my bondage customers and as well as a cage which was a bit like a parrot cage; in as much as it had a drop down black-out cover, I had a box which was like a padded blanket box and was completely dark and quite air restrictive.

The doorbell went and I let in my gentleman and ushered him into the bathroom. I did check my watch because I had expected Carol to have arrived, but I wasn't too fussed and just got on with the job in hand. This particular customer liked to be naked and tied with a rope starting at his shoulders and then being wound around his body down to his knees. Normally it would have been down to his ankles but as there was only me to help him into the box, I felt that was being a bit ambitious. He also enjoyed restricted breathing so I used a rubber hood which only had two holes in the front, into which two tubes were pushed.

Ready for the session to start I flicked him with end of a riding crop, struggled a little getting him into the box without literally throwing him in, checked his breathing tubes and then slammed down the lid and then locking the box and then locking the dungeon door behind me, went to the kitchen to retrieve my tea. I'd just sat down when the phone went off and for a moment, I thought I had a heavy breather on the line. I was about to put the receiver down when Carols voice broke the silence with what I will call a stage whisper.

"Don't put the phone down, it's me."

"I thought you'd be here by now what's up?"

Another long silence. "Help me" ……

"Carol are you all right. What's the matter? What's going on. Where are you?"

There was another long silence and then, obviously trying not to be overheard, she explained her situation.

Though having said that, her explanation was very strange.

Apparently, she was in the bathroom of a flat or Hotel room (she wasn't sure?) With the telephone cord under the door and she had managed to lose her handbag and purse, had no idea where her shoes were, but for whatever reason she wanted to try and leave where she was, without waking the man she had awoken beside who was still soundly sleeping?

She wanted me to bring her a coat and shoes, enough money for a taxi and some breakfast. One thing I'll say for Carol was that no matter how hung over, how many pills she'd popped or even if she was on her way to bed, she could ALWAYS eat a fry-up.

I was irritated and as she didn't even know where she was, I suggested she just leave, hail down a cab and come straight to the dungeon where I could give her some money for the taxi and we could sort it out from there, but she wasn't having any of it. She started to snivel a bit and said she really wasn't up for this particular walk of shame and threw everything she had ever done for me, at me, alternating between trying to play my heart strings, to being vaguely threatening!

When I started trying to get out of it and pressed her as to her whereabouts, she sounded almost cross?

"For fucks sake Roma, how big is this town???" We were living in Brighton?

Ultimately it was decided that I would go down to the seafront in front of the 'open' pier with shoes, coat etc.

And I would wait for her there. I must stress that this was before everybody and their dog had a mobile phone so it meant that I had to stand there, until she turned up or I lost the will to live!

I sorted out a coat and shoes and shoved them into a carrier bag before grabbing the dog and heading out into a miserable grey drizzle and a biting wind. I don't drive and always walked everywhere, but on this occasion even Bruno looked askance at me. I really can't remember what time I got there but after lurking in a doorway for nearly an hour I was fed up to say the least and then I saw her.

She appeared head down battling the wind wearing a chiffon blouse that was literally stuck to her, a short skirt that seemed to have shrunk because her hold up stockings were on full view and weren't doing a very good job of holding up and no shoes so there was more hole than foot in those same hold up stockings. The temporary hair dye had left orange streaks all down her face with the rain and she had more black make-up under her eyes than she would ever have had on her lashes. In that moment however I didn't know whether to laugh or cry, because despite myself I felt so sorry for her. Without another word I pulled out the coat and wrapped it around her, dropping the shoes onto the floor for her to wriggle her toes into and managed to get a taxi instantly. I bundled her into the cab and gave the address. I saw the cab driver looking in his rear-view mirror but his expression never wavered and I wondered how often he had picked up others who had looked similar?

When we got to the dungeon Carol went straight into the shower and came out looking far more relaxed and happier in a big pink, fluffy dressing gown but I could sense that there was something on her mind. I was waiting for another revelation because she still hadn't mentioned breakfast and that meant that something else was wrong. She made herself a cup of coffee and sat down avoiding eye contact. I waited. I didn't see the point in giving her a telling off because actually what she did with her life wasn't my business and I say that kindly, not in judgement or some sense of superiority.

I had to let her tell me in her own way, but when it came, it really wasn't something I was expecting. Carol was a single lady. She worked hard and played hard and was careful about her sexual health, always using a condom if it was simply casual sex.

In this instance, as always, when it had come down to the nitty gritty she had used a condom. The problem was that when that particular coupling finished….no condom? Apparently, they were both pissed enough to believe it was somewhere in the bed sheets and actually thought it was funny, but after a bit more foreplay they had sex again…and the same thing happened. Eventually sleep put an end to anything else happening, but when Carol awoke the missing condoms were at the forefront of her memory. Apparently, she had practically taken the bed and surrounding areas apart but she couldn't find either of them and she didn't want to wake him up and risk him either wanting sex again or just shrugging his shoulders because it wasn't really his problem.

She carefully explained that she had used the shower as a douche, she had struggled to get her fingers up inside herself to have a feel and had even tried using the handle of the bog brush to see if there was anything there, all to no avail.

Our eyes met and I let out a low moan. "Really?" I asked

But she was already nodding before I'd finished the word. Feeling slightly numbed by the very thought of what she was asking me to do, I quickly got myself together and called a black cab. When it arrived, Carol didn't even bother to get dressed, she just threw a long coat on and I bundled Bruno and her into the back, locked the Flat door and almost in a stupor gave the cabby my address.

When we arrived home, I tried to busy myself, but Carol was sort of hanging around me and I realised I had better get it over and done with.

"Get me a very large, stiff drink" I said to her, "and then lay on the bed with your legs in the air!"

She gave me a really mischievous smile, went and got me the drink, which I downed in one and as she approached the bed she said, "try not to enjoy yourself too much!" Then in a movement which actually left me in awe of her suppleness, assumed the position.

It's very difficult to explain exactly how this felt but I had had three sisters and like most siblings, quite a range of topics had been whispered about after the lights went out.

I don't remember any sexual interaction, but I probably just didn't like any of them enough to have experimented in that way. The only thing akin to this was probably delivering my first lamb who was attempting, fruitlessly to be born with one leg hooked back up against the ewes' ribs. I had been amazed at the amount of space inside her womb allowing me to un-hook the leg and the lamb to be born and yes, sorry Carol, but that is what comes to mind.

She didn't help matters by saying things like, "ohm that's nice, just fiddle around there for a bit". Despite myself all of her silly remarks kept making me laugh and when I finally found a condom and fished it out, she jumped off the bed and did a victory run all around the bedroom. It was a victory but it was also a stark reminder that her suspicions had been correct and that there was another one up there, hiding in some of the funny little fleshy folds and apparently not overly willing to re-surface.

I don't know how long I was fishing around for, but I was ready to throw in the towel. Not literally of course and although she was getting more desperate, she had started to understand that if I really couldn't find it, it was a hospital job. I struggled probably for about another half hour and then demanded she get dressed, because we were off to A&E.

Like all emergency waiting rooms, by the time she had been through triage and then placed in some sort of queue, it felt like I was about to have another birthday and then suddenly a nurse called her name and she grabbed my hand and dragged me into a consulting room and then froze…

At that moment we were faced with probably the most handsome, fit specimen of masculinity, either of us had ever seen and I silently offered up a prayer thanking God that it wasn't me having to ask him to fish around and find the illusive condom. He asked all the obvious questions and as Carol answered her voice became quieter and her face became redder. When he inclined his head towards the examination couch she looked as if she were going to the gallows and as soon as she was in the right position, she screwed her eyes tight shut and left me to make the small talk. He really was a beautiful looking man and when he smiled at me and winked just before he took on the quest, my knees wobbled. There was a wicked little flicker in his eyes and when he mentioned to the nurse that he needed a light, I had to steel myself and supress the desire to laugh.

Once he started poking around, he found the offending object, removed it and then offered her a course of antibiotics and the morning after pill. I had clocked his name on his badge and made a point of using it when I thanked him on Carol's behalf. Her humiliation complete I thanked Dr Webb and we left and took a taxi home.

She made dinner and we shared a bottle of champagne, exploding into fits of laughter as we re-lived the events of the previous night and what had happened during the day. Carol was great fun and like me she could always laugh at herself. We stayed up until about midnight and then let the dog out before heading to our respective rooms.

I was tired but something in the back of my mind was plaguing me. I tossed and turned and was finally just dozing off when I sat bolt upright. A chilling reality had me wide awake and moving at a speed that would rival a greyhound. As I pulled on clothes, I called for a taxi bellowed at Carol and started heading for the door still holding one shoe. I started doing that weird God bargaining thing.

Please, God, I'll never eat chocolate ever again as long as Mr. Smith is still alive...

I had completely forgotten with all the fuss and bother with Carol, that I had locked a punter in my bondage box and then completely abandoned him. Carol threw something on over her 'jarmies' and as we headed out of the door towards the taxi I was gabbling about the danger of the situation and that our customer may have expired. As I opened the cab door Carol hesitated,

"What?" I asked.

She looked sideways at the driver and in a hushed voice asked, "should I go back and grab the chain saw?" I had no idea what she was talking about so just hauled her in beside me.

The bondage box was a multipurpose piece of equipment for varying levels of restriction. Some were just placed inside and the box would be locked. For others there were slits in the side of the box so that I could add leather straps for both the wrists and the ankles. There was also an optional strap that went around the throat, something only the very experienced sub requested.

On top of the box itself I would usually dress the sub in rubber or PVC depending on the size of the person and what is commonly known as a gimp mask. They come in several styles and I always had three or four clean and ready to use. They are usually rubber but I had had a few made in leather. I personally found the type that only has two breathing straws pushed up into the nostrils, risky and distasteful, but a lot of heavy bondage users loved them.

I think because I have a personal fear of suffocation i.e. Being starved of air whether by drowning or some other form of being denied breath, I find it difficult to understand why someone would find this type of domination pleasant, exciting, sexually arousing?? But we're not talking about my own predilections. The mask I am talking about truly restricts the air that a person can breathe in and if for some reason the straws become dislodged a person may suffer brain damage or even death if they cannot get enough air.

My man in the box was wearing such a mask. We practically threw the cab fare at the driver and then struggled against each other when we both tried to get through the flat door at the same time. We were falling over each other trying to get the dungeon door open and get over to the box but once we both stood beside it, we both hesitated.

"Can you hear anything?" She whispered. I shook my head and then with trembling fingers unlocked the box and opened the lid.

His snoring resonated around the room and as we woke him, he apologised profusely for dozing off?

Without saying anything we lifted him out, removed the mask and then unwound the rope. His lack of movement for so many hours had left him wobbly and disorientated and I am ashamed to admit that I just wanted him off the premises as quickly as was humanly possible, so I almost bullied him into getting moving and taking a shower. What is strange was that he never, ever asked about that day, even though he came on a fairly regular basis and it had been daylight when he had arrived and dark when he left?

Carol had her own explanation. She worked out how much it would have cost him if he had had to pay for the amount of hours and thought that he had decided just to keep 'schtum' rather than risk having to write us a cheque.

One would think that having a scare like that would have seared the memory into my consciousness and that it would never have happened again…but it did and not just the once!

13. 13 PUPPET ON A STRING

When I look back at the years Carol and I knew each other my strongest memories are the amount of laughs, loves and experiences we shared. She was a beautiful

looking woman, statuesque and truly confident in her abilities, but like all of us, she had her weaknesses and I often felt that her demons stalked her more than I ever realised.

She was almost viciously protective of me, family and her friends and if you were going to get into trouble, she had your back. Unfortunately, the trouble one found themselves in actually nearly always had Carol stamped all over it, but she wasn't averse to cleaning up her own mess or yours if you needed her. She came from a large

Irish Catholic family who probably wouldn't do well in that particular country because the bulk of them couldn't get their ears around any accent other than Mancunian and I confess that though I usually have a good ear for accents, when I visited Ireland, I couldn't understand most of them either. The interesting thing about her family was that they took up two streets and lived in practically every house in the row. They were all in and out of each other's kitchens or any other rooms for that matter. It used to make me laugh that if someone wanted the loo badly, they'd run along the row until they found one that was empty. Far too claustrophobic for me, but they seemed happy with it, except when it came to Christmas.

Carol needed an out and I was happy to give it to her because we had worked together in Manchester and I genuinely liked her. I have memories that can still make me laugh out loud but in all honesty most of the time 'you would have had to be there' comes to mind. She was genuinely funny and even after all these years, I miss her. The life she chose when she went back to Manchester wasn't the way I would ever have wanted to live, but like so many others our friendship fell by the wayside once she went home. I hope with all my heart that she found happiness and if she ever reads this, I want her to know she played an important part in my life and I'm a better person for knowing her.

When Carol came to work with me, she brought with her some implements and a few customers who had visited her when she had owned her own dungeon. Interestingly it was her dungeon they used in an episode of 'Cracker'. One of her customers was a very nervous man who seemed to be on the brink of a nervous breakdown every time he visited. I commented on this but she just shrugged and I guessed she was just used to him. I did question her as to what his predilections were but she thought for a moment and answered that he was into a bit of everything. I confess that I doubted her but as he never asked me to attend to him, I didn't waste much thought on him.

We were two single women when we were in Brighton and that did have the advantage that we could offer something a little different to our 'special' customers and make good money doing it. One particular day Carol came off the phone just as I had dismissed my customer and I could see the wheels turning in her head.

"What's up?" I asked.

She thought for a few minutes and then said that 'Mr Ferret' (this was the name I had given the hyper nervous customer of hers) had a few days off and wanted something special to be cooked up for him. He was taking her to Brighton races on the Saturday but was arriving Friday afternoon and she wanted something to occupy him Friday evening. After a bit of toing and froing we finally decided that he would take both of us out to dinner (there are some lovely restaurants in Brighton) but that there would be certain conditions that he had to fulfil during the course of the evening.

When he arrived, Carol showed him into the bathroom and then showed him the cage that would be his bed for the night. We shared a bedroom with en-suite facilities beside the dungeon and the room was large enough to hold two double beds. When we worked evenings or on all-nighters we always stayed at the dungeon and not my home.

Carol had asked him to present himself to us when he had showered and dried himself. When she got anywhere near him, he was twitchy to say the least, but she didn't seem to notice. The first thing she did was make him bend over and without lubricant, like lightening inserted a butt plug, which made him scoot to the opposite side of the room. Her response was to roar at him and he returned to her literally with his knees knocking. Deftly she attached the necessary straps and made sure that it would remain in situ. Then she got hold of his cock and proceeded to tie coloured ribbon around it, even I winced at how tightly she pulled in the knot and then she ran a long piece of plastic fishing line around his cock and balls and threaded it under his clothing so that she could tug on it secretly, obviously causing him pain…agony would probably be a better word but who was I to judge. When he realised that the leash of fishing line was how she could control him even at a distance of a table between them, all of the colour started to drain out of his face. Before we left, she handed him his written instructions and then painted a very graphic picture of what would happen to him, should he fail to obey her properly.

In the taxi we chatted as if he wasn't there, however Carol couldn't help giving the string an occasional little tug, just to keep him interested as we travelled towards our destination. The first show of power occurred just as we entered the restaurant. Instantly a waiter offered to take her coat and as cool as you like she said, "Hold that a minute will you" and handed the end of the string to me as she removed her coat. The waiter really wasn't sure what, if anything, had happened and after taking my own coat and Mr Ferret's, proceeded to show us to our table. This again caused some subtle problems for Mr Ferret, in as much as it was important to stay close to Carol and make sure that the waiter didn't get tangled up in his string. While they danced around each other Carol took her seat and obviously gave Mr Ferret another little pull. I say little, but obviously not to Mr Ferret, because his knees slightly buckled and the supressed scream that hit the air, actually sounded like a strangled squeak. He almost threw himself into a chair opposite Carol and next to me, and was now visibly sweating.

Our waiter looked a bit perturbed but continued as if he had noticed nothing at all except when it came to handing back the menu's. I noticed how gingerly he took the book back from Mr Ferret as if he didn't really want to touch it, but then by now there were visible droplets of sweat running down his face and stinging his eyes that even made me shuffle my chair a bit so that I wasn't in quite such close proximity.

Carol and I placed our order and a bottle of champagne, but when the waiter turned to Mr Ferret, Carol gave a dismissive waive at the waiter and said

"He will just have a glass of water"

He hesitated for just a second and then returned with the champagne in an ice bucket and the ordered glass of water, which he placed directly in front of the copiously perspiring Mr Ferret. The glass hardly had time to skim the table as he downed the water in one.

Carol glared at Mr Ferret and proceeded to order another glass, making sure that both he and the waiter knew he wouldn't be getting another one. I have noticed in similar situations how when something strange is occurring within a confined space, everybody can't see a thing and should they catch your eye a steady stare is usually enough to make them concentrate on who they are with, instead of what else may be unfurling at someone else's table.

The waiter never attempted to direct anymore questions towards Mr Ferret and was attentive enough it to be acceptable without hovering around us like a fly. Two bottles and an excellent three course dinner later, we were both enjoying ourselves and feeling far more relaxed, but Mr Ferret was obviously becoming very unhappy and I gestured to Carol with my head, to intervene.

She looked at him with a slightly irritated sneer and barked, "What?"

He looked down unable to meet her eye. "I'm so sorry mistress but I need the toilet"

Carol banged on the table with her hand. The hand that had the loop of the fishing line curled around her fingers. "Well you shouldn't have been greedy with your water, should you? Anyway, I fancy a brandy. Roma?"

I agreed, but I confess that because Carol had been drinking before we went out, I just checked my watch secretly, to keep an eye on the time we were making him wait. Four or five brandies later Carol was in an extremely convivial mood but I had decided not to indulge after the third just to keep the edge on the situation should anything go awry. By this time Mr Ferret had turned a sort of grey/blue colour and the shirt around his neck was ringing with sweat. His eyes kept dancing around the room like a trapped animal, as if looking for some way out and I felt that it was really time to call a halt. I asked for the bill and Mr Ferret practically ripped off my hand to get to the bill, obviously recognising that this was perhaps the end of his ordeal. Carol made sure that he left a hefty tip and like a cat, slowly raised herself from her chair and stretched. It was too much.

Frighteningly Mr Ferret started to physically crumble before our eyes, and so grabbing my coat I started shoving him out of the door without realising that Carol was still holding the string. He screamed. It was a sound that actually sounded as if he were being murdered. Without being able to stop what I could see unfolding before me, I watched with horror as Mr Ferret started to urinate in his trousers and then lose his balance causing him to plunge forwards down the few steps, screaming horribly as he fell towards the pavement.

I turned to Carol and hissed, "Drop it", which thankfully brought her back to life and made her drop the end of the tie which at least helped to subdue some of the gurgling yelps that Mr Ferret was unleashing. She looked down at him and then looked at me and smiled.

"Well he's not dead, is he? Not making that fucking racket"

I refrained from answering and then as if it couldn't get any worse, it did. An ambulance appeared screaming towards us with a Police car in tow. There have been times in my life where despite my obvious inclination to just kick off my shoes and leg it, under the circumstances I had to take responsibility and attempt to retrieve the situation. My story to the Police and the Ambulance paramedics bordered on the ridiculous, however if we all stuck to it, I hoped that we may just get out of this drama unscathed.

I initially just started to apologise claiming that it was actually 'Mr and Mrs Ferret' who I had joined in some sort of celebration, who had had a little bit too much to drink, but everyone was completely fine and we'd just be on our way if that was alright. It wasn't. The spotty individual who had obviously just passed his exams to become a paramedic, completely ignored my protests and dragged a trembling Mr Ferret into the back of the Ambulance and started ferreting (excuse the pun) in his clothing. Before Carol or myself could intervene, he had covered Mr Ferrets lap with a blanket and had started to remove his trousers, guessing from the animalistic groans he was making that this was the area he needed to attend to.

As if in slow motion I saw the paramedics face as he discovered the fishing line tie twisted skilfully around Mr Ferrets' meat and two veg and the pretty ribbon ties. With a slightly strangled tone he called over the policeman who also became quite pale as he looked under the blanket and then at Carol and myself. I jumped in before anyone could ask a question and in a vaguely conspiratorial tone shrugged and launched into an explanation.

"Look officer, they're both consenting adults and although WE may find it odd, they're both okay with it. It's a game…err she sees it as a…sort of puppet on a string", I stammered, "like Punch and Judy "I said shrugging.

Carol growled behind me, "there was a nosey fucking copper in that too!" She hissed.

"Ask him" I said, talking slightly louder and giving Mr Ferret a smile that suggested he had better agree. He groaned and nodded slightly, just relieved to have somebody taking care of him. The two men looked at each other and then at Mr Ferret so I jumped in, sensing that miraculously I might be being believed.

"He's embarrassed. Wouldn't you be? It was just a silly sex game that went a bit wrong, wasn't it Carol?"

Thankfully she had also sensed that we were probably about to be allowed to leave and so she consented to my explanation and tried to behave like the doting wife, clucking and gently touching Mr Ferrets brow. The policeman looked at the paramedic and gestured with a nod of his head,

"What are you going to do with that?" He asked, gesturing at the blanket.

"well, we'll go to the A&E and get it removed there. It'll probably have to be surgically removed" the paramedic said, and then seeing the look of horror on the policeman's face, he corrected the mistake. "The tie thingy, not the…." His voice faded away to nothing and the policeman took that as his que to remove himself from the ambulance and distance himself from the whole ugly scene.

We travelled in the back of the ambulance and soon arrived at A&E. Despite wanting to go home as soon as possible we were now committed to the rubbish I had cooked up and as Mr Ferret was actually staying with us, we were duty bound to stay at the Hospital until we could get him home.

As always there was the endless wait although Mr Ferret had been whisked away immediately when the staff had heard what had happened to him. I assume that they wanted to remove the tie before the pressure made his cock drop off?

We had been there about an hour when a junior Doctor appeared and said that the offending object had been removed and that Mr Ferret was being discharged as we spoke. When the ferret sheepishly, Carol caught hold of his arm and started leading him to the doors leading to the outside. We had nearly reached the exit when a voice as smooth as silk called, "Mrs Ferret?"

We turned and like a knight on a white charger, Dr Webb strode forwards holding a little prescription bag.

"Oh, hello", he purred, "We meet again!"

Without a shadow of a doubt the nice Doctor Webb had obviously remembered the lady with the lost condom. Now, to add to the already distorted view he had of Carol, he now thought she was married to a man who actually looked like a ferret, and with whom she played rather odd sex games.

Her smile froze and after exchanging a few pleasantries so as not to appear rude she almost dragged Mr Ferret to the exit.

As she hit the pavement, she decided to open the rather heavy prescription bag and instead of finding a large tube of soothing cream, she had been given back the butt plug, nicely washed and dried.

I trotted along behind, a whole load of thoughts bouncing around in my head. I could not believe that I had actually got away with such a ridiculous explanation, but there was something that I could believe with very little prompting. Mr Ferret, once he was better, was definitely going to pay!!

14. HIT BURNT HAIR

As I mentioned before, we were invited to visit fetish clubs and parties all over Europe and the USA, with Germany being the leader worldwide in clubs for the S & M scene. I hadn't realised until we got another invitation via email, that Carol had actually never taken up the offer of one of these invites. She had received them but I think as she was an unknown quantity to the promotors and vise-versa, she had decided that she wouldn't go.

Well we fancied we deserved a night off, or on, depending on how you look at things and it was actually really nice to be going with a fellow Dominatrix instead of taking a slave. The budget included a maid which was great because it meant that he got lumbered with the cases etc and making sure all of the hand implements were packed. It is odd but we all get used to certain implements, as if they become moulded to the shape of your hand, but one has to limit how much baggage you take with you. In the early years I had tried to take too many things with me and had, to my anoyance ended up leaving some of them behind. With a maid it was his responsibility to see that everything we brought with us,, in which case left with us, so it was a more relaxed feel to the evening.

Shopping for a new outfit for Carol and my maid was fun and although I was starting to get a bit tired of all the questions, it was nice to see how excited they both were and regardless of it being just one of many dates that I had covered, their mood was infectious.

We arrived in Berlin at around 8.30 in the evening and took a taxi to our Hotel. It was nice and comfortable and we all decided that we would have dinner in the Hotel restaurant rather than wander the streets looking for somewhere to eat. After dinner we had a few drinks at the bar and then retired to bed saying goodnight to our maid who had a single room on the same floor and then proceeded to enter the room we were sharing. Carol was one of those people who climbs into bed (if she is on her own) lays her head on the pillow and instantly starts gentle snoring. However on this particular night Carol was sitting up in bed with a book in her hands.

"What are you reading ?" I asked trying to see the cover of the book.

She held up the book for me to see and I was a little surprised that it was a German phrase book. I had already told her that practically everyone in Germany spoke English but she explained that she had taken the language whilst at school and had actually advanced enough to take an exam in it. I confess that I was impressed. I too had studied German at school but in my case the word studied wasn't even remotely applicable. I don't think that I had ever learnt how to do more than count to ten and use the phrase, "this is a chair"!

I would have to agree that this is probably the most useless phrase ever. To any normal person they would be able to see that it was a chair, unless of course they were an alien and if they were an alien I really don't think we would be discussing chairs?

Either way my enquiry seemed to have both started a conversation and ended it in the same breath. She turned over and snuggled under the covers ready to sleep and I decided to do the same.

When invited to these types of gatherings there were different roles the Mistresses and Masters could take. A lot of the German contingent were happy to sit on thrones and get served their drinks etc and do very little. I had learned early on that if you made the effort to pick out someone and used them as a showcase for your abilities, the next time you got paid more, affluent mashcocist's would fly over to attend your dungeon for a private session and you gained a reputation that actually meant you didn't have to work too hard and could end up enjoying yourself.

We spent the day wandering around the shopping precincts, enjoying the buzz of being in a foreign city. It was a beautiful warm day and it was lovely to be outside, sipping champagne at lunch, watching the world go by. I've always been a 'people watcher' and I can happily waste hours just being in my own head watching peoples body language and facial expressions. Sheila had said it was my study of other people that made me a good Dominatrix and I think she was probably right.

As the day wore on and evening beckoned so I helped my maid into his corset and did his make-up and wig. On these sorts of occasions I relaxed a little with the maid or slave, so that whole experience was more 'bonded'. It was good to prepare for the evening in a relaxed manner and to take our time so that we looked 'perfect'.

There is obviously an underlying sexual atmosphere at these types of party/club and it is not uncommon to witness certain acts with an extremely sexual bias as well as full penerative sex. In many cases the people attending are not looking for a mistress or master but have come with a partner and just enjoy the 'scene', enjoy exhibitionism, or are just curious and open minded about what goes on in this type of club. There is usually an area, always with dim lighting, where those who wish to induge in overt sexual play or penetrative sex are pointed towards by the promoters staff. I do not criticise when saying this, but in all honesty for every one Dominatrix dabbling in sexual voyerism/exhibitionism there will be at least 4 Masters doing likewise. Many Masters are Homosexual which means that generally there is a more promisicuous element to the relationship. I say this without prejaudice, but I have always beleived that the male brain IS attached to his cock and that it is because women say no, that men don't have a different partner everytime they have/want sex. Put together two males who are attracted to other males and the thinking is alike, hence the more partners most gay men will have experienced to the amount of partners the average woman has in her lifetime.

I have met Masters who admit that although they seriously love female submissives, very few women are willing to pay for the experience and so if they are to make a living 'on the scene', they have to accept that the bulk of their patrons will be male.

One of the things I pointed out to Carol was that if she wanted to go and have a look at this area of the club, it's not something I frown upon, but to be careful where she steps, as the floor can be exceptionally slippery!!

Carol was happy to take my lead and when we arrived (at least an hour after the club had opened and at least one bottle of champagne down) we were greeted with an actual fanfare. We had been advertised as ' very experienced and coming from the UK', so a Line of exceptionally fit men, dressed as slaves with washboard stomachs and oil all over them, lined our entrance and as we descended down into the belly of the club the waves of humanity parted to let us through. I could see Carol was not just impressed but ready and willing to play her part. When we felt comfortable and had been purchased a couple more drinks we were ready to join in. One of my party pieces was to pick out a hairy male and to set alight to his body hair, making sure I used my gloved hand to stop the flame reaching his head. It looked really impressive but providing you picked the right man who had a gap between his body hair and his head hair, it really wasn't dangerous but appeared quite dramatic. The flame once lit, would literally climb up the back like a forest fire and would leave the area completely devoid of hair, without burning the individual.

Carol and I got on with our own showcase of talent and were rewarded with submissives grovelling about our feet begging to be chosen. We were in an area used for Mistresses and Masters to show off their abilities, similar to an arena and of course we were not the only ones putting on a show. We alternated between the 'show-ring' where we gave demonstrations and milling about the club seeing what else was going on. Carol went onto the dance floor but ultimately kept tripping over the slaves who kept throwing them selves at her feet. She got fed up with keep kicking them in the head because it also affected her balance, so gave up and we went to the bar instead. Having relaxed for a while, both of us were thinking about calling it a night, but we wandered back to the arena with the idea that we would both perform one last attention grabber.

I gave a spirited demonstration with a collection of canes and then finished with a sponsored nipple piercing. (I had trained in this but would never have done it publicly in the UK)

Carol looked on smiling, vaguely casting around for somebody to use in her final demonstration. A quite tall, attractive male approached Carol and after a few words she came over to me. She introduced him as ,"Treffen sie verbranntes harr" meaning 'please meet Mr Bernard' and proudly used the German language for the introduction. I saw a seconds hesitation on behalf of Mr Bernard but he obviously changed his mind about deciding to say something and he allowed her to clip on his lead. Immediately she had him drop to his knees to lick her boots and my own before deciding what else she would do to him. Mr Bernard was a very hairy individual, the type of hairy that I would probably have avoided in view of the amount of champagne I had swallowed, but I wasn't really concentrating because I had felt I had done enough. From when we entered we had been busy for well over an hour at a time and had alternated between the ring and the rest of the club. I decided to take a breather and grabbed a gentleman and posed him correctly so I could sit on him and give my feet a rest. My Stilleto boots were not uncomfortable but I had spent a long time on my feet, what with the earlier shopping and being busy most of the evening. Mr Bernard was on his knees with Carol standing astride him and I watched as our maid handed Carol a small bowl of ice cubes. Almost casually, Carol started feeding Mr Bernards arsehole with ice cubes which was causing a little bit of interest from the assembled crowd.

I confess that I invariably ignore the orifice at the back end because despite how clean the gentleman is, it doesn't stop his arse from behaving in an unpredictable way. I have a very strong stomach when it comes to most things and I have always picked up my own dogs pooh, but human faeces and it's smell immediately affects my gag reflex. Carol, on the other hand had an even weaker gag reflex, but didn't seem to associate stuffing things up mens arseholes with what would normally come down an arsehole? I had been caught out a few times by discovering pooh on an object that had been retrieved from a mans rectum. It always totally disgusted me, so I decided that playing with bums wasn't on my list of practices on offer.

Carol, having fed the last cube in with a flourish, almost bounced onto his back, mimicing my own seating arrangement. I did say earlier that Carol was quite a 'big girl' and as she plonked down on the gentleman, the shock of the sudden weight landing on him made him expell a sort of cough come huff!

To add to the moment he instantly farted as she landed on him and I watched fascinated as ice cubes shot out of his arse like a machine gun with incredible speed. In a split second one hit another mistress on her cheek as she worked on the other side of the arena. Instantly she realised what was happening and dived behind a pillar to avoid being hit again, leaving her submissive to bear the brunt. Carol and I exchanged glances but decided the best tactic was to ignore it. I had to stifle a laugh, as did she, especially when we noticed that there was quite a gap in the crowd directly behind Mr Bernard's bottom. Confident as always, once the hub-bub had subsided a little, Carol stood up to her full height, jerked Mr Bernard into an upright position and before anyone realised, had set alight to the hair on his back, starting at the crack of his arse. As I mentioned earlier, it's quite important that one concentrates on the job in hand when performing this trick, but her delay as she used the flame to light a cigarette had the flames climbing his back, his neck and then onto his head before she had even dragged on her ciggi!

Panic? well I'm unsure who panicked more, him or Carol, but thankfully an alert submissive threw his pint of beer over the poor man leaving him in a cloud of smoke, dripping with beer and minus hair on his back, neck and a large streak over the top of his head and no eyebrows!!

Without waiting I stood up and bellowed at him to go down onto his knees and thank the Mistress for her time and her attention. For a moment I thought he was going to blow his top, but I think that the amount of people surrounding us saved the day and slowly, his eyes burning into my own and a slight twitch pulsing at the corner of his mouth, he did as he was told and lowered his head to the floor. I said a silent prayer that we were in an area without mirrors.

As casually as possible we signalled to our maid and left the arena and climbed the stairs to the exit. Somebody sourced a taxi for us almost immediately and once safely ensconced in its interior the laughing started. When we reached our destination we piled out with tears streaming down our faces and left the maid to deal with the fare, (our entourage were always given money to cover these sorts of expences). In our room the whole thing was acted out between us accommpanied by more shrieks of laughter and more tears.

When the mirth finally died down a little, our maid asked Carol what seemed like a rather odd question, "Did you know that was going to happen...in view of your introduction?" he asked.

We looked at each other and back to the maid as Carol slowly shook her head. The maid realised that an explanation was in order.

'Well I speak German fairly well and you didn't get it quite right if you didn't actually mean you were going to do that?" He noted the confusion on Carols face and asked, "what did you think you said? "

Carol shrugged and said, 'Please meet Mr Bernard ? "

" Ah, well in that case what you should of said is, 'Bitte treffen sie herrn Bernard ', but what you actually said was, 'Treffen sie verbrannts haar '"

Carol shrugged , "Well what does that mean ? "

The maids smile twitched, "You said, Hit burnt hair! "

I was still giggling when I drifted off to sleep.

15. BOIL IN THE BAG

The balance Carol and myself made for a good working relationship and flat mates was complimetary. So many things suited us both, we laughed at the same things and cried together when something hurt either or both of us. We were comfortable in the knowledge that we looked after each other without poking around in eachothers private business unless it was invited.

There was a substantial difference between the two of us and that was when it came to indulging ourselves during our private down time. Carol had me waiting in the wings when it came to alcohol and drugs. She could start with a couple of joints and a few glasses of wine whilst getting ready and from there on there was no boundries to her indulgence and she had a bottomless capacity to embibe.

To my shame, more than once she gently looked after me whilst I had to put my face down the toilet bowl or lost my legs on the way home, but one of the reasons I became a Dominatrix is because I like to be in control. I can, hand on heart never remember an evening where I became so intoxicated on anything, that I didn't know where I was or how to get home. I may have forgotten the specifics of the journey but like a homing pidgeon I couldn't 'let go' until I was safely tucked up in bed. There was always that point where mentally I drew back and I would essentially start sobering myself up so that I felt more in control. I have also had a life-long hatred of throwing up and what it entails and there were times when I would take the dog out at stupid o'clock with a packet of frozen peas stuffed down my top to help me sober up. There is nothing like frozen boobs to concentrate the mind rather than take the risk of trying to lie down and the room starting to spin. At times two of my dogs, if I grabbed the leads while it was still dark, would run and hide under the bed determined that if I felt the need that was fine, they just weren't coming with me!

As mentioned previously, Carol was what one might call 'statuesque' and I think I am correct in saying she was probably about 5' 7 or 8" so she liked her men BIG. She had a particular love of big, strong, hands and wasn't attracted to 'submissivre' men when it came to her private life. One of the things I teased her about was the delicious Dr Webb at Brighton Hospital A & E, who must of been at least 6' 3", was exceptionally good looking in a 'James Bond' sort of way and had hands like soft shovels, with long, strong fingers.

Carol had gone home for a weekend to Manchester but returned on the Sunday, instead of her usual slot around 11am on Monday. She would normally return with a raging thirst and a pocket full of stories about her weekend. I was relaxing on my bed with a book and dogs wrapped around me when I heard her key in the lock and checked my watch. Thankfully, in view of the way the evening panned out I was exceptionally grateful that I had already eaten. It was early evening and as she came through the door with her case, I thought she looked rather pained and was moving strangly. She gave me a cursery hello and then went straight to her room, coming out minutes later and going into the bathroom and closing the door behind her. This in itself was strange. Both of us were in the habit of bathing or having a shower with the door open, so that we could chat during our ablutions. I could hear the bath running and then the sound of groaning once the taps had been turned off. For a few moments there was complete silence and then a splash followed by a string of expletives. I got off the bed, tapped on the bathroom door and gingerly stuck my head into the room enquiring if everything was alright. The hot water and the steam had turned her face crimson but the expression, with her teeth clenched together had me really quite worried. I gently tried to ask what was wrong and tentatively entered the room and sat on the lid of the toilet hoping she would explain.

"Oh Roma," she moaned, "there's something wrong with my bum".

Without thinking I found myself trying to peer around her to look at her arse.

"It's so painfull, but I just can't see what's wrong. I thought a hot bath might help but I don't really know what's there? And I just can't take the pain".

My heart sank. Carol was funny, gregarious, a really good Dominatrix and kind as well as beautiful, but she was absolute rubbish around any form of pain. When we had first started working together I had put her on Evening Primrose Oil for her PMT and had then purchased a mammoth supply of Buscopan for period pain. Carol's PMT was unbelieveable. I had never knowingly suffered from it, but if I had I would have hoped someone would have done for me what I did for her. In honesty if I hadn't done something about it I probably would of murdered her. When she started to be hormonal her mood was aggressive, confrontational, angry and a couple of times I was actually a little nervous around her. She was a big girl and could of bounced me into the next world without effort. Initially she wasn't that happy about me insisting she take the tablets until I stepped in and practically held her down until she had swallowed them. I was grasping at straws when I purchased the Evening Primrose oil but the change was phenominal. It was like living with the 'nice Carol' all the time and interestingly she admitted that she was much happier and more serene since she had started taking it. During the whole time period we lived and worked together, she took her pills every day, for which I was grateful.

When she had lifted herself out of the bath, gingerly dried her nether regions and laid on her bed with her legs in the air, I instantly saw the problem. She had a huge black and red boil type of thing next to the opening of her arsehole squashed between her bum cheeks, which looked very sore and was almost pulsating. She spotted a look of worry cross my face and instantly started badgering me to tell her what was wrong and to do something about it. I explained what I was looking at and suggested we head for A & E, but after much protestation on her part I fetched a bowl of hot water with TCP in it, a wadge of cotton wool and gingerly tried to bathe it into exploding. Her screams were frightening and I was seriously worried about what the neighbours might make of it. After an unsuccessful hour of trying to make it burst with more and more hot water and TCP, with her shrieking and tears rolling down her face, I literally threw in the towel. The agony the boil was causing had finally beaten her into submission and she dressed without underwear and sort of hovvered over the taxi seat as we went to the A & E.

When we approached the desk, Carol just stared at me with baleful eyes so in hushed tones I explained to the lady on the desk what was the problem. I noted that the woman did exactly what I had done, which was a slight lean forward and round, as if she actually expected to see something visible on Carols bottom through her clothing. It must just be a human-being's curiosity and the subliminal instinct to try to see what it is that is being talked about. Carol noticed it too and looked back at the woman with mildly disguised hatred and I remember thinking, 'thank goodness she's on Evening Primrose oil!'.

I smiled at the lady apologetically and almost in an aside she leaned towards me and said, "It must be very painful?"

Carol snapped back having heard what the woman had said, "It is, so instead of fucking about, perhaps I could see a Doctor?... Please do NOT ask me to sit down "

The lady on the desk literally wound her neck in and vaguely gestured at the waiting room which was chocca-block with bodies spouting blood, dribbling drink, talking to inanimate objects in madness and screaming children. I have had to attend various A & E departments in different places and I have always been perturbed that there never seems to be any 'normal' people there. What is it about Hospitals that brings out all of the 'odd people?' I'm so grateful that whilst growing up I never became enamoured of the idea of becoming a nurse, 'because I wanted to help people'??? Give me a straight forward pervert any day!

Something had obviously been said about Carol's problem and had caused various members of the staff to decide that if they were going to have a giggle it would be better to see it in the flesh, so to speak. Within a very short time of Carol shuffling about glaring at people, a nurse appeared and called Carol's name. She immediately grabbed my hand before following and in a strange way I was quite glad. Having looked the problem in the eye so to speak, I was quite interested to know what they intended to do about it.

Carol stood during triage and we were then shown to a cubicle where the nurse asked her to remove her underwear, climb onto the bed and wait for the Doctor in a sort of kneeling position. When the nurse left, she was kneeling with her arse in the air and a sort of paper sheet over her, with her head down resting on her arms. In all honesty I had never seen her look so miserable, to a point where I moved closer to her and gently held her hand. She glanced up at me and gave me a wan smile just as the door opened and Dr Webb strode into the room.

"Good evening Carol," he said, "what have you got for me this evening?" For a split second it crossed my mind that it was amazing that he could recognise her from that specific angle, until common sense clicked in and I realised he would have seen her notes.

She raised her head slightly and despite myself I found that I had started to smile at her next comment. With a huge sigh she said, "Don't you ever take time off?"

The Doctor and I shared a grin. "Now, now Carol", he intoned. "Don't be like that. I'm here to serve".

In my own head I answered, 'oh no you're not. Not in the way we mean anyway!'

Bending for a better view he let out a sort of whistle between his teeth. "Hmm that's a beauty! Have you been constipated recently?"

Carol looked at me with pleading eyes. I shrugged, "I don't know?" I said lamely, "Have you?"

She looked away and with a tiny voice said 'yes'.

Dr Webb started to pull on some rubber gloves and went to the door and called for a nurse. When she arrived, they both donned rubber aprons and put on safety goggles. To be honest I was starting to feel that maybe I should have been offered protection too as they approached her nether regions with what looked like trepidation. The nurse proffered a small kidney dish and held it against Carols flesh at arm's length as I watched Dr Webb unleash a brand-new sparkling scalpel. I must have looked on with an expression giving rise to anxiety, because Carol looked at me with fear in her eyes and said, "What?"

As she did, the Doctor moved forward knife in hand and Carol let out a blood curdling scream and squeezed my hand with such ferocity that I thought she was breaking my fingers. I also started to squeal loudly and both the

Doctor and the nurse looked at both of us with an air of anticipation, as if they expected Carol to leap off the bed and wrestle the knife away from him, whilst I flattened the attending nurse with a karate punch.

The boil unleashed its anger in an explosion of pus and blood and the smell was so awful that despite myself I wretched.

In the silence that followed I watched as Carol almost seemed to deflate with relief and I checked that I could still bend my fingers. I wasn't initially listening as I watched the disgusting pus oozing into the kidney dish whilst holding my nose, until I caught something about having to do that every day and heard Carol say, "Roma can do that".

Dr Webb turned to me and smiled as he gently poked and prodded what had turned into quite a large hole on Carole's bottom.

"It's a fissure caused by straining to use the toilet. The faeces become hard and impacted and where the patient is pushing, it causes a small tear in the wall of the anal canal," he explained. "When it tears, a small amount of…err pooh, seeps into the tear and causes a nasty abscess. The resulting puss has to go somewhere, so the bacteria extends the canal to release the build-up of toxins hence it erupts very close to the anal opening. Eventually it would of burst on its own but unless it is drained properly the abscess can keep returning or the problem of septicaemia rears its ugly head."

I couldn't help but glance at Carol when he used the phrase about ugly heads, but I controlled myself and said nothing.

"You can understand," he continued, "why it's important that it is kept clean and dry and that it has to be packed daily with the antiseptic gauze I'm going to give you." He must have noticed my facial expression because he followed with, "If you want, we can send around a district nurse every day?" but Carol was having none of it. In a firm voice she politely refused anybody else fiddling around near her arsehole and assured Dr Webb that I would be happy to help out my friend and do the honours. After a reasonable wait I was given a carrier bag full of dressing packs, plastic tweezers, sterile wipes and rubber gloves, which I refrained from mentioning that we always kept plenty of at home.

Once I got used to gently pushing a sort of tube impregnated with iodine into the hole left by the fissure it really wasn't that bad, providing I didn't allow my brain to fully acknowledge that I was staring at Carol's arsehole. It was surprising how long it took before it completely healed but eventually it did. Carole asked me one day towards the end of treating her, "Do you think it will cause a scar?"

I frowned. "Probably I suppose, but I don't think it will affect you wearing a bikini or anything like that?"

She grinned. "Did I say Thank you for looking after this for me?" she asked. "There was no way I was saying yes to someone from the Hospital to come and pack it. It might have been him?"

She didn't need to tell me who she meant.

"They were going to send a district nurse, "I said, "The Doctor wouldn't be the one to come here and do it. He's a Doctor. Do you think he trained for seven years so he could come out and dress your arsehole?"

She shrugged, "Hmm, well it would be just my luck that in this instance he volunteered" she said. "Let's be honest, every time I have had to go to A & E who do I get? You can't tell me he isn't making sure that he treats me and not some other Doctor doing it. He doesn't work in that department on his own, does he?"

I slowly shook my head.

"Well are you telling me that you don't think there's some sort of connection there?"

I burst out laughing, "what sort of connection?"

"Well you know. I think he wants to get to know me properly. Thinks there's more to me than meets the eye"

"I'll tell you what he has found out about you, "I laughed, "you're full of shit!"

Despite herself she started to laugh as well. We were good mates who probably went above and beyond for each other. Even after all these years I can think back to moments we shared and find myself actually laughing out loud at a memory of when we were together. It was funny then and still is. I hope she is happy. She should be if life does reward those who deserve it.

Carol. I salute you!

16. DARK SARCASM IN THE CLASSROOM

After Carol went home, I never again worked with solely one person. I had various ladies and two gentlemen come to me for training and they paid for the privilege. They learnt how to run a dungeon, use the implements, keep the books, learn the law and how to earn a living doing something that you actually have to love, if you're going to make a success of it.

During this period, I met a man who stole my heart and then most of the money in my Bank account. He was damaged goods with a hang up about why his mother left the family home when he was young. He didn't trust women, either consciously or not, so he went through life hurting them before he could get hurt. To my shame there was such a sexual chemistry with him that I ignored all the warning bells going off in the back of my head and was stupid enough to marry him. I'm not completely sure, because once something is done with, I see no point in labouring over it, but I think we lasted less than two years. In total I had 3 legal husbands' during my lifetime and two long term relationships, but when it came to love I am no different from anybody else. I have loved and been loved and I have broken my heart and maybe broken someone else's heart. That side of my life is just a story that possibly you could apply to your own life. Up's and downs, laughter and tears. Nothing special.

When I didn't have a trainee working with me, I had a couple of ladies who I could call upon to work alongside me as well as a maid. Initially it was a bit of an unsettling time and I had a lovely girl come to work with me who turned out to be a raging alcoholic. Not good for business. Another woman I interviewed was so obviously a man but refused to acknowledge it, that I decided I wouldn't be comfortable around her. A lady who was a dwarf who discovered that she could make a fortune laying on her back only once or twice a day because there is a recognised fetish for wanting to bonk someone who was born with achondroplasia and many other weird and wonderful human beings who help make up the diversity of our planet.

About once every 6 months I would do a school day, where the rest of the dungeon was closed and a school room was set out by me with exercise books, inkwells and quills (a type of pen made from a bird's feather) blotting paper and test papers. School days were actually a lot of hard work for me, but I had gained a reputation as being, possibly the best Mistress at this type of domination, in this country and abroad. School was held in the garage which was attached to the main building by a walled courtyard.

I had travelled around second hand shops, auctions etc. so that I could purchase proper school desks and a real sliding blackboard. 'Pupils' had to arrive ready for lessons sharply at 8am. Any lateness wasn't tolerated and late comers forfeited the right to be spanked. That sounds strange but of course this is probably the way the readers mind works as against the way a 'caners' mind works. If I didn't have rules the whole day could fall into a type of anarchy, which would mean I didn't make my money and the punters wouldn't come back. My school days were so popular that I no longer had to advertise them and had a waiting list of probably about 30 people at any one time.

My school was girls only. In the past I had tried a mixed school but ultimately, with the amount of preparation involved and the underlining sexual aspect that this brought to the table, I had decided it wasn't something I wanted to do.

The 'pupils' usually started to arrive around 7am and my maid and a 'helper' shepherded people through the shower, dressing rooms and handed out filled satchels with their Girls names in the name plate, in preparation of the day ahead.

Just like any school, uniform had to be worn and as an extra they were expected to bring with them PE kit and plimsolls. Anyone who couldn't do PE had to bring a note and the lesson was held in the courtyard regardless of the weather. There was a morning break where every pupil was given a drink of milk taken outdoors unless raining and lunch consisted of something like mashed potatoes (with lumps in), fish fingers and peas followed by tapioca with a blob of jam in the centre. All meals were served more tepid than hot, a tribute to my own school days. For the school day we used the large Kitchen as a dining hall. Using pasting tables and small stools we could seat 8 comfortably or ten at a push. During break times we had sectioned off a portion of the courtyard with my garden shed which for the day had a sign saying bicycles on it and if anyone wanted to smoke, this area was where they took a chance of doing so, hoping not to get caught by the 'assistant teacher'. It was these little things that made a school day so popular with the punters. We rang a bell to signal end of break and the day finished at around 4pm. Mornings consisted of English before break and PE after. Then lunch followed by mathematics, a short break and then a test. The test would be set with a range of questions covering English, Math, History and Geography and there would be punishment metered out with no specific regularity, to keep things interesting.

One of my customers who never showed an interest in any other type of S & M had in fact been a teacher at a grammar school for over 20 years and he told me that my attention to detail and the quality of the exam questions were what brought him back every time. He had even been to Spain for two weeks' holiday at a 'Boarding School', run by an English Mistress who had located abroad, but he said that though it had been 'interesting', he wouldn't be going again. He never explained why and I was far too polite to ask. When he had missed the date of a day pending, he was desperate to be included and tried all sorts of bribery to be allowed to attend. As I liked him and he was a good customer I squeezed him in at the last minute.

As I mentioned, when I did a school day, I closed the shop for transvestites and the dungeon because of the amount of work involved. I no longer advertised because they had been so successful that all I needed to get customers was word of mouth and regulars but leading up to a day, people fought to be included. There appeared to be nothing different on this particular school day to any other. I was working in Manchester so like every day in Manchester, it was raining. I knew all of the participants, 12 in all and there were no issues regarding lack of uniform, PE kit, plimsolls etc.

As there was 12, we split them into 2 groups of 6, with myself taking one group and Margaret taking the other.

Margaret was a lovely lady who had the first pair of green eyes that I had ever seen. She came from Northern Ireland and was an ex scrub nurse who had worked in Ireland during the troubles. She had 3 grown up children, a cat and worked for me part time. She was as competent as I was in all aspects of our work but couldn't dole out punishment. She completely understood that some people wanted it but she didn't want to do it herself and her miscreants were brought to me so that I could do the honours.

If I remember correctly it was just after lunch when there was a rather insistent knock on the shop doors. Margaret saw a man in a suit peering through the glass doors and automatically went and opened them. As she did so, a blue van slid open its side door and with what looked like as many as 10 police officers all trying to get out of the van at once, with some vicious elbowing and pushing they almost fell out of the van and charged the front door. As they proceeded into the shop Margaret watched as two more vehicles spewed policemen all over the pavement and whilst some appeared to be running around to cover the back door, the bulk of them squeezed into the shop, through the connecting door and into what appeared to be 2 classrooms.

I so wish I had had a camera to photograph the expression on the faces of the two detectives and the rabble in blue, as they stared at grown men sitting at their desks with pen and paper, wearing little, navy skirts, white shirts and school ties. Wigs were plaited into single and double pigtails, pony tails with the odd 'bob'. It was difficult to decide out of the two groups who looked more surprised?

It was as if there was a game of statues being played out, with everybody frozen into position, until my maid for that day strode over to the detectives, removing his wig as he approached and said extremely calmly,

"I'm their solicitor. Warrant please?"

Margaret didn't hesitate. She clapped her hands and said, "girls take five minutes in the garden please?" and after only a moment's hesitation some filed out of the back door, across the courtyard and took shelter in the garage. Others slipped downstairs with me and lingered in the dressing room whilst I got back upstairs hoping my sudden absence hadn't been noticed. As the searches began officers were followed around to make sure that they searched but didn't plant anything. The warrant stated that they were looking for evidence of a disorderly house i.e. a brothel, but there were no condoms on the premises, even in my private quarters, no money (people paid up front before the day so it had all been banked) other than a float in the register and no makeshift bedrooms or cubicles. It was obvious that the bedroom's upstairs were in my private quarters and the policemen didn't appear to be enjoying themselves very much, especially the policeman who had been sent upstairs and returned with my old Chihuahua hanging off his trouser leg growling her head off.

Interestingly, despite heading off downstairs, they didn't find the door, half disguised by a curtain to the dungeon; but my instinct was that they really didn't want to hang about or suffer the embarrassment, of asking men in schoolgirl uniform to move out of their way. As they regrouped shaking their heads at their superiors they all looked like they wanted to be anywhere else but on my premises...!

The detectives had read me my rights and insisted that I accompany them back to the station. Just to be bloody minded they insisted on handcuffing me and placed me in the back of a police van with the slide looking into the cab closed, in case I reached through and grabbed a policeman by the throat and took him hostage???

How I was meant to achieve this with my hands secured behind my back? I cannot begin to understand, especially as it was taking me all of my effort just to stay sitting on the bench instead of sliding off and finding myself rolling around the floor of the van until we got to our destination. The driver was almost throwing the van around and of course the position of the handcuffs prevented me from hanging on.

Just before I had been loaded into the van, Mr Lewis had stood on the doorstep still in uniform, wig in hand and shouted to me,

"No Comment. I'll be with you soon as I've got this lot off". He was absolutely true to his word.

As far as I am aware there are no laws against adults of either sex dressing up as schoolgirls and taking mock exams, providing they are not doing this with actual underage schoolgirls? and even that scenario could be a tricky one for prosecutors to handle?

I wasn't charged and was bailed to appear in two months' time, which never happened because I was never charged with anything. Mr Lewis drove me home at about 9pm and I was taken aback that all bar two of my schoolgirls, were waiting for me as well as the policeman who had been stuffed into the dungeon in his school uniform, when I had realised what was happening. The other schoolgirls who had seen my signal and followed me down, had deliberately placed their chairs in front of the door behind the curtain in the hopes that the coppers didn't want to move them. My policeman who we had rescued, was obviously very grateful and relieved that we had acted so quickly.

His only comment about his superiors said it all.

"Pricks"

17.   NO SUGAR CANE

Two points I would like to make here, just to clear up a few myths about my world. Men interested in the school scenario or even just S & M were NOT all ex public school boys, neither were they all Judges, MP's, bankers and the like. People into S & M do literally come from ALL walks of life and though I personally did have a Judge, an MP, and a police commissioner plus a few Councillors on my lists, but I also had bin men, builders of various levels, shop workers, actors etc. There really isn't a 'typical' customer. If you can imagine it, somebody somewhere is selling it and making a living out of it, and that is a fact.

I personally can spot a submissive from 200 yards, no matter what 'cloak' he's wearing.

The other myth I am about to de-bunk is for those already on the scene and who would like to try the cane, but don't because of marks. Being whacked with a cane is a very specific experience and should only leave 'stripes' if the customer requests it. I could apply the cane in such a way that the cheeks of the buttocks turned scarlet for about an hour after the spanking without leaving any marks at all. I do believe that all 'caners' would actually like to see in the mirror, evidence of what they have endured. Taking the cane is one of the most painful forms of punishment there is. When I was a school it was still common practice to be given the cane for certain infractions, either across the hand or on the back of the legs. When told that a caning was imminent the child was asked where they wanted to receive it. No more than three strikes were allowed by the school authorities, but I witnessed a boy at my junior school who received five on the back of his thighs and marks were left. I too received the cane on two occasions. Once across the palm of the hand and because to me it was excruciatingly painful; the next time it came up I chose the backs of my legs, on my calves. In both instances I received one strike but if I concentrate, I can still feel the sting and because I have experienced it, I have a healthy respect for 'caners'.

The average appointment in the dungeon was an hour or an hour and a half, but there were short term stays that could be as little as fifteen or twenty minutes. These were mostly the 'caners' because they usually rushed in, paid, bared their bottoms and were savagely caned until they apologised for their weakness and left. Caners often brought their own implements and I too discovered that different lengths and weights produced different marks. A good Mistress can use a cane without leaving any mark other than that which will fade in about half an hour, she can also flay the skin of the arse presented to her.

These little appointments were extremely lucrative but surprisingly tiring. The art is to start as a tap, working up to striking and then speeding up the gap between each strike whilst becoming gradually harder. It takes on a sort of rhythm that should not be interrupted. Some of my customers made my arms ache for about an hour afterwards and I confess that more than once I kept eyeing the clock working on the basis that if he didn't give up, time would!

Pouring scorn on my victim and at times making them egg me on could sometimes shorten the amount of arm ache I was left with. It did not escape my intellect that the service I was giving was actually pretty painful for me. Repetitive strain injury I think it's called?

The cane can be used almost like a 'tickling stick' being wielded very gently and producing a sort of gentle vibration against the skin. It is an implement that handled with skill, can produce a huge variety of levels and there are different lengths and weights to produce different results. A lot of Dominatrix grab hold of a cane and just plough in, or others have been shocked by the amount of damage they have unwittingly caused and then never put any force behind it because they are scared. This isn't what the active caner wants and although this implement was one of the hardest for me to learn, once you have learned how to use it, there is then the range of results it can produce. A Dominatrix that understands and handles the medium can earn a great deal of money. I met a lady who had paid her dues as a Mistress and had chosen to retire, however because the caners, generally don't need 'the look' or the atmosphere of the dungeon, she supplemented her pension with periodic 'regulars' who had been going to her for years.

A great many caners are proud of their stripes and it always amused me how at the end of a school day the patrons would show off their welts with pride to each other. A large proportion of caners were married and so it was rare that they could be marked, however I think every single one of them, without exception would try to pay for magnificent holidays for their spouses, with a girlfriend of their choice at least twice a year. The minute the wife was on the plane, they would hot foot it round to me and they would be ready to take their stripes with pride. Whilst in Manchester I had a customer who literally came every week, sometimes twice weekly. Mr Scott as we will call him did not attend school days. He was a very thin, fragile looking Scotsman with glasses like milk bottle bottoms who looked like you could literally blow him over, but when it came to the cane, none matched him. I would guess that he was well into his 50s and I assumed that he was either single or that he was never seen naked by his wife. He had a very bony, saggy bum with no real padding on it and he was a spontaneous ejaculator, so you had to be careful where you stood in case anything escaped. He never really gained an erection and had a horrid little dick like a small maggot that he didn't even have to touch. He always prevented himself from making a mess with a large wad of kitchen towel that he brought with him and disposed of, off the premises. He always smelt of soap, even before he got into the shower.

After a session, this man's bottom would be bloody and bruised with thin strips of flesh hanging from the welts all over his arse. In this instance, 'black and blue' only partially described his bottom after a session. The bruising he tolerated was yellow, green, grey, purple and was never completely free of bruising by the time he wanted to do it again. He had obviously been having this type of punishment for years and the scarring and splitting of his skin was just a part of what turned him on. When he pushed himself and believe me, he could, he would bounce up and down, knees nearly reaching his chin as if he was in the cast of River Dance. When this happened, he would expel little noises, a sort of 'wha.who.wiw. whoa.wum.pa! I just ignored it.

He had often praised me for my ability to catch him just under the cheeks at the top of his thighs. An area that really stings and is difficult to get to whilst caning. I personally believed that the punishment he had taken for years had slightly desensitised his butt cheeks and this area was still relatively sensitive.

When he spoke, it was almost a whisper with a strong Scottish accent and he always lowered his eyes. I couldn't tell from this whether it was out of respect or shame. Sadly, a great many submissive's' are very ashamed of their needs, but when it all gets too itchy, they have to get it scratched.

As I said, this chap had been coming to me for years so had often paid, quite literally to put food on the table, so I was a bit perturbed when I hadn't seen him for about three weeks. He was one of those who for some reason had given me his number, but I was loathe to use it. One day I was in the town centre when I spotted him sitting on a bench in a raincoat and trilby looking for all the world, like the loneliest man on the planet. I didn't have to think about it, when I wasn't in the dungeon I wasn't a Mistress, so I went and sat beside him on the bench and it seemed that he was grateful to see me and happier to explain the problem in those circumstances, than come to the dungeon. It turned out that at 62 he had lost his job. He had worked for the same tiny company since leaving school, and it had finally gone bust leaving him afraid for his future.

Now I wouldn't want any of you to think I'm a soft touch, but this man had been seeing me, often paying for a full hour and sometimes only lasting 15 minutes, for well over six years every week and sometimes twice a week.

I've always been disgusted at the lack of loyalty people display these days in many circumstances and I felt it was time to give something back. As an aside I was given a strong sense of me from my mum. I haven't talked about her much for so many reasons. I made an arrangement with him that for the foreseeable future he would only speak with me on the phone and would come once a month free of charge and when I was training somebody to use canes. The agreement was that I would ring him and use him as the Guinea pig when assessing a novice. He was so taken aback and so grateful that a little tear escaped from the corner of his eye as he took my hand in his and thanked me. Such a small thing really that made a world of difference to him. He stayed with me until sadly he was the victim of a fatal hit and run accident. He had no-one, so I went to his funeral with my maid and a girl who sometimes helped in the dungeon. He had bought his plot and headstone in readiness, probably because he knew there was nobody to take care of those sort of things for him at the end.

Eighteen months later I had a cheque from his estate for £2000. He had left the rest to Dr Barnardo's who had apparently brought him up and given him a home until he was 18. I couldn't help but wonder if that was where he picked up his fetish for the cane? I don't know if corporal punishment was allowed in those homes but as I mentioned, caning was an accepted form of punishment in my school and maybe it's a bit like training a dog? Any attention is better than no attention and receiving the cane in front of your peers is definitely a way of drawing attention to yourself? Something that was unattainable from the 'house' mother and father because of his shyness. I don't know and I'll never know. There was so much about him that will forever only be a smidgen of a memory because until his death, I really knew nothing about him. I only learned that he was an orphan, because it came up when he included me in his will. I don't know if he was a foundling, if he was the child of an unmarried mother or if his parents were dead. I had wondered about doing a little research on him, but ultimately, I had to ask myself why? There are things closer to home that are just waiting for me to do some digging, especially now that both of my parents are dead. But even that has me thinking, 'do I really need cans of worms?'

18. JAMMED ROLY POLY

I had never been approached by anyone with a walking disability and because my building was on so many different levels, when I was faced with the question, I wasn't sure if it was feasible. The gentleman who telephoned to ask about an appointment, seemed determined to visit no matter how impractical, so despite me being brutally honest about what would be available to him, he insisted he wanted to make an appointment. He had told me that he used a wheelchair, but when I said that there wasn't wheelchair access, he reassured me by telling me that he was capable of using two sticks as long as he wasn't rushed.

It has always been a rule for me to 'go with my gut,' and if I am to be honest my gut was screaming at me, 'NO, NO, NO!

I believe it was because within me, I felt an edge of guilt that just because someone was 'different' why should that mean they were turned away? Being 'different' was my bread and butter and I just felt that we could give it a go and if it didn't work out, I could always refuse, apologise and return the fee. I made a point of phoning around to make sure that I had someone experienced with me, on the day that he was booked in. As the day approached, I became more and more 'jumpy' and the night before he was due, I hardly slept at all.

I will call my number 2 on this day, Brenda and although I hadn't worked with her often, when we had worked, she had been on time, good at judging the punter and although she was quite limited; only using a few implements, those she knew she wielded well. She also had all her own kit and was quite comfortable playing second fiddle. She had the most striking features with beautiful bone structure, large dark green eyes and the longest, thickest lashes I had ever seen. She also had a figure to die for, but wasn't the innocent 'novice' she came across as. The circumstances escape me but for some reason I had to leave the dungeon for a moment. When I returned the customer was in a half Nelson and was literally begging to be released. The stupid man had completely read her wrong and had thought that with me out of the room it might be worth it, to take advantage of her. He really hadn't read the situation at all and after being tortured by me and threatened with my dog, he dressed hurriedly and left.

A couple of years later he attempted to be seen in my dungeon again but when I said No, he just turned tail and left.

The day started badly and proceeded at break neck speed into a catastrophe. The first problem was a phone call from my maid apologising profusely but informing me that she wouldn't be joining us. There was no time to find somebody else but the call actually gave me the heads up that Brenda was late and I could see no way of contacting the customer to explain that I wanted to cancel. In desperation I headed outside to see if Brenda was rushing along the road towards me, but as I attempted to mount the small set of steps the light had suddenly completely disappeared and I was shrouded in darkness. Looking up I realised that the sun had been blocked out of my vision by the bulk of a huge man in a bespoke wheelchair that resembled more of an army tank? He must have weighed somewhere in the region of 25stone and when he said that he could manoeuvre using a couple of sticks, I had a vision of two reinforced telephone poles groaning under his weight. Before I could say a word, he lifted his huge body out of the wheelchair and clung on precariously to the small handrail as he tried to propel himself forwards down the steps. I didn't know what to grab to help stabilise him, but was terrified that he might lose his balance and land on me. I had a terrible vision of being found dead from flattening by this whale of a man, who had then expired himself on top of me and nobody having found us for five days!!!

Suddenly I realised that Brenda had appeared behind him and was also trying to work out what to grab, but my instinct told me that something was very wrong. Before I had an opportunity to get my head around the situation, Brenda managed to lose her footing on the step and as she kicked forward, grabbing onto this man mountain to prevent herself from falling, she inadvertently kicked him in the back of his knee and the whole unstable mound wobbled and shook as we grabbed him and tried to prevent him from going down! At the last moment he managed to save himself, but the horrible creaking noise the hand rail was making as he leaned himself against it, actually had me praying out loud. The property was an old one and the front door was unusually small. The two of us pushed and pulled and tried shoe horning him in sideways, but I had convinced myself that he was now going to get permanently stuck in my hallway. Secretly I was thinking that if that were the case no matter what, I wasn't going to feed him. That way he would lose weight and I would only have him as an unwelcome house guest for a couple of weeks. I could see myself using his fat rolls like a climbing wall so that I could enter or leave the premises.

By the time we had managed to get him into the bathroom I was physically sweating and had decided to head back to my own shower to freshen up before working out how to get him back out of my dungeon, up the stairs and into History.

When I reappeared, I caught Brenda swigging neat Vodka out of a bottle in her bag and realised that though upright, she was very, very drunk. I took a deep breath and attempted to make sense out of the words she was slurring at me, but I couldn't get it. In both anger and frustration, I gave her a tongue lashing that if she hadn't been drunk, she would have remembered forever. As it was, she had forgotten two minutes after I had finished, but she completely understood when I told her to 'Get out and go home'!!

She shrugged and started to stagger towards the front door when she stopped; and swaying slightly told me in a very loud voice, that because the customer was 'So fucking fat!' rather than try to squeeze him into the shower, she had told him to get in the bath. My heart sank as I leapt forward and pushed her out of the front door. When she left, I sank down onto the carpet, put my head in my hands and took deep breaths. My imagination was running riot and I told myself that nothing in reality, could possibly be worse than the various scenario's banging about my brain. Steeling myself I turned the handle of the bathroom door and entered, stopping in the doorway I thought I heard myself let out a strangled squeak, but decided that it must have been somebody else?

It was like staring at a monstrous vat of lard that shimmered and slimed in huge pools, one on top of the other.

It was difficult to work out where one limb started and another stopped. The huge blob of tumbling flesh was distributed between the bathtub and the floor and until he turned his head and spoke to me, I couldn't tell which way up he was. I was determined to remain calm as I apologized but explained that a domination session just wasn't going to happen. He didn't seem terribly upset because I think he had worked out for himself that it really wasn't practicable, but my relief was short lived when he attempted to manoeuvre in the bath and all that happened was a tsunami swooshing out of the tub and a sort of sucking, farting noise from within as a ripple effect moved across his bulk from one side to the other.

I suggested that it might be easier if he could pull out the plug, but he seemed incapable of getting past his own roles of flesh so I found myself paging through fat to attempt to get my arm down, and around and pull the plug myself. When I finally released the plug after having had to hold huge layers of fat out of the way, nothing happened. The suction seemed to of grabbed a plug of his skin, sealing the hole that was also weighted down by the mounds of flab above it, therefore doing nothing to release the remainder of water or to help with any type of movement of the man in the bathtub. In a frenzy I started pulling and pushing, grabbing and twisting and trying to lever him out of the tub. I used ropes, pulleys, two bottles of cooking oil, tubs of coconut oil and a winch. Nothing, not a sausage. No matter what I tried, I had not been able to produce even a hint of a movement. As if to tease me, periodically everything would shudder and make sucking noises, but not even a hint of movement was achieved.

By now the time was slipping past and I knew I had to think of something because the fat man was definitely an unwelcome distraction in my bathroom and leaving him there wasn't an option. After trying everything I could think of, with a heavy heart I telephoned my local pub and asked about a couple of builders who I guessed would be in there. Explaining my predicament was horrible and I could hear the tale being told in the bar as I explained and the sound of peals of laughter as it was repeated. Luckily most of the regulars knew how I made my living, but knowing something and witnessing it are definitely two different things. After what seemed like an age, two of the young men from the pub turned up and after fits of giggles, attempted to remove the gentleman from my bath. After being thwarted by the situation for about half an hour, one of them got on the phone and within five minutes another two blokes turned up to help. The same scenario played out, peals of laughter followed by the sound of grunts and bangs as they tried to defeat the suction and get fatso out. Again, someone asked to use the telephone and whilst we waited, I made tea for everyone and passed round the biscuits.

Despite the piggy eyes staring out of the flabby face longingly when the chocolate biscuits were whisked under his nose, I made certain that nobody gave him so much as a crumb. I was gradually starting to believe that he was going to be an unwanted house guest forever or I gave in and called the fire brigade. By six o'clock in the evening, there were enough builders on my property to rival Taylor Woodrow's, and I still had a ridiculously fat man in my bathtub. I decided that it was time to get the fire brigade, but one of the guys saw the expression on my face and realised that I would probably have to find a new property once the firemen had attended, because reporters always followed them and this would definitely be a 'story' with local interest?

They decided that they would give it one more go and remarkably there was a sudden loud farting noise and the fat man was hauled out of the bathtub landing like a huge blancmange onto the floor, layers of blubber following more layers. I caught an atmosphere of sheer terror as they realised with horror that it was possible; they were about to be engulfed by a sea of fat and then palpable relief when the blob taking up most of the floor came to rest in a wobbling heap.

My rescuers stayed with me and once he was dressed, they then proceeded to get him out of the flat and up the stairs. Interestingly he paid me handsomely because his 'thing' was humiliation.

I attempted to share out the money with the guys but they wouldn't have it, so we all went down to the pub and I paid for all the drinks. Brenda did work with me a couple of times more, but sadly she was an alcoholic and would stay off the booze for a couple of months before falling off the wagon again and being out of it for six months. I also decided that unless I changed premises, unfortunately I wouldn't be taking any 'disabled' submissive's.

I've often thought of that day and having been squashed and run over by very fat people on motorised vehicles, I get a sort of chicken/egg question running around my head. Do they become these huge, flabby parodies of themselves because they are disabled and cannot exercise, or is it their inability to say no to food that makes it become too painful and difficult to walk so they get these scooters so they can get out to buy more food?

19. THE RELENTLESS TIME

As I mentioned earlier, a couple... sorry, I should say a few times during my career I left somebody 'hanging about in bondage' because I just simply forgot they were there. Bondage takes many forms and in this particular case, the gentleman was wound round with rope and seated on a stool whilst his legs were bound together and were suspended from the ceiling with a rope that just prevented them from touching the floor. His hands were handcuffed around his back, he had a hangman's noose around his neck and a couple of weights suspended from his ball sack. I should mention that the noose was simply a visual stimulus and that even if he had tried to top himself with it, it wouldn't work because it wasn't actually attached to anything. Obviously, a piece of theatre that from the submissive's point of view looked very real, but not actually harmful. There was also an added little piece of excitement because if the submissive found the weights on his nads too much, he could always wobble himself off the stool so only his legs were suspended, taking into account that his Mistress wouldn't actually try and hang him…would she?

On this particular day the dressing service for the trannies was remarkably busy and the second dungeon was also fully booked, so I had very little opportunity to do anything other than the most cursory glance at my 'friend's suspension' and bark something nasty at him, just to let him know I cared!

I have to say this, though I am glad that I cannot see the readers face when they read my next statement, but what happened was actually the submissive's fault. People paid for a length time, unless it was some sort of different service like an overnight stay or attending a booking to a club with mistress, that she had been invited to. Generally, I was good at judging the time and as time was money that was a bonus, but in this instance, it was the sub himself that caused the problem. At the allotted moment I went into the dungeon to release him, but he asked if he could stay a bit longer. I left him and checked that the second dungeon had only him booked in, so it was effectively his until he had had enough or it was time to close the shop. He was more than happy, so I adjusted some of the pulleys, changed the weights to something a little less heavy, removed the noose but covered his mouth and eyes before leaving him, locking the door, taking the key and slipping it into my pocket while attending to my other jobs. Now this is where I suppose I may have to take a little of the blame. When a dungeon was in use it was locked and the key kept on the Mistresses person until she was finished with that particular client. Then the key would be placed in the lock but the door would be open and maids etc. could gain entrance to do the cleaning and such like. At the end of the day, whoever was last in the dungeon to clean would then, when finished close the door, lock it and hang the key in the key box. Once it was home time, unless I said differently, If the door were closed and locked it would be assumed that the room was clean, and that the key had been placed where it should be.

We started finishing at about 4pm as I insisted everything was clean and tidy for the following morning. I always wanted to start a new day with everything ready to roll, with nothing left over from the day before other than the ironing. This meant customers wandering in and out of the showers, getting dressed, paying their bills, the maids placing everything in the washing machines (I had two industrial machines), my dungeon clients being released, if not by me then by my assistant and things being finished by the time I wanted to lock up. I was wielding the hoover in the trannies 'day room', when my girl popped her head around the door to say Goodnight. 'Everything done' I asked, to which she happily assured me that it was and left. When I had finished the carpet in the shop, I removed the takings from the till, waited for my lift and then locked the premises and pulled down the shutter.

Once home the takings were placed into the safe, the dogs were taken to the park and then when I returned, I started dinner. At this time, I had a husband but he did nothing around the house, wouldn't even think of starting or even making the evening meal and moaned continuously because I expected him to take me to and from work. I see no point in writing about yet another disappointment in the 'love' department so we'll sort of skate round this, other than mention his whereabouts when it's relevant to the story. When we had eaten and watched tele for a bit, I put the dogs in the back garden for a last wee and we went to bed at about 10.30pm.

When the telephone started ringing, initially it just didn't register with me that it was the phone. Looking at my watch I realised it was 1.45am and that it was still dark outside, which brought me around and I answered quite quickly. Apparently, the shop alarm was going off and the Police were in attendance, so could I please join them as soon as possible. Having woken my other half, I dressed and grabbed a coat and headed out to the car. The penny hadn't dropped. In fact, it didn't drop until we arrived at the premises and were greeted by three police cars and a police dog the size of a medium sized horse. As I had exited the car, I felt my fingers curl around the dungeon key and I knew what had set off the alarm. Once I had got the shutters up, this snarling, dribbling beast was encouraged to enter before me to flush out any burglars. In panic I desperately tried to prevent the Police or their huge canine from getting anywhere near the interior of the shop, using my body to physically block the doorway and sticking out my leg in the hope that the dog would take the bait, bite me, thereby ending the situation. I started babbling that I was very sorry but that I had forgotten to set the alarm properly and that I was certain I was not being burgled because I would have known if that were the case??!! And anyway, there was nothing to burgle unless the burglar were a transvestite and under the circumstances that would be unlikely. If the burglar were a cross-dresser, then the chances were that the police would already know of them because they would have discovered this predilection when they had been arrested before and had been searched? Perhaps wearing stocking and suspenders under their kit? And on that basis when the alarm went off, they would have immediately scarpered because the police would know who they were looking for by the items stolen and, on that basis, nobody would still be in the shop!!!

The expressions on the faces in front of me, including my husbands, was an expression of both concern for my sanity and complete disbelief in my explanation. I can't remember when I actually stopped speaking, but before I had finished, some of the police had given 'that look' to each other and shrugged their shoulders before wandering back to their cars and the others were just standing in front of me with their mouths open. When I finally got into the shop, I insisted that my husband stood by the door to prevent anyone from entering behind me and I took the stairs two at a time till I stood panting at the dungeon door.

Mr X was laying on the floor, stool on its side, legs still suspended but the weights no longer hanging and he had managed, probably by rubbing his face against the wooden floor, to have pulled his blindfold down over one eye. Removing his gag, he immediately started apologising, but I wasn't listening because I was unwinding him and attempting to confirm that I had returned the circulation to his body. Trying to get him to remain upright was stupidly difficult because he had no feeling in his feet or legs, or his arms and hands so he couldn't even hang on to something. I ended up calling my husband who placed his arms under his armpits and sort of bobbed him up and down in the hopes that he could be shaken into feeling something. I really don't know how long it took, but I think my memory of up to two days was an exaggeration? Memory can be a funny thing?

When he was finally able to stand on trembling legs and was looking a little less blue, he confirmed that the feeling was returning to most of his body, but that his nose was very painful. Once into decent lighting and to keep him quiet, I attempted to examine his nose but as I grabbed it, he screamed so loudly, that unceremoniously I covered his mouth with my hand and schussed him. When I let him go, glaring at him, I gently examined his nostrils and spied a huge splinter, more like a plank really? lodged securely up his nose, probably acquired whilst trying to remove his blindfold? My husband was getting restless, so I chivvied him into his clothes, said we would discuss payment at another date and drove him home. As he left the car struggling to remain upright, I suggested that he might have to go to A & E to get the splinter removed, before driving away at relatively high speed!!

On another occasion we had a customer who's thing was to be peed on in the face and I had had made a special chair with a removable box (for cleaning) beneath a solid seat a bit like the old Victorian style of toilet seat. The idea was that the mistress could urinate on the customer without the embarrassing loss of dignity of pulling down her underwear and then wiping in full view. When Carol worked with me I took on almost all of those who wanted this service, because I had very good bladder control, was capable of drinking large quantities of liquid and holding on to it until it was needed and knew how to control the flow so I didn't splash any of it on myself. The problem that arose was that some of Carols 'personal' customers were desperate for her to do it, rather than me and that she was being offered silly sums of money to do it. Obviously, she had attempted to do this before more than once, but as soon as she looked at the smiling face of the customer looking up at her, she found that she wasn't able to pee at all. The more frustrated with herself she became the less chance she stood of even pushing out a dribble. She could ultimately stand aside, run taps and hear the evidence, as well as watch me do it without a hint of needing 'to go'. The minute the customer vacated the premises she would fly past m, throw herself onto the toilet seat and piss like a Donkey. It was the amount of cash she was being offered that was so difficult to pass up and as they weren't offering me the money, the ball was in Carol's court.

I had commissioned the box for both of us and used it myself until Carol left. A couple of times a maid or customer had emptied the box but had underestimated the quantity of urine I could produce. Having watched them struggle and spill some of the contents, I generally reverted to how I had done it before I had had the box but it was a multi-purpose object that earned its money virtually every day, so there was no problem.

When the box finally arrived, Carol looked at it, tried it for size and smiled at me. In the weeks that followed she spent her days and evenings trying to control her bladder and peeing regularly into the box. Finally, the day came when she was ready to offer the service and having picked the chap who had offered her the most money and would take her out to dinner afterwards (a double incentive) she was raring to go. By now we no longer had two dungeons, but as his appointment wasn't until 2.30 and I had been fairly busy the day before, I was happy to take a day off. Now normally his appointment would have lasted an hour and after having showered he would have handed over a bunch of cash and been told to go away until he picked her up for dinner. I had been out for lunch, done a bit of shopping and visited my dressmaker, planning to arrive home whilst Carol got ready to go out, have a drink with her and she could share with me the intricacies of the session. I walked into the flat and the first thing I realised was that someone was in the dungeon with Carol. I steered past what we called the business area and walked through leaving my coat on the hook and heading towards the kitchen to get a bottle out of the fridge. In a sudden rush of air and leather, Carol appeared as if the devil were on her tail and said almost in a squeak, "I can't do it! I don't know how many times I've tried but I can't do it!"

I stood in front of her looking stupid before I got my head around what she was saying. "When did you start trying?" I asked.

"about 3 o'clock"

"What?"

"Well maybe a quarter past or something, but I can't do it!!" she wailed.

"Has he been moved at all?" she shook her head and I was astounded that he had remained prone, occasionally seeing his Mistress grimacing at him through the hole, being left again, seeing her return, but still no water sports!

I immediately told her to get me a large glass of water as I struggled to change into something more suitable. Once ready and having downed a bit more water, I hesitated and asked what had gone wrong.

"I just couldn't" she stammered. "Every time I went to sit down, I looked into the box and could see his face looking up at me!"

"Well what did you say?" I asked looking at my watch.

"Nothing," she said. "I didn't say anything. Every time I saw him looking up at me, I just shouted at him not to say anything and I tried. I tried every time I sat down but I just knew he was staring up at me and I couldn't…"

Pushing gently past her I walked back through the flat, Carol hot on my heels and quietly opened the dungeon door, trying to decide what I was going to say.

His stillness made me approach slowly but when I peered into the box, I could hear him snoring gently and it was obvious that he was fast asleep. Putting my finger to my lips I picked up an empty pint glass on the side, dimmed the lighting and motioned to Carol to sit. After a second's hesitation and me miming, 'zip it' when she attempted to speak, I positioned myself and peed in the glass without spilling a drop. I carefully held the glass and motioned to Carol to open her legs in such a way that I could pour the contents into the box and it would appear that it came from her. The urine splashed all over the punters face, waking him up and forcing him to cough and splutter. I confess there was a bit of splash back but I felt that under the circumstances it was only fair. I slipped out of the dungeon without him being aware that I had ever been there. Back in our private quarters I showered, changed into a dressing gown and curled up to watch tele whilst sipping champagne. By the time Carol joined me she explained that she had postponed dinner with her customer until later in the week and she flopped onto the couch beside me, either of us spoke for a bit but then she raised her glass to me and said, "Roma". We both smiled.

20. CRAP PARTY

I suppose that I have given the impression that all of our bondage customers were old and sleepy, but it is a fact that quite a few gentlemen invariably dozed off when left in bondage for any length of time. As with most things, bondage comes in different forms. Some like to be placed in something like a bondage bag and others require far more skill, being tethered with ropes, chains, straps and the like. Some require the Mistress be present whilst the submissive wriggles and squirms and in some instances objects, while others like to be constricted to a more or lesser degree and then left alone. Some enjoy being secreted within the dungeon in a predicament which allows them to witness the mistress as she attends to another client. This can be some sort of restricted view, like a keyhole or just sounds. For some, bondage is the route to receiving physical abuse, spanking, paddles and for the hard-core, having their scrotum nailed to a piece of wood, their nipples pierced, the surgical 'umbrella' inserted into the penis, needles passed through the bollocks, sometimes with thread! There is also the misnomer that all men into this world are in their late 50s which actually couldn't be farther from the truth. On several occasions I insisted that proof had to be shown me to confirm the boy asking for an appointment was 18 and there was one bizarre night where myself and 4 other professional Dominatrix were invited to a party, where we were paid to play in the couples own dungeon with their son and his mates because it was his 21st Birthday!

Lots of unusual elements are explored by the submissive on the road to sexual gratification. I will not pretend that the Sado/Masochistic world is about playing cards or gardening, it isn't and it is a fact that like so many secret passions, the more it's done, the more it's needed. As the submissive experiments with the various methods and choices, it is a fact that for him the play becomes 'harder'. The longer he/she is allowed to dabble, the more difficult it will be to reach orgasm, though this area is reached much faster with men than with women. I stated right at the beginning that this lifestyle for the Dominatrix is completely sexless; but if she should choose to allow a sex object, to become a 'partner' then it is because his looks are attractive to her and that his place is totally about pleasing her. This type of relationship takes nothing away from the Mistresses status, however most

Mistresses are not attracted to 'weak' men and the type of roughty-toughty male, who is brimming with muscle and testosterone, loses his charm the first time he grovels on the carpet in front of her or squeals if she steps on his hand. This again is the big difference between the male counterpart and ourselves. Masters use sex and the demanding of it, as part of his control that he wields within his dungeon. Oral sex is just that for the Master. No frills and a more or less guaranteed ending. 'Queening' as it is known (not to be confused with the homosexual form of Queening which can also be called rimming and requires the submissive to 'tongue the arsehole') is simply oral sex, performed on the Dominatrix with the intention of her coming to orgasm. It is acceptable because she enjoys it and enjoys the climax, however long it takes. One of my Dominatrix friends seemed to always have 'her' personal slave stuffed up her dressing gown, if for some reason you visited, and could hold a conversation as if she were eating beans!

I could never get my head around this because for me, reaching orgasm requires the lady to lose control and that wasn't something I wanted to do with a stranger. I would happily piss on them, fart on them, fart in their mouth, torture them and draw blood, but I couldn't get myself to allow that type of intimacy for money and definitely not for pleasure. In my private life I hadn't orgasmed until I was in my late twenties and once, I had discovered it I still had difficulty 'giving in to it'. I'm afraid my best friend and a guaranteed sexual partner without all the fuss, was my fingers.

As I said at the start, a good Dominatrix learns all aspects of her trade, perfects them, tries them and then decides what she will or will not do. Of course, in my dungeon, over the years, I had some spectacularly beautiful men and internally I might sigh for what might have been, but then I just got on with the job. I have been asked and it has even been mooted that the mistress DOES get off on the persona and the power that she harnesses in her dungeon. However, it is because women are notoriously difficult when it comes to having any type of orgasm, that she does not recognise it as a sexual thrill?

Men come in various different ways and that isn't meant to be a pun. There are spontaneous ejaculators, premature ejaculators, no stiffening of the dick ejaculators, no discharge of any description ejaculators, quiet ejaculators, screamers and so many variations on a theme. It is a part of the Mistresses job to acknowledge how, why and when a man may reach orgasm. It is also her duty to explain to the customer what the 'form' is concerning his ejaculate and to what extent he is expected to clean up after himself. This is because, however hard you try (uh! Another pun) various bodily fluids can escape and possibly place you at risk, so rubber gloves are always worn and if torn are changed after washing your hands. Sometimes a rubber apron and or face mask can be employed as protection too. I was fairly laid back about the types of fluids that may leave a drop or blob on the floor, furniture or even your gloves but I would not, under any circumstances deal with pooh! Neither would I expect any of my girls or maids to do so either.

If you think about it, most 'liquids' that could possibly be spilt are fairly benign. Blood, ejaculate and even urine can actually be handled fairly safely. There is nothing about pooh that is benign. It is a waste product that stinks, smears and can flick off in particles if banded about and those who want to feel it in their pants, rub it on themselves or worst of all eat it…. should be taken outside and shot!

There is no possible excuse for wanting to be around excrement and the individual who chooses this as his fetish, doesn't deserve to exist on the basis that at some point during his life he WILL want to involve somebody else and my fear is that for some reason I unknowingly put myself in harm's way and that person becomes me!!!

I had travelled to London to a very nice apartment opposite Lords Cricket Ground for a private party, with Carol, a girl called Judy and a friend of Carols who was working as a Dominatrix but who I really wasn't 100% convinced that she, wasn't actually a he? It didn't help that they were called Sam, but Carol was convinced of the ladies' credentials and had worked with her in the past. It was actually Sam's client but as soon as we arrived, I had that feeling that something just wasn't right. The submissive came across to me as a dirty old man and when introduced to us he made some sort of inappropriate comment to Judy and winked at me.

We looked at each other and as soon as he turned his back Judy gave me a signal and asked where the toilet was. We both went to leave the room at the same time but before we could exit, he leaned forward and pressed a wrap into Judy's hand. Touching the side of his nose he winked again and said "I'm sure you lovely ladies would enjoy a livener?"

Before I got out of the room Carol elbowed her way into the Bathroom before me and shouted, "best get some of that champagne out of the fridge and some glasses. Need to get in the mood". She stood between us and rubbed her hands as Judy chopped and made lines. In a split second she had snorted her portion and was nagging for more but Judy and I suggested that it was probably for us all to share, though the idea of Captain Birdseye in the lounge, high on Cocaine wasn't a good thought. We looked around and then back to each other. Carol took the initiative and chopped the rest of the powder and divided it between the three of us. Judy stopped Carol from bending down to snort.

"What about Sam?" She asked sounding genuinely concerned. Carol stared at her for a few seconds and then dived in with her nostrils flaring. We looked at each other, giggled and then followed suit.

When we returned to the lounge Sam showed us into a bedroom through a door next to the kitchen and said that this was where we could change. Sam had obviously changed whilst we were in the loo and on the dressing-table was a bottle of bubbly and 4 sherry glasses. Carol wrinkled her nose, took a swig out of the bottle and went into the kitchen. After a short interlude she returned with glass tumblers and shared out the bubbly. We could hear Sam and our host in the lounge but to me it wasn't sounding right. Carol leaned in to us and said, "I think she's knocking one out for him?" and grimaced.

After downing the whole glass, we shared a look of disgust between us and slowly filed into the other room.

We were being paid very, very well for the evening and he had booked a hotel for the three of us. Sam had informed us of the arrangements but didn't seem to be staying at the same Hotel. We had been paid on arrival and given the Hotel details, so we decided we would drink and party as much as possible using his drink and drugs and watch the time until we could leave. The following day we were meeting my lovely friend for lunch at Fortnum and Mason and as we had planned to stay at my mum and dads, we would pop there before getting ready and going to a club in the evenings. Home Sunday.

The evening sort of started with a whimper and went on to die quietly. We were sitting around, occasionally using a cane or paddle but really watching from the side-lines as Sam and the grinning, drooling Host interacted in a manner that occasionally had me looking away with embarrassment. After about an hour the doorbell went and as Sam went to answer the intercom our host, who to me was just a horrid addled old man, lunged at Judy from his chair and attempted to get his hands full of her tits. She moved out of his reach easily, but Carol, angered by his impertinence, elbowed him with full force in the side of his head, catching him on the temple. The force of her blow left him slumped down in his chair.

Sam walked in, all smiles leading another octogenarian in by a collar and lead, a shabbily dressed tranny who had his wig on backwards and 'something' squeezed into an outfit of PVC that couldn't cope with the height of its thigh length boots. In a strange form of introduction, she attempted to speak to her friend still slumped in the chair. Obviously, no reply, but before she could investigate, Carol blocked her view and interaction, by intimating that as he was so old, he was probably just having a nap and to leave him be.

I can't actually tell you what occurred during the course of the evening because it alternated between incredibly boring and mind numbingly boring. We kept sneaking a look at our watches and once we had finished off the last of the bubbly I realised that Carol was giving us the signal that it was time to leave. We all changed in a heartbeat and were just about to file out when a strong smell of shit wafted into the room. We all looked at each other and crinkled our noses before slowly realising we had to get out via where the smell seemed to be coming from, which meant entering the room. We entered squashed together moving slowly and with care. What greeted us had to be seen to be believed.

Our original host was now awake and was standing in the centre of the room minus his trousers and pants, a stream of what looked like pooh leading from the chair, which looked as if someone had thrown a curry at it, across the carpet to where he was standing. Sam was being given one up the arse by the transvestite, who was going at it like a demon, as Sam stared blankly out of the window and I noticed there was the hint of a flaccid little willy bobbing about under her skirt. Fleetingly my consciousness acknowledged that my suspicions had been correct, however the stench overtook any other thought than how to get out of there and I looked away! The octogenarian was naked, looking like there had been some sort of seismic shift on his body making him look fairly acceptable from the shoulders until one realised that there was skin hanging in folds down his body, placing his nipples just above his hips. It appeared that he had probably gone down onto his knees in front of the host for the purpose of sucking his dick, but even if he were blind and deaf there was obviously nothing wrong with his sense of smell. I think that if he hadn't been on his knees, and at a disadvantage when it came to getting up, he would have removed himself from his position in front of the host?

I vaguely remember his eyes catching mine, pleading silently with me to help him get up, but I was unable to involve myself because the final vision, had myself, Carol and Judy screaming and fighting each other to get out of the flat into the hallway.

The thing in the PVC who we now knew was definitely a man, was also down on his knees behind our host licking the horrid, yellow parchment which was the skin stretched over the bum cheeks of our host. As Mr PVC lowered his position his tongue streaking out like a snakes towards the arsehole, Captain Birdseye let out a terrible fart which seemed to reverberate around the flat. This was followed by a stream of pooh which spurted out of his bum hole like an exploding geezer, hitting the PVC friend full in the face with liquid pooh. There was a collective retch from Judy, Carol and myself and as we gasped for air and battled each other to get out of the flat door, the smell engulfed the whole area forcing us to try not to breathe until we could find fresh air.

Carol always used the lift but, in this instance, she was the first to find the stairs and pushing open a window hurled like a dragon breathing fire straight out onto whatever was below her. Judy was next and she spaced her eruptions of vomit with gulps of air obviously trying to control herself, but fighting a losing battle. I have mentioned that I would rather run naked round Wembley stadium than be sick, but the heaving and retching of my partners was too much. The smell of pooh and vomit confirmed that I was definitely going to hurl and once it happened, I was sure that it would never stop. When we had finally managed to hang on to whatever was still in our stomachs, we descended the stairs gingerly, looking over our shoulders as if we expected to see that revolting spectacle following us down the steps. Even being sick is an art and though we all felt rather empty and had a nasty taste in the mouth, we hadn't spoiled our clothes so we decided to walk to the hotel to allow the fresh air a chance to make us feel better. We spent the evening in the Hotel bar speaking very little, but all of us periodically retched and we had to struggle not to allow retching to become like yawning? All for one and one for all!!

21. CATALOGUE OF ERRORS

There is something about watching somebody else, who being showcased, has everything that could go wrong, go wrong!

It is a sad fact, which some comedians have cashed in on, that human beings tend to laugh at somebody else's misfortunes, but I think my laughter comes from knowing that that which is unfolding in front of us, could be happening to us? Part of the laughter stems from relief that it isn't you. In a strange way you empathise and sometimes just that someone else is getting it in the neck, is just funny?

I believe that I am lucky because I have always been able to laugh at myself, possibly from insecurity but hopefully because if something is amusing, it just is. My twin was the first to laugh at something happening to somebody else, but could see no humour in a situation which may have somebody laughing at her?

An example. When we were at school and being bullied (which was mostly her fault) I was sitting in a classroom on my desk trying to muster the courage to nibble one of mums sandwiches, with two or three others and my twin. This was at the time where I was just starting to get a reputation as someone who would fight back, but in truth these girls scared the shit out of me. A huge black girl, big for her age at 5'.8" and as wide called Ivory (her parents obviously had a sense of humour?), who had tormented me since we had arrived, sidled over to us and I assumed wanted to join in our conversation.

I have no idea how we got onto the subject but she started going off on one about who she hated and what she would like to do with them? I desperately wanted to appear like a co-conspirator so started to do the same but without specifics. She was terribly intimidating and leaning forward, her face inches from my own, kept pressing me for a name. I could feel the fear wafting off the others and I was starting to sweat, as her eyes searched mine. I was aware that I had started to stammer and that my mouth had gone dry. I have always said that under pressure, I would have revealed all of the names of the 'Resistant's' to the Germans during world war two, if someone had been stupid enough to try to make me a spy? My own instinct (thank you mother!) was to tell the truth.

As her eyes bored into mine and my sphincter trembled, without hesitation I blurted out, "Ivory!"

There was that split second where I was either about to be stomped on, or I could try to deflect the result of what I had just said. In desperation I started to howl with laughter (which did actually resemble howling rather than laughter) and slapped her on the back. Fortunately, my friends picked up on my cue (probably because they had been in conversation with me before she had arrived and were trying to avoid the guilt by association?) and laughed heartily, supposedly enjoying the joke with 'our' friend Ivory. Looking blank for a few seconds, Ivory finally believed I had been playing a well-meant trick on her and joined in the laughter.

My sister loved telling that story because she had seen my failure rather than the resulting triumph, a pattern that stayed with her throughout her life. When we were adults and she was visiting, some of my friends turned up and shortly before she arrived, I had been to the toilet. Let's just say that it was impossible to open the window and I had only just come out when my sister arrived and desperately needed the loo, so ploughed straight in. I hadn't even used air freshener so I made some comment to my friends, expecting her to say something when she came out. She did, but it wasn't what was expected…

"that's lovely perfume you're wearing" she said smiling at me.

"Really?" I said. "I've just had a shit?" which had my friends rolling about with laughter. She left before anyone had a chance to say anything else with a face like thunder. She had perceived that the laughter was directed solely at her. And therefore, it wasn't funny. Sad…

The point is that by being able to laugh at yourself you can sometimes make good, what may have been a dreadful situation. I was once in a club in Amsterdam when a young woman approached the working area with a slave and a bull whip. These long-tailed whips are very difficult to use and having tried it myself, I have to take my hat off to those who have mastered the art. Because of the danger these whips if incorrectly used, the working area is always cleared before a demonstration can take place. This young woman had obviously practiced endlessly and though she did little more than allow the end of the whip to lick the slaves bare back, her ability was impressive. She finished to huge applause and was soaking up the atmosphere when approached by a 'would be Dominatrix' with another, slightly heavier and longer Rodeo whip. These whips look the part so some 'dabblers' carry them because they give a good impression and as I have mentioned before, there is an element of theatre at this type of gatherings.

I said earlier that personally, if I become an expert with an instrument, it is the action with that particular instrument that gives me expertise! I was intrigued when I saw the Dominatrix take the new whip, balance it in her hand for a moment and then nod her head to the person who had handed it to her. She took up the slight sideways stance that these long whips require, especially if handled by a female, and waived her slave out of the circle. I could see her weighing and re-positioning the handle until it felt right and then suddenly, she lifted her arm and sent the long part of the whip away from her with the speed and snap like the strike of a snake. Instead of allowing the whip to curl back on itself, she deftly lowered her arm into a position so that the body of the whip slithered across the floor, losing momentum as it travelled, and curled into a heap at her feet. The audience went mad, clapping and whooping until she actually looked embarrassed. People were chanting and stamping their feet to make her do it again and I personally believe that she was forced into another demonstration without being allowed to get her head around what had to be done. To add to the pressure, somebody had pushed her slave out into the ring to be her target, which brings with it a whole different set of movements to bear on the outcome.

It seemed like we were suspended in time, and in slow motion I saw the whip snake out and start to return wrapping the body of the whip around the subs neck, lifting him off his feet and dragging him as he was being strangled, towards his mistress. She dropped the handle to interfere with the strength of the curl and as she did so the tip of the whip, having returned, moved to a position where it wrapped itself around the heel of her boot, taking her down with the slave already screaming and wriggling, into a pile on the floor. The melee that followed had to be seen to be believed as people just started jumping in, presumably in an attempt to help, on top of each other, squashing and crushing and shouting, arms and legs everywhere a seething mass of humanity totally out of control. Above the noise the slaves voice could be heard screaming for help to breathe and I just stood, glued to my position, eyes wide and probably with my mouth open.

Suddenly I became aware of somebody beside me, because a bony elbow bounced off my rib cage, forcing me to pay attention. Standing there, was a very small Dominatrix, dressed from head to toe in expensive leather, paddles and hand whips dangling from her belt, beautifully coiffured steel grey hair, hanging on to a Zimmer frame. She looked up at me and smiled.

"I'm glad I woke up in time to see this" her voice crackled. "He's not dead because I can hear him screaming over all that noise and I'm as deaf as a post"!

She put a bony, long fingered hand out sporting several diamond rings that glittered in the half light. She had the most beautiful, educated voice and may have been educated at Rodiene or had the same nanny as the queen? Her hand very lightly took hold of my arm. She started to chuckle "we never had to do this sort of thing when I started out. You either had it or you didn't? That young man," she said bobbing her head towards the melee, "is either going to be strangled to death or far more likely be suffocated by the amount of people that have landed on him?". She looked up at me and vaguely waived her hand towards the bundle of people. "This isn't where you earn your living. You do that at home. She..." she said, signalling with her finger, "The one under all of those people. She doesn't have to do this shit! I'd rather hang up my whips than deal with this rabble."

I was waiting for her to continue but as I waited, I saw her head slowly sink towards her chest. As seconds passed where I could hear her breath become more regular and deep, she suddenly snorted and raised her pale blue eyes to mine. "It's as much as I can do to stay awake" she said starting to cackle, "but I always get the money first" she said. And she gesticulated towards the heap of people, " Fuck that!" Was her parting comment as she slowly faded back into the crowd and staring at the heap of people still rolling around on the floor, I just had to laugh. Humour can be found almost anywhere, but I do have to wonder if the participants in that particular exercise ever saw the funny side to it. What had made me laugh was the observations and the language used by the beautifully spoken, old lady and still does!

22. ALL CHANGE

I ran my businesses, the dungeon and the dressing service, in tandem for a long time, but as the years went on, I'm afraid I became completely tired of the lies I had to tell or worse listen to the lies men told themselves that I was expected to go along with. My business was successful because I was a damn good make-up artist, had purchased all of the right things to wear that will give a man the curves of a woman. I chose expensive, stylish clothes for all occasions but within six months I realised that most Transvestites do not actually want to look like a woman, they want to look like some sort of parody of a woman. It did not matter what they saw in the mirror, or more to the point what I saw in the mirror, because whatever they saw, it was light-years away from reality. One of the services we offered was to take the Tranny out on the bus, go shopping in a department store, take tea and then return to the shop. It had seemed like a great idea to make money and give people the excitement of going out dressed up, and we charged a reasonable amount for the privilege. In theory I felt that although I expected some stares, my ability with make-up and dressing was good enough that they would pass. Also, the fact that those able to afford this were usually over sixty and it is a fact that as we get older our faces tend to become less pronounced as male or female. Old ladies sprout facial hair and old men lose facial hair (although men's ears just get hairier) and it really is the hairstyles and the clothes that tells us at first glance what sex we are looking at. Working on these ideals I failed to foresee the horror I would have to subject myself to, to earn the dosh. I soon realised that actually you couldn't pay me enough to fulfil this promise of 'going out for tea'!

Why did men anywhere over fifty and in some cases young men, ALL want to wear stockings and suspenders, tops so low that if the breasts had been real, they would definitely have flopped out. Skirts so short you could see the cheeks of their bums, stiletto shoes that they were incapable of wearing and bright red lipstick taken way over the actual width of their lips? The long blonde tresses that accompanied this look was actually alarming and the knowledge that they had stuck their penis up between their legs with gaffer tape made one decidedly queasy. I actually wondered if the strange 'gait' employed when wearing stiletto shoes was actually a combination of the shoes and the Gaffer tape ripping out clumps of pubic hair as they tried to walk?

Changing their perception of 'what a woman thought like' and how they looked became something of a tired conversation which after hours of argument made not a jot of difference.

I had a young woman working with me as Saturday girl and during college breaks, who was incredibly laid back and yet had a large, confident personality. She was a slip of a thing, pretty, a 'goth' wanted to join the Police and she was someone who I would have trusted with my life. Like all of us she had her weaknesses, usually controversy around her partners (often my own problem) but we got on well and she had a 'bucket of balls' (not literally, although she did joke that when she walked behind some of our staggering trannies she half expected their testicles to drop off and she'd have to kick them away before anyone noticed?) She had a wicked sense of humour and I believe it was humour which kept us able to cope with so much of the nonsense that our Transvestites spouted. Honestly, there was a list of beliefs of which nearly ninety percent of them sincerely believed, either one, some or all of them???

1. They actually thought like women and therefore had more empathy with others. Possibly, until they felt threatened emotionally or didn't get their own way???

2. They had better dress sense because they had this female ability to choose the right colours etc. and knew what men wanted to see???

3. They looked after themselves more than the average woman???

4. That there was a huge myth about childbirth being very painful because we are designed to give birth and their female intuition meant they could see that the fuss was caused by the fear that the father would prefer the child???????

5. They know what women are about, which was one of the reasons they wanted to dress like them??

6. If their wife understood they could dress up together, but this wouldn't mean that they would want to dress more, or go out??

7. That 'dressing' was benign, a hobby, it wasn't done to attract a sexual dabble with somebody else. A persona to hide behind to satisfy sexual curiosity???

8. It meant that they 'listened' more without offering their own version of what should be done?? (pardon…I just chocked on my tea!!)

I have to stop, because this would end up a real feminist rant, but working alongside these types of views made even my feminist hackles rise. Men who came to us were liars and manipulators and initially used me, my staff and my business to blag their wives that what they were doing was perfectly normal and the amount it cost them? Well that was their business. Time and again these sad ladies entered the shop with their respective spouses almost dragging them in front of me, so that I could tell them how 'normal' Fred was really!

I remember coming up from the dungeon, dressed in my 'shop' attire and finding Cathy sitting in the lounge with a husband and wife, obviously 'selling' the idea again, that her partners desire to wear women's clothing could be taken as a compliment, was just a tiny little wrinkle in an otherwise perfect marriage and please do look round so you can understand better and realise how safe the surroundings are i.e. not a venue where somebody could indulge in sexual practices, unless of course he's in the dungeon, but we won't mention that! Most of these visits were precipitated by the poor woman coming home unexpectedly and finding their spouses either parading around their bedroom dressed in their clothing or worse, just their underwear.

When she spotted me she stood up and introduced the woman to me, I already knew the man, so I said all the right things with a smile and noticed how, once his wife was engaged with me, he sidled off to the cabinet of false breasts and purchased a pair from Cathy, all the time keeping watch so his wife didn't spot him. When he returned to the conversation, he held the paper bag slightly out of sight to his wife's periphery vision. Cathy again joined the conversation as we moved towards the door and together, we waived them off, all smiles hopefully having reassured the woman that everything was fine. As we stood on the threshold Cathy lifted a hand to wave goodbye and said under her breath, 'If I

EVER came home and found my other half in any of my clothes, I'd fucking hang him!' Sadly, I agreed.

I feel a twinge of guilt regarding my eventual animosity towards this sector of fetishist because there were some customers who I genuinely liked as did my staff, and I had no problem with the way they scratched their itch and who I would still call friends. My problem really was that these 'Ladies' were very definitely men, the worst type of men, and they thought like men, were arrogant and selfish like men and mentally believed they were 'better looking than the average woman and without a shadow of a doubt they were always obviously right', on the basis that men are…of course?

One of the Trannies, we'll call her Ethel, could actually pass for a female pensioner and quite an attractive lady to boot. I liked her a lot and so did my staff. She had kept herself very trim and visited the gym almost daily when she wasn't visiting me. She wanted to dress and make-up like a stylish woman of her age and because she was slight, about five foot six inches and walked carefully in lower heels, whenever I had taken her out nobody really paid her much attention. The only real giveaway was if she spoke because she had a very deep, masculine voice so if she was spoken to, I usually explained that she had a problem with her throat and it had taken away her ability to speak... Inevitably the person would then start shouting at her? I didn't get it? She had a problem with her voice not her fucking ears? Why do people do that?

Anyway, she had booked to go out on a Thursday afternoon and as Cathy was working, I asked her to accompany her. I did not foresee any problem as, like me, she liked Ethel and, on that afternoon, as it was drizzling. Ethel was wearing a plain raincoat over a skirt and twinset, silk scarf around her neck (hiding the Adams apple) one of those pocket rain hats that tie under the chin and neat little kitten heels with trim that matched her handbag. I can't remember what Cathy was wearing but she had toned down her Goth look and when she did these jobs for me, she always posed as the Granddaughter. I think I mentioned earlier that there is an element in most of these things of Theatre and as Ethel had never married, she enjoyed pretending she was 'granny' and always treated whoever took her out to 'something nice'.

They left at about twelve and I expected them back at around three thirty, so when it got to about five, I felt a flicker of concern. These days with everybody owning a mobile phone it would have been easy to contact one of them and do a check-up, but although this isn't that long ago, mobile phones were not around so one had to wait. At six o'clock I was definitely starting to feel bothered by the absence of a call to explain the delay. When it got to a quarter to seven, I was really starting to worry, and then the phone rang.

"I would like to speak with Mrs Ives-Murray" said a man,

"Speaking" I replied and as I spoke something in my head gave me warning bells.

"This is the duty sergeant at Collingwood Police Station"

…

Groan, "How can I help?"

The ensuing story could only have happened in my life. I did have to go down to the station but the actual story was told to me by a very unamused desk sergeant, almost a monotone with long pauses for emphasis. Thankfully I had a better version when I got them both back to the shop.

Apparently initially everything had gone well. On the bus nobody stared or nudged their friends and Cathy chatted enough for both of them. She was very good at holding a conversation with herself so that it looked like the other person was speaking. Example:

"I'm sorry I was late Nan but the alarm didn't go off, anyway you're always up really, early aren't you? Well I know you are…' natter, natter, natter.

After the bus trip they went into Debenhams, mooched around the make-up department where Ethel purchased some overly expensive make-up for Cathy, then strolled around various departments finally deciding on a cashmere twinset for Ethel. From there they went to a jewellery shop where she purchased a gold bracelet for Cathy and a string of cultured pearls for herself. Both purchases, including the make-up was placed in the same bag as the Debenhams bag that held the wool twinset.

After leaving the jewellers they decided to head for a quaint tea shop that served home-made cakes, where we were well known and it was safe to take some of the 'not so passable' dressers. There was no warning, but as they opened the café door an unknown male tried to snatch Ethel's carrier bag. His expectation was probably that this was a frail, sweet, little old lady who had something in the Debenhams bag that was bound to be worth something. For all Cathy and Ethel knew, he could have followed them after they had left the jeweller's, either way he had made a terrible mistake!

Ethel did not let go of the bag and in the ensuing struggle the two of them went round each other struggling to take control of the carrier bag. As they whizzed around Cathy leapt onto the back of their assailant and stuck her fingers up his nostrils, pulling his head backwards, and sunk her teeth into his ear lobe!

I was surprised too!

Screaming like a banshee the perpetrator managed to grab Ethel's hair and as the wig left her head and came effortlessly away into his hand he started shouting for help? With that Ethel kicked off her shoes, felled him with a half Nelson and as he hit the pavement, Cathy punched him square in the face, causing his nose to flap away at ninety degrees and blood to cover all three of them. Ethel had not remained quiet during this confrontation and as he fought his assailant, he had let go of plenty of expletives in a deep, obviously masculine voice. Neither Cathy or Ethel saw the squad cars pulling up but as several officers attempted to untangle the three of them, Cathy said later that she heard the mugger claim that they had attacked him because he had refused the sexual advances of Ethel? She immediately started shouting above the sound of everybody else that Ethel and herself were innocent and they needed to arrest the man with blood pouring from his nose and ear and being held in a headlock by the man in a dress.

I was asked to attend the station to verify the earlier part of the story and that 'Ethel' was a very nice gentleman who just happened to like wearing ladies' clothes and was known to me because I provided a service for Transvestites.

I also had to vouch for Cathy who the 'mugger' was trying to get 'done' for assault, but thankfully he had a lot of form as a mugger and I think some of the policemen at the station were quite amused that he had picked on the wrong people, for once!

Ethel and Cathy related this story with pride and we all got involved with the hilarity of the situation.

23. NOT EVERYTHING IS FUNNY

There were many funny moments and I did meet some lovely people, but as I said before, things happened which finally made my decision to walk away. Dressers used to pay for a photograph and we had a huge board which the customer's added their photo's to, if they could not risk taking them away with them. We had a customer who visited probably once every two months. A nice enough chap, in his early thirties, single, not too outlandish in his dressing habits, just generally an ok customer.

It was a busy day and a gentleman with an up-right demeanour and a slightly puzzled expression entered the shop. Barbara, another part-timer, was speaking to him and as she leads him into the lounge area to the board with the photographs on, she looked visibly shaken. When I caught her eye, I saw her gently excuse herself and looking worried she approached me.

She told me the gentleman's name and said that he had actually come to speak to me, but had asked if we had pictures of his son, dressed as a woman, before he was brought to me. She told me that his son was dead and that he had a letter which had led him to me? She shrugged her shoulders and obviously wanted me to take over, so I approached the man, introduced myself and took him upstairs to my private sitting room, where I offered him tea or coffee, but he declined.

He had been some sort of officer in the British army. He had married and had one son, who was the gentleman we had known as a Transvestite. I am not going to use his 'dressing name' I see no reason to. The gentleman's wife had died when his son was seven and he had left the army to be a hands-on father. He had believed that they were close, they holidayed together still and enjoyed a lot of the same things. They no longer lived together but were living close by to each other and spoke probably every day. He sat opposite me and I watched a whole host of emotions cross his face as he looked at me. When he started to talk tears rolled down his face and yet he held his composure.

His son had started dating a girl two years prior. He quite liked her, was unaware of any problems, saw her probably as much as he saw his son and was completely ignorant that anything was amiss the weekend it happened. Saturday he and his son went to local football and then to the pub for an hour. His son said he was seeing his girlfriend later; he couldn't remember what else had been said it wasn't important. Nothing was out of the ordinary according to his memory. On the Sunday the three of them were having lunch together at his son's house but as he was just about to leave the phone rang and his son said he had woken up late so dinner would be an hour and a half later. He couldn't remember if they had discussed him using his key but it was his habit to let himself in and then shout his arrival before going forward, so that he didn't walk into anything embarrassing. The son also asked his father to pick up a couple of bits for him from the supermarket.

He watched motor racing for an hour, left, went to the supermarket and then walked to his son's house for lunch. He did not notice whether the girlfriend's car was there or not.

When he entered the house and the first thing, he saw was a pair of heeled shoes on legs very slightly swinging, suspended from the bannister above. His first thought was the girlfriend and without hesitating he rushed up the stairs to find the top of the noose which was around the neck of a woman wearing a very pretty summer dress, with long blonde hair. Sometimes the shock actually prevents a person from seeing what is actually there. He managed to take the weight of the body, release the noose and drag the body back onto the landing. He ended in a sort of heap on the floor with the body in his arms and as he brushed the hair out of her face, he found the distorted features of his son, fully made up, eyes wide open.

I cannot imagine the horror and then the grief that must have washed over him at that moment. He had been a soldier so had met death before and recognised it in his son. He said the rest was a bit of a blur but he had phoned the emergency services, and just as they arrived, the door being open, he saw an envelope pinned to his son's skirt with the word Dad on it, so he quickly ripped it off and put it in his pocket. He said that he horrified himself, because if he had thought clearly, he would have ripped the female clothes from his son's body and washed the make-up from his face. He was tormented by the shame he had felt when the Ambulance men saw how his son was dressed and the double whammy of being ashamed of the shame because his son was dead and it didn't matter how he looked.

He looked down into his lap and went silent. I got up and poured two stiff Brandy's, handing one to him before sitting back down. He mumbled a thank you, took a few sips and with a huge sigh continued. Nobody knew about the letter but him.

Apparently, the girlfriend had arrived earlier than expected the night before and had caught him in women's clothes. There had been a row, tears and she had left saying she never wanted to see him again. His letter from his son never mentioned his dressing other than to say that that was why his girlfriend left. After writing a few things that were deeply personal to him and his son, the only other thing in his letter was to say that if he wanted to know why he had committed suicide to find, Roma and he had given my address but no number.

He sat and looked at me waiting for my response but I did not know what he meant. I had never had an in-depth conversation with his son and though I could guess that the break up with his girlfriend was because she had caught him in ladies clothing, I still couldn't see my involvement in his suicide?

I started to explain that I was confused, but a sudden burst of anger from this man meant I was going to have to be very careful how I handled this.

"You made him like that didn't you?" he shouted and raised himself slightly from his chair.

"You got rid of her and made him be a pervert to make money out of him. Were you having sex with him? Were you? Tell me? I want to know how you killed him!"

I stood promptly and crossed the gap between us so that I was standing over him. I could feel his anger and grief like a hot wind emanating from his head.

"I did NOT kill your son" I said clearly, in a tone that was firm but kind.

I explained my business, how it worked and told him that though I knew his son it was not an intimate relationship and sorry, but I knew very little about him. I knew nothing about his girlfriend but stated he may have seen me 'council' women who wanted to understand why their loved ones dressed in women's clothing. I told him that I didn't know why, I just explained that some men were wired a bit differently, it wasn't dangerous, unless they courted danger, and that there were far worse 'habits' than dressing up as a woman. Having been in the Army he would know that as a fact and it was my observation that squaddies always seemed to want to dress up as a parody of a woman, at the drop of a hat!

He crumpled in the chair and wept, his grief raw and endless. I went down on my knees beside him and tentatively touched his shoulder. He almost fell into my arms and I cradled him as he cried. I could feel my mascara stinging my eyes but I wasn't going to let him go until he wanted me to. I've no idea how long we stayed in that position other than to say my legs had gone to sleep and I did worry that if and when I stood up, I may actually end up crumbling into the chair and into his lap.

Which I don't think would have gone down well. Thankfully a member of staff knocked on the door before entering and whilst he was distracted, I managed to stand very slowly. When he was a little more 'together' the lady who entered the room, asked him if he wanted to talk to her about his son, because she had known him and actually, she knew him, the father too. He looked rather worried, until she explained that they all went to the same church.

After a few seconds he realised who she was and seemed comforted that she worked in my business. She gently took his empty glass and then held his hand.

"Would you like to pray?" she asked and went down on her knees in front of him. He nodded and slid off the chair to kneel beside her his head bowed. I quietly left the room.

The reason I have included this is because I was so very angry, that it had a huge bearing on me closing down the business. How dare he take his own life and drop the guilt firmly into my lap. I do not feel sorry. Suicide is a choice that I have always believed we all have a right to, but unless you are going to write a letter that explains your reasons, just do it!

I found out later that he had actually expected his girlfriend to find him. He wanted her to feel guilty for the rest of her life for ending the relationship. It was his way of giving her the ultimate guilt trip. People always assume that suicides by the nature of the act, shows instability and that the person is not in their right mind.

This really isn't always true. I have personal knowledge of two suicides which were planned meticulously and that I had been aware of before it happened. I had talked in depth to both, before the deed, and was convinced. I understood their reasoning and gave them the acknowledgement that they were perfectly rational and had the 'right' to die if they really had, had enough.

The anger that I felt was raw. I was disgusted that this selfish, stupid man, took it upon himself to play God and planted me firmly in the frame. I felt so sorry for his father who was left alone, completely unable to digest the horror of finding his son looking the way he did, with a letter that explained nothing. It forced him to come and find me, to enter a world that he had no real knowledge of and to try to share his grief with strangers. I was disgusted and removed all of his photographs from the board and burned them. My staff member left the shop with the man, who attempted to apologise to me as he were leaving. I didn't let him, but I hugged him before he left and then asked someone else to cash up and close the shop for me. I went upstairs and cuddled my dogs whilst I got slowly pissed on champagne. That night I cried myself to sleep.

.

24. POP GOES THE...?

Sometimes in the dungeon despite your best intentions things just go wrong. We're all fallible and so is the equipment we use and sometimes the funniest moments are times when something that should be inanimate, suddenly isn't? I've had canes break; paddles decide to suddenly paddle away from their handles. Padlocks that won't open, either before use or far worse still, sometimes after. Rubber splitting in the wrong place or at the wrong time, boot heels breaking, a long whip catching you on the back of your leg. Just so many things, just the same as in other walks of life, that can and therefore will, go wrong.

I remember once being in the dungeon and although I didn't realise it, I was heading for a nasty dose of flu and I felt a bit achy and my head felt 'woolly'.

Now I explained earlier that for customers who wanted me to pee on them I would wear an eighty percent denier tight, that had a cotton gusset, that with care could be cut out without damaging the tights. I didn't want my bits on show and I didn't feel it was right for the customer to see me pulling down my tights and pants, then wipe myself and pull everything up again. I know it sounds ridiculous, but though I had no objection demeaning the sub by pissing on him, I felt it was demeaning to me if he watched me go through the ritual that all women go through to go for a piss.

In some instances, I would use the second bathroom which had subdued lighting, a beautiful, extra-large, roll top bath and I would position the sub lying in the bath, hands shackled to the lifting handles. I used to wear a special leather mini skirt that was short enough to show my legs but tucked my bum up nicely and then I would step up and balance on the side of the bath in a position which made it very easy to pee and direct the pee where I wanted it to land. Usually on the customers' forehead or his dick, depending how I felt. I was also pretty good at breaking my flow to keep them guessing or because they were taking too long to ejaculate. This type of customers nearly all wanted 'to come'.

Anyway, as I said I wasn't feeling on top of my game but was still working. We had a customer for being peed on and the session was quite normal until it came to me pissing on him. I've no idea what or where my head was, but he started wanking and I started peeing…and that's where it all went wrong. I hadn't changed my tights? I also couldn't control my bladder and stop, so there I am above this gentleman with piss running down my legs inside my tights getting very squishy feet with me looking down in horror, hoping like mad he still ejaculated? In desperation Judy sank a jug into the toilet bowl and chucked it in his face which had the desired effect. Still standing on the edges of the bath, despite the punter still lying in it, I peeled off the very soggy piss filled tights and dropped them on his upturned face. Carefully making sure I only stepped onto the bath mat, I dried my feet and I left the bathroom heading for my own bathroom to shower. Judy dealt with the customer who was demanding his money back because I hadn't actually peed on him. She was a sensible girl and went and found a clear plastic bag, gingerly folded the tights and offered him my piss filled tights instead of my pissing on him, pointing out how often in the future he would be able to use them for wanking. It worked and he left a happy bunny.

I also recall one particular moment when I was working with Sheila, a day I shall never forget though trust me I have tried!

On this particular day I was working with a girl who had stepped in for her, as she had been called away. The gentleman was a bondage customer who wanted us both in the dungeon with him. It was his birthday and he was treating himself to the luxury of two Mistresses rather than just the one. He wanted to be gagged and strapped up, then placed in a rubber cocoon and on top of that shackled down on the bondage bed. He liked to be periodically sat on, whilst trussed up, which I confess had made me slightly nervous before we had even started.

Ordinarily I wouldn't have given it a thought, but the lady I was working with, though extremely agile was a dress size 20. I'm not really sure what a person who wears that dress size actually weighs but I think it's roughly about nineteen stone and I had doubts how long the customer would cope with her sitting on his diaphragm? I had to assume that he had seen this girl before because she basically took control from the moment the session started and as she had been the one to brief me when he had first arrived, it was logical that he had seen her before. What slightly worried me was that he was a tall, thin, very weedy man whose flesh wouldn't recognise a muscle if it tried to find a home in his body and he had more in common with a twiglet than a man who liked to be sat on?

It would have been extremely unprofessional if I had nodded towards my 'sister in leather,' behind her back and whispered, "Are you sure?" even though I wanted to ask. Ultimately, I kept my mouth shut and just got on with the job in hand.

After we had both gone through the preliminaries it was time to truss him up and even that posed a slight problem because his wrists were so skinny, we both ended up stabbing at implements to create more holes. When he was firmly secured, she eased herself up onto the bondage bed and sat astride him on her knees. As she lowered herself slowly down onto his lap, we heard him sort of slow grunt as the air left his lungs and then a sort of strangled noise as she leaned forward and pressed herself against his chest. Just as he started to slightly struggle, she gently let the pressure up and leaned backwards releasing his lungs and then wriggled herself downwards, so that she was sitting on his crotch.

"Naughty, naughty" she purred, slinging her leg round and sliding to the floor as if dismounting a horse. When she was standing beside him, I jumped up and replaced her, sitting slightly shy of his knob and when I felt him relax, I battered that area for him with a paddle. Little grunts and sighs kept escaping from the gentleman, which was normal, and whilst I pushed down hard on his pubic area, she battered the soles of his feet with a cane. The rubber obviously absorbs a lot of the momentum, so to make it hurt the Mistress has to work twice as hard.

I will never understand the use of 'poppers' (Amyl Nitrate) but they are extremely popular within the Gay scene and quite commonly asked for in the Dungeon. They didn't do it for me but then I'm female. Like most things, I have at one time or another tried using it, but it really wasn't something I enjoyed. It was used at one time for the treatment of Heart Attack and or Angina. It speeds up the heart and produces a high for about 15-20 seconds but I found that my head would pound almost as soon as the high wore off and I just didn't like it. Men try to use it at the moment of orgasm, as it intensifies the feeling, but I've never used it at that moment so maybe I don't know what I'm missing? The chemical comes in a small bottle and is sniffed to achieve the effect.

This particular gentleman would always climax at some point towards the end of the session and had requested that at his signal he be allowed to take a sniff of the little bottle.

Things were hot-ting up and we were working towards the finale. I think I already explained that ejaculators have to pay for an extra half an hour so that they can clean up after themselves, so we would work towards the hour. If nothing happened then it was tough, they still had to pay. I was seated on the bondage bed at the head end and I had removed the nose portion of the mask in readiness. Now when I used poppers I tipped the bottle onto a piece of cotton wool and used the pad for the customer to sniff, but my compadré in this instance waived away the pad and just took the bottle. She was now sitting on his chest and regulating his breathing, as she held the little bottle of poppers.

Just at the penultimate moment the legs at the head end of the bondage bed buckled inwards sending me sliding backwards into a heap, but I managed to quickly shuffle sideways and land on my haunches. To my horror I watched as the other girl was thrown forwards and at the same time practically emptied the bottle of poppers up the nostrils of the punter, which caused him to start to fit so violently that the legs at the other end of the bed shattered under the thrashing and crashing. The other girl was suddenly being thrown about like she was on a bucking bronco. Straps were ripped free and I was terrified that as he thrashed around under her weight he was going to hit his head and cause himself some serious brain injury, that is if the poppers didn't kill him, or cause irreparable damage to his brain first! If you have ever seen a fish in the bottom of a boat having been hauled out of the water, that was exactly how he looked?

And then suddenly it had all stopped. She was literally slumped in a sort of sideways heap off to the side of the punter but seemed very disorientated and after saying her name a couple of times and getting no response, I wondered if she had maybe hit her own head during the fuss? In desperation I rolled her out of my way and started removing straps that weren't broken, zips I could reach and tearing at the rubber to get to the customer underneath. When I exposed his head and removed the mask, I was greeted with a grin like the Cheshire cat in 'Alice's adventures in Wonderland.'

He was still slightly gasping for breath, but the first words out of his mouth were, "How much to do it again?"

I kept my cool and explained that as the bench had been broken and we had other customers, I was very sorry but, 'times up!'

Just as he was heading towards the shower Sheila came in through the front door. I waited for her friend to give an explanation, but she was more worried about the bruising on her knees and the fact that she had cricked her neck, so I was left to give an explanation of sorts. Sheila peered round the dungeon door and stood for a second just staring at the rubble, then she turned to me and asked if anyone else were expected. I explained who was due so she found her book and made a couple of calls but just as she had finished the customer came out of the bathroom. He smiled broadly and started to praise myself and my work colleague asking if he could book again while he was there?

Sheila smiled, "of course you can" she said, "but I can't promise that we'll have another bed that can be broken?"

He looked from her to me and back again. The penny dropped and he started to make excuses as he backed towards the front door. Sheila saw him out herself and closed the door behind him.

"Just another day at the office" she said almost to herself, but I pulled a face.

"I bloody well hope not," I said.

"Tsk, tsk Roma," she said heading for the fridge, "You wouldn't know what to do if you went back to working in an office!"

We both knew she was right.

25. ONLY IN MY WORLD

When I was running the business for Transvestites, one of the women who worked for me part time used to run a clinic, possibly the only one at that time in the country, for transsexuals, offering counselling, hormone therapy and regular appointments with a surgeon able to do the reassignment surgery. Now if I thought some of the trannies were a bit un-hinged, I'm sorry but the Transsexuals and those who haven't actually decided to go all the way through to surgery, are quite frankly as mad as a box of frogs!

I know that I will be jumped on from a big height (and if you saw the size of these 'women' it's not something even remotely enjoyable) and I had better clarify my comments. I guess that because I have my own mental problems, I feel I'm allowed to comment on what I believe in many cases, is actually some sort of delusional condition. I know that as I write this I am not being politically correct, but I have formed my opinions from 'inside' the world of Transsexuals and Transvestites and as far as I'm aware this IS still a country where we have a freedom of speech and a God given right to our opinions, even if some people do not like them. As long as we do not use our opinions to try to incite hatred or form some sort of action against those we disagree with, I believe we do still have a right to air our opinions and a right to hold them.

I am not for one moment stating that there are not accidents of nature. I believe that there are conditions from birth that have placed a person to feel like they are in the wrong body and I have met these people and am happy for them when they achieve their goal of being able to be who they believe they are. My problem with this is that firstly, (after all these years no doubt things have changed?) The outlets for hormones were private, as were the visits to psychiatrists, gender 'specialists' (some of whom didn't even have basic nursing qualifications) and Doctors and I am afraid that having the cash to 'change' or in some cases deliberately turning themselves into half-n-half's for me personally, just didn't seem right. I will clarify this again before I get thousands of emails wanting me stoned, I AM talking nearly forty years ago, so I am SURE it's not like that anymore. But then it was and there were a great many people being handed out 'hormone' tablets that were extremely unstable individuals, who thundered through life hurting those who had loved them and ramming their 'sexuality' with as many graphic examples as they could muster, down your throat!

I actually feel this about all minority groups. Gay's, Fetishists, Bisexuals, Bestiality, non-Binary, Straights (not a minority but thought I should include us) and all variations. I have no desire to know what turns you on, who you have sex with, how you have sex with, or anything else concerning your sex life. I don't open conversations with, "I had a good fuck last night with a Goose", obviously trying to bring about a conversation, and I don't want to know somebody else's bedroom secrets, unless for some reason I ask?

So, as my shop was open for transvestites and employed a seamstress to make bespoke clothing, longer sleeves, the longer body, wider neck etc. and I employed a woman who ran a gender clinic, it was obvious that my business would attract attention within the Transsexual lifestyle.

The first thing that bothered me was that far too many, who presumably were either of independent means or on some form of benefit, would turn up and literally abuse my hospitality. I didn't charge for teas or coffees, because I felt it should be a part of my service, but these 'people' would arrive and literally stay until I had to politely ask them to leave. Some even had the Gaul to bring a packed lunch with them! They would also use my premises to 'hold court' and tell the Trannies that they didn't understand the actual desire to dress as women because what they really needed to do was move away from their loved ones and go and live as a woman. I heard, more times than I've had a hot meal, that if they did this, they would realise that they really wanted to have sex with men, not because in any way they were homosexual, but because they were stifling their real desire to have sex properly as a woman.

Interestingly, having been around pre-op and post-op transsexuals (remembering we're going back a bit) when asked pertinent questions, admitted that not only do the hormone injections affect the mental wellbeing (they can cause nasty mood swings) but they can drastically damp down the sexual urge and if not the urge, the ability to have an erection. Once operated on, IF they find themselves in a relationship and want to be intimate, many find that the tube which replicates the virginal tract, is too short and too painful to have what a 'woman' would call normal sex and if they can have sex in the normal fashion, there is no clitoris, or it has been put in place but the nerve ends die, so the sex itself actually has no feeling, meaning that they are never going to have another orgasm. I think today there is probably still a bit of a lottery when it comes to being able to 'feel' during sexual intercourse and possibly be able to orgasm? When you could find someone, who told the truth about their surgery and what they could actually feel after the op as completed. Most admitted that the need for the continuous use of an instrument to keep the vagina open was upsetting and unpleasant and that the hormones that they would have to take for their lifetime, prevented the sexual feelings they had expected to be able to feel after surgery.

Most men have a deep seated 'need' for sex and the completion of the sexual act, the climax. I discovered really quite quickly that despite insisting that they 'thought like women', sex seemed to still be a topic of conversation and something to be sought after.

Things have changed a great deal since I was around Transsexual women and a survey of male to female in 2018, of the 22 asked all stated that they did have some sensitivity, however there was a huge learning curve when it came to these women achieving orgasm, or similar as they needed to understand their new genitalia and how to stimulate it in a way that produced pleasant sensations. The male penis is easy to stimulate, with very little stimuli needed to arrive at satisfaction, women, surprise, surprise! are far more complicated.

Another factor is who and where the operation happens. In the UK and America, the cost of the operation is still prohibitive, hence the 'plastic surgery' migration to the Eastern European countries for breast implantation and clitoroplasty and vaginoplasty, but each operation is a separate surgery. As a rough guide, breast implants seven thousand pounds, clitoroplasty eleven to twelve thousand and vaginoplasty five thousand four hundred pounds making a total of thirteen thousand four hundred pounds sterling...yikes!!! and I have no intention of jumping into the NHS debate, even mentioning it has me running for the duvet to hide under!

For the sake of argument, I will call this couple, Barbara and Ann who were two post op transsexuals who lived together as house mates. Barbara was, I'm afraid, not the best advert for gender reassignment. She had had her surgery in the USA when she turned fifty. She was six foot one and insisted on wearing really high heels because she could walk in them, which I have to agree but her stride was more than a metre. She had shoulders like a quarter back and had grown her hair long to comb over her bald spot, a bit like president Trump? She insisted on wearing skirts about four inches above the knees, no tights and she hadn't really got the hang of things like shaving her legs, shaping her eyebrows and worst of all did nothing about the veritable rain forest hanging out of her nose! The hormones that she would have to take for the rest of her life, were expensive which meant she dabbled with the dosage and occasionally walked around with a five o'clock shadow? She had paid for breast implants which were huge, she had hands like shovels and a terribly deep voice with a Manchester accent. Her favourite colour was pink.

Ann was about forty-five, only about five foot five but her dimensions meant that her width was about the same. She, very sensibly, wore long skirts (well, long in relation to Barbara) had her own hair cut in a bob ending just above the ears, which unfortunately made one look for a tonsure? and tended to emphasise her five chins. She never wore make-up, but always had well-manicured talons. I have no idea whether she had breast implants because one rolls of fat just sat on another, in fact the only way I knew she had legs was because she wore skirts.

Sadly, Jabba-the-hut comes to mind and her favourite colour was Sunflower yellow.

I can hear the hissing from here, but is there no way that a person who believes that they have been born in the wrong body should be persuaded to leave well enough alone and recognise that, sorry, nature was cruel but you're being unrealistic asking us not to stare, laugh, be embarrassed? I didn't dislike these women, well not at first, and went out of my way to try to help them, as women. I went out with them, socialised with them, supported them and stood with them when someone picked on them. Having said that, unless there was twenty of them or they were a man mountain, my money would always be on Barbara.

If they looked after their bodies, skin etc. which a great many do, one could feel a certain respect for having the balls (oops.bit of a bad analogy) to stare the world in the face and go for it, but I found that the Trans who didn't work at it, like women do, just shouldn't do it!

The main topic of these two women was how to get a man. Ann did slightly better in the dating game because she was smaller in height and some men when very drunk will 'go for a fat bird', but Barbara and her aggressive sexual advances would if being realistic be better to find a man in a coma. I would listen in horror when out with these two girls, at their patter and modus-operandi when they saw a possible target. Despite being women, they still treated the challenge of finding a mate like men, worse irritatingly persistent men. I remember once being in a rather run-down wine bar when both of them zeroed in on a man slightly slumped at the bar. Both bought him a drink which he gratefully accepted and attempted to hold a coherent conversation, the nature of which I couldn't hear. Periodically some sort of joke must have been made because the two ladies would burst out into very loud laughter, while their new friend gave a sort of grimace which was either that he was trying to smile or trying to stop himself dribbling. As he visibly started to wilt, Barbara took one side and Ann took the other and with a huge wink and a thumbs up to me whisked him quickly out of the bar before he collapsed completely. I finished my drink and decided to walk home and as I started walking, I thought to myself, "I really wouldn't want to be in his shoes tomorrow when he has to do his walk of shame??"

I had a friend who, and I know this sounds weird, had no idea that she was pregnant. I'm not talking the immaculate conception, she knew she was having sex, but during the pregnancy she had had what she considered to be normal periods, no morning sickness and just didn't know, having never been pregnant before. She was a bit overweight, but I am not talking obese and was in the shop with me (she worked part time) when she said that just recently, she was suffering from wind. Not just the normal farts, she elaborated, but really stinky loud farts which she was apologising for in advance. She had also started to suffer from indigestion and was chewing Rennies like sweets. On that day we were fairly quiet and Margaret and I decided, having opened every window that could be opened, that the sounds were like explosions and the stench unbearable so we would be happy for my friend to go home. Both of us were actually relieved when she left and were making bad jokes about her, when Margaret said, "I know this sounds sort of odd, but to me she looks pregnant?"

I looked at her like she had lost her mind so she just shrugged and changed the subject. In all honesty I would have no idea as I was sterilised at nineteen and in fairness to Margaret, she was an ex-nurse and had had two children, so she certainly had more experience than me, but at the time it just seemed ridiculous. Now I have just informed you that I was sterilised at nineteen which was rare and for me very fortunate. I never wanted children and I don't have a maternal bone in my body, unless it's covered in fur and has paws or is an Octopus. I have never had an Octopus but I would truly love to form a relationship with one of these exciting, intelligent beings that's DNA is not found anywhere else on this planet and has three brains!

I had been to see my GP at fifteen and begged to be sterilised stating as a certainty that I never, ever wanted to have a baby. She told me that if I was as sure at twenty, as I was then, she would get it done for me. Just shy of my twentieth birthday I visited my Doctor, reminded her of her promise, stated that I would rather have a leg chopped off than have a child and went into hospital within the week. Job done!

Margaret and I had both had a phone call to say that my friend had been rushed into hospital the night before in a very serious condition. She was so poorly that when she was told she had preeclampsia it just didn't mean anything and she drifted off under aesthetic grateful to sleep, while a healthy baby girl was removed from her womb by caesarean section, weighing seven pounds something. I was flabbergasted but my shock at what had happened was nothing in comparison with my friends. When she came around and was greeted by beaming nurses trying to make her get her tit out and feed this small, angry, very loud, orange coloured alien, she was horrified and insisted it be removed from the room, so she could go back to sleep. I am told that a caesarean is quite painful, but the pain my friend felt was the total lack of knowledge of her pregnancy and a desperate lack of acceptance that she was now expected to be a mother. Her family, though surprised, were ecstatic that she had delivered a baby girl and couldn't understand why she was being so 'silly'? When she telephoned me, she was in tears and very, very distressed because everybody was pushing her to stop being awkward and get on with loving and looking after a new baby. She said she felt nothing. No maternal instinct, no love or desire to love a baby, that as far as she was concerned, somebody had accidentally left in her room. I got it. I was probably the only one who did and so I made arrangements to visit her in Hospital, organising Barbara to get me there by car. Now I specifically expressed to Barbara that because of the circumstances I didn't feel it was right for anyone to be with me, which both her and Ann agreed was probably best.

I'm not one of these people who say, 'I hate hospitals!'. In fact, I think it's a stupid thing to say. Even if they clarified it with, I hate hospitals because bad news, horrid things etc. happen in them'. Duh? Good things happen in them too. People's, bones mended, babies are born (wanted ones hopefully) lives are saved, and they don't smell 'funny' anymore. When I was a little-un they had a very distinctive smell, carbolic maybe? And that could be the source of 'hospital phobia', but it is no more. Now hospitals smell of a variety of things, especially in A & E on a Friday or Saturday night?

Talking about smells, I wonder if like myself, there are people who miss the smell of paint? When I decorated in the past, part of the satisfaction when you have finished is the smell of the paint, informing your nostrils and everybody else's that you have worked hard and things are fresh and clean. Even in my sixties I still have to do my own horrid painting and at least before there was proof, I had worked until my tennis elbow screamed!!

Well I left Barbara and Anne in the hospital tea shop, (Anne was happy anyway..buns!) and when I got up into the ward I had to ask where my friend was because she wasn't obviously visible. A nurse led me to a bed with the curtains round and whispered that her reaction to her baby was very bad for other new mothers, so the curtains were kept closed. As soon as I stepped through the curtains my friend spread her arms to hug me and started crying in such a painfully emotional way that her sadness reached out and grabbed me around my heart. We clung together for what seemed like forever and all the words she couldn't say to anybody else, all the feelings that nobody else could understand, and all her physical and emotional pain washed over me like a shroud. When we finally separated, I sat on the edge of the bed, told her who was downstairs in the coffee shop and tried desperately to make her smile. I don't know how long I had been sitting there but suddenly a nurse appeared with an incredibly noisy, wriggling bundle which appeared to have a wrinkled orange as a head and a gaping gash, which I assumed was how the baby could make such an awful noise. Without a word she held out this small, living object to my poor friend in the bed. She turned away and I could see tears welling up in her eyes again and then ridiculously the nurse lent over the bed and said, "you hold her for your friend?".

I didn't mean to, but I physically recoiled and at that second Barbara burst through the curtains like Superman, the curtain clinging to her six foot shoulders like a cape, blocking out the light and boomed,

"I'll take it Mar'm!" holding out her huge hands to engulf the screaming baby. The look of shock horror on the nurse's face was a picture.

It was the first time since I had been there that I saw my friend break into a smile and then let out a little giggle. I was so grateful to Barbara at that moment.

26. FIGHTS OF FANCY

When I had the business for trannies one of the weirdest things to me was the rivalry, between the transvestites and the transsexuals. As I said earlier, one of my staff ran possibly, one of the only clinics (in those days) for pre-op transsexuals, which meant that my hospitality initially was offered to those who were visiting the clinic, as a matter of course. Unfortunately, as I mentioned before, I ultimately resented the way that these women tried to take over my 'lounge' drinking my tea and coffee, without offering any sort of contribution to my business. I think with hindsight that I should have clarified what my business was for, who it was for and sadly probably not employed the lady so involved with the Transsexual side of this coin.

Initially the 'squabbles' between the two factions was vaguely amusing because the topics quite frankly was banal, but I started to notice over time that these petty arguments were getting louder and longer and at times were poisoning the atmosphere of the 'community' that I had built up around my business.

One of the endless rows was about whether Transsexuals or Transvestites were born with the 'female' mind, which in my books was ludicrous to the extreme. Time and again I tried to explain that the 'sisterhood' women shared was made up of life experiences and the way people were brought up, not only by parents but also the way society views the different roles of the sexes.

Nurture, in my own thinking is a very small part of what makes us who we are, unless of course you are talking extremes i.e. 'concentration camps in the last war'. There is obviously differences and I would advise reading 'Women are from Venus and Men are from Mars', because it really does help us view these things in a more constructive manner. However, for me the idea that these men, actually 'thought' like me by nature of my sex, was rubbish.

This particular day I had, 'Mary', 'Angela', 'Patricia,' and Alan in for the dressing service. Alan never bothered with a 'female' name as he had only come to 'dressing' at the ripe age of seventy-six after his wife of forty years died suddenly of a ruptured aorta as he handed her a cup of tea. The only make-up he wanted was face powder and a tiny bit of blusher and lipstick. He had purchased a wig from me but wore his wife's clothes, almost like a tribute to her memory and he insisted on paying for the time he spent with us (I think he was lonely) whether he dressed or not. Angela was an ex paratrooper who had had problems adjusting to 'civi-street' after being invalided out of the regiment. I never asked what his injury was and he never volunteered it, but initially he had ended up behind bars for a few nights after being involved in fights. He sincerely believed that when he discovered dressing it had helped quell a lot of the anger because it had made him read about 'women'. Woman's issues, their role in politics and the history of that role. Women in the armed forces both in the United Kingdom and globally. Women's roles in various aspects of working life and the more traditional roles of home and family both historically and in the modern world. He was great to 'debate' with, had a wicked, very dry sense of humour and I really liked him. Mary was unfortunately one of those dressers who wanted to look like a 'tart', but was actually very nice and very well educated and Patricia was a family man with six children and another three with his first wife. One of his favourite jokes was that he had no idea where they had all come from and if he caught you just standing around, he would say, "don't hang about near me, you'll get pregnant!"

All of my ladies were made up and 'dressed' and I was sitting doing Angela's nails (we stuck on false ones with a glue that just dissolved in water) when the entry bell on the door went off to signal someone entering the shop. Before I had a chance to move, Barbara's voice boomed out a hello, accompanied by Anne's squeaky greeting right on the tail of her friends. When they appeared in the lounge, they had a very nervous, I want to say, 'straggler' with them, who unnerved me by the way his eyes darted around his environment, as if looking for something to steal. With four seats taken, leaving only two available chairs and the small stool I had been sitting on, Barbara plonked herself into the centre of the couch using her large frame as a sort of battering ram against the two ladies already sitting there. The stranger made herself comfortable in one of the easy chairs and Ann hesitated, obviously wary of the stool but realising that if she wobbled her way into the only available chair, it may look rude. Exasperated, I deliberately mentioned that we were short on milk as I walked into the shop, which went completely above their heads because as I left, I heard

Barbara trying to persuade somebody to make her a coffee.

I've no idea what set everything off, because I didn't hear any raised voices, but suddenly there was an almighty crash and Ann came flying through the air, and like a ball, practically bounced onto the shop carpet on her back. As I rushed into the lounge it was like a Saturday night in one of the Irish pubs I had worked in, only in this instance the 'straggler' was attacking Patricia with the stool, and in the pub, all chairs, tables etc, were bolted to the floor. Even the fruit machines were locked down with huge chains and padlocks. As my eyes registered the scene in front of me, my brain refused to acknowledge what was actually happening before me. Barbara's nose had taken a bashing and she was grappling with Angela like she was performing some grotesque, bloody dance, whilst Mary was on the floor, skirt up round her chest, sinking her teeth into Barbara's calf. Alan was cowering in the corner holding up a cushion as some sort of defence and as I started registering who was where, Ann came back into the room screaming like a banshee and landed on Mary, causing her to exhale violently and leave her teeth in situ, as she tried desperately to climb out from under Ann's weight!

I saw Margaret running around being as much help as a chef during a fast, and I heard myself shout above the noise,

"Margaret, call the police"

It was a bit like the words in a pantomime, 'abra-cadaberer' which makes everyone stop to see what is going to happen. It all stopped and as people untangled themselves, I pointed towards the front door and aimed my voice towards the Transsexuals.

"OUT! No fucking argument. Out!"

I wouldn't allow any explanations. In my view despite all the bollocks these men gave me, the resulting fight was to me, just a typical male way of settling a dispute. Over the coming days I received various bunches of flowers (another typical male method of trying to win back favour) and some staggered phone calls trying to test the water to see if anyone was forgiven. I still have no idea what made these men behave in the way they did whilst claiming to have a 'female' brain and actually I didn't care.

As I explained earlier, I really did try to remain with a foot in both camps, which was why one evening, I agreed that a pre-op Transsexual could kip down on my sofa in the shop for one night, if I am honest, I really liked his dog... He had turned up after hours with a German shepherd and a pillow case with his clean work clothes, saying he had seen his ex-wife after having disappeared for five months and had, had breast and hip implants abroad in the time he had been away. During his absence he had left her without leaving any money for herself and the children, not even for the dog. The only thing he left behind was a stupidly ambiguous note and a promise that when he returned all would be revealed. When he finally went home, he had changed his occupation as well as his 'shape' and she had told him to take his dog and fuck off!

This was a woman who in one week had discovered that her husband of five years was taking hormones to prevent facial hair, didn't see why his children of four and two should have a problem with the years of transition he would be facing and couldn't understand how much he had damaged the woman who loved him. He had already grown his hair long and it was full and glossy which must have been even more irksome as his wife suffered from Alopecia.

It was these sorts of situations which ultimately made me turn my back and walk away, but at this time I was still trying to understand and not judge. When it got to about two in the morning I apologised and explained that I had to be up early and really needed to go to bed. My back door was, for me, quite weird. It had a two-inch thick steel plate on the inside which made it incredibly heavy, three dead bolts, a mortis lock and a Yale, as well as a security chain. I had been told before I rented the property that it had previously been an Undertakers??? As the daughter of an undertaker, I really couldn't imagine what could be that precious that the type of security the door was fitted with, was needed? Unless there was something about the local residents which I had not been made aware of?

Anyway, If I'm honest I didn't want to be involved but at the same time I couldn't see the dog out in the cold, so I said he could stay. At about four in the morning I was initially woken up by his dog jumping on my bed and one of my own dogs grumbling. Initially I thought she was complaining about the 'guest' snuggling up on the duvet but when I shushed her, she actually started to growl properly and was looking towards my bedroom door. Unfortunately, I am one of those people who if you wake me, I will have to go to the toilet before I can even consider going back to sleep. I never put lights on because I had good night vision and anyway it has a tendency to thoroughly wake one up, so it was avoided if possible. Sitting on the loo, I realised that I could hear something strange near the back of the shop and possibly whispering, so I sat quietly straining my ears to hear. I was just starting to think I had imagined it when again I heard this odd sort of stretching noise and muffled whispering. I picked up my tiny Chihuahua and popped her back into my bedroom and closed the door. She was as brave as a lion, but she didn't have any teeth left and only weighed two and a half pounds so I felt safer doing this on my own. My immediate instinct was to think that as I had only used the single lock on the back door, my night guest had somehow arranged for somebody to come to the shop to see him at stupid o clock? Irritated, but wary of jumping to conclusions I quietly padded along the hall to the top of the stairs and peered down into the darkness. I had been there a matter of seconds when I spied the shapes of two people creeping along in front of the stairs towards the shop area. Very quietly I descended the steps and to my right the back door was partially open in such a strange way that I couldn't work out at that moment, what was wrong with what I was looking at? The bottom half of the door seemed to be bent inwards whilst the lock still held. Turning left I picked up a baseball bat that I kept hidden away at the base of the steps and as I entered the lounge area, I deliberately hit the bank of switches with the flat of my hand, illuminating the whole downstairs area. For a split second myself and two men wearing black hoodies froze into a tableau of confusion as we all blinked against the brightness of the light. Suddenly there was a bit of a rustle and my house guest appeared stark naked, with curvy hips and size c breast implants, long flowing locks and a five o'clock shadow and a raging stalker, in all its morning glory!

The potential burgers looked from me to the vision standing in front of them, still only half awake, and as one let out a sort of guttural howl the other joined in with a very girly screech. As one, they turned on their heels and rushed at the back door, falling over each other as they both tried to squeeze through the previously made hole at the same time. It was like watching a car crash as these two idiots resorted to fisty-cuffs in their bid for freedom and as one managed to get one half of themselves, an arm and maybe a leg, the other would drag him back and try to crawl over him to freedom. When the police arrived my house, guest had covered up in a very pretty pink dressing gown and my two assailants were insisting that I and my friend in the dressing gown, should be the ones arrested on the grounds that we were... Well whatever we were, it wasn't normal?

27. DIEING TO MEET YOU

One of the things I always joked about was the 'what if' scenario of a customer dying in the dungeon and I very nearly found out. I will call him Dave for the purposes of telling you the story. He was a tall, well-built man in his mid-forties who ran a building business and had an office along the sea front in Brighton. He wasn't hard up and had built his house in Falmer, settled on fifty acres, in beautifully landscaped countryside. The house had seven en suite bedrooms, a library, indoor swimming pool and a gym which he used every day, as did his wife who was a stunningly beautiful woman from the East End of London.

He had made his money by building a huge development on the docks of London and then switched to a more environmentally friendly style of building, providing country style houses in land designed to embrace and encourage wild life. He was tall, very good looking, charmingly flirtatious, but left nobody in any doubt where his heart belonged. He had known his wife since school and though they both wanted children they deliberately left it until they were financially secure and they had done all the silly, dangerous partying together in various deadbeat countries. They had lived in squats and stayed as guests in stately homes and despite various separations of a day or two, they had spent the last thirty years loving and laughing together.

I really, really liked Dave and I really, really liked the way he talked about his wife and children. His sincerity and respect for all women came across not only in the dungeon, but in the way, he spoke about women generally. When he was near the dungeon and had half an hour (which usually turned into an hour and a half) he would ring and if I wasn't busy, he would pop in with lunch for me and whoever I was working with. I cannot lie, there was a little pang of jealousy when he waxed lyrical about his partner, but only because I don't believe I have ever been loved that much by anyone.

In the dungeon Dave was one of the more extreme submissive's. He was into bondage, whips, canes, razors and extreme torture. He had asked me about erotic asphyxiation but I was wary of offering this service to anyone I liked. That probably sounds strange, but my thinking was that although I had given this service a zillion times, a Dominatrix who doesn't recognise the dangers of the practice shouldn't offer it. My thinking was that if things went horribly wrong, nobody knew where the punter was. Men don't make random chat about going to a dungeon after work, or enjoying having their scrotum nailed to a block of wood?

This was the 'what if' scenario that if you run a dungeon you would be very silly if you had not had some thoughts and ultimately ideas on how to take control if the situation did arrive and things went horribly wrong.

Once when piercing Dave (something that was common to the way he enjoyed his particular type of fetish) he appeared to have some sort of adverse reaction to either the piercing itself or an allergic reaction to the needle used. I was just finishing the piercing itself, when I noticed that he suddenly became quite pale and his hands began to almost imperceptibly tremble. Without causing alarm I instructed him to take deep breaths and placed him in a position near an open window for fresh air and ordered him to sit so that if his legs gave way, he wouldn't have far to fall. The incident passed quickly and within moments I was taking the usual steps during a paying session, but I recognised that something had occurred and I was keen to bring it up with him after he had showered and dressed and as was his usual custom, stayed to have a coffee with me.

I asked him what had happened and at first, he seemed to be reticent about discussing it. After I pushed it, I soon realised that in actuality, he was almost unaware of anything being amiss. I ended up having to explain exactly what I felt was wrong and see if he knew what I was talking about. It became clear within a few short minutes that it seemed that there was actually more to worry about than I had first thought, because not only did he have no memory of what had happened but he admitted to me that actually if he were honest, he couldn't remember the session at all.

Over the years my passion for animals has led me down some strange and unusual paths and it was one of those paths which made me try to understand epilepsy. Over the years I have owned two dogs that were epileptic and rehomed several with different levels of epilepsy when I ran a rescue, and needed to be able to explain what needed to be done when a fit occurred. I had never heard of something called 'missings', which were a mild type of fit where the animal appeared to be behaving normally unless for some reason you needed to get them to do something. Despite this appearing to be relatively innocuous, when one of my dogs wandered onto a dual carriageway during one of these phases, I realised that in many ways this type of fit can be more dangerous than a full-blown epileptic seizure.

I didn't try to fanny around the subject, I asked him outright if he had ever had any type of epilepsy and if so, what was the actual diagnoses. He was more than a little 'put out' by my questions but he did understand why I was asking and said that he had a medical coming up, so would bring it up with the Doctor when he kept the appointment.

In many ways that was the last I thought of it. I felt as a 'friend' I had to flag it up to Dave, but once that was done it honestly just dropped out of my mind and if something else hadn't happened around me, I would probably have never given it a second thought. I cannot tell you when the next odd moment happened because it was actually so covert that it wasn't until a fair bit later that I put two and two together.

It was a Wednesday and when Dave called, I had already had two customers and Carol had had three, so we were pretty busy. He asked if I had time to have a sandwich with him for lunch, which I was more than happy to accept. When he arrived, Carol had just finished and I could see the conundrum instantly. Should she eat now and run the risk of letting the customer out with red sauce and crumbs all over her chin and mouth area, or just wait till until he left. No real competition, she grabbed the sandwich out of Dave's hand, winked and closed the door. He opened the chilled bottle of wine and poured into it into three glasses and we chatted as we ate and sipped our wine. Carol re-appeared and sat down at the table, reaching for the glass of wine, when Dave gently pushed a serviette into her hand and nodded smiling.

"You don't want the crumbs in your glass and ruin the flavour of the wine, do you?" Carol spluttered some sort of funny retort and started fishing around for the second half of her sandwich. During the conversation, I can't actually remember what we were talking about, but Carol stopped mid-sentence and after a few seconds asked, "Are you alright Dave?"

There was no response. It was as if the air stopped moving and the colour had drained out of his face. His eyes were fixed into a strange stare and had that look which makes us say, 'the lights are on, but there's no one home. Carol raised slightly out of her seat, bent towards him and gently put a hand on his arm. Carefully she gave him a little shake and after a second or two, he shook his head, blinked, smiled and said,

"sorry?"

She frowned, pulled a face and asked, "what are you on?"

He looked confused and slowly shook his head. "Nothing, Really, Why?"

Her expression softened. "You just went away with the fairies, me old mate…"

She settled back in her chair and took another mouth full of sandwich. "Didn't you feel that?" she asked. "You sort of zoned out from us. Ever happened before?"

Before he could answer I butted in. "Yes actually, in the dungeon that time. Remember?"

He shook his head. "No I don't. Did you say anything to me?"

"Yes. We had a conversation about epilepsy? I suggested you see a doctor and you said you had a Doctor's appointment soon for a check-up and that you would tell him?"

Dave looked even more bothered. "When did this happen Roma?"

I shook my head. "Your last appointment. I can give you the exact date if you want me to. It'll be in my diary?"

He looked a bit concerned. "I had my medical the end of last month and came out fine. Everything normal," he looked down at his feet. "Nobody else has said anything…I wonder if it's just here?"

Carol humphed, "Cheers! Anyway, according to you, you wouldn't remember if anyone had said anything anyway… you don't remember Roma saying 'owt, do you?"

A sudden smile crossed his face and he winked at me. "I'd remember if you took me into your arms, kissed me passionately and went fiddling for my wallet," he grinned.

"Huh!" she said, "Yeah you would, but it wouldn't be your wallet I'd be after!"

We all chuckled and the conversation carried on in a suitably naughty manner.

Dave used to visit us in his capacity as a punter roughly once a month and twice during the month of his Birthday. As a mate he would sometimes pop in a couple of times a week or even more and then he would disappear for a few weeks for work or a family holiday. When I said, 'as a mate', neither of us had known him before he started visiting as a punter, but he was a real charmer and often hung back after the appointment for a chat and a laugh and sometimes we went for a drink after work. He spoke often about his family, his wife and his love of them and regaled us with funny stories from his past. He had often given us a lift home, lift to the Doctors, dentists, hospitals, even shopping a couple of times. When he stepped in to the dungeon, we all wore different hats, but somehow it was easy with this particular customer because he had been visiting Dungeons for over twenty years and knew the rules.

Dave had called in the morning to make an appointment around lunchtime, but had then rung back to change the appointment to last knockings and booked an hour and a half. Nothing strange, a normal day and when Dave arrived there was nothing to suggest that anything was going to go wrong. Carol didn't like blood, well actually she didn't like blood, pooh, urine and semen?? Odd choice of career really? So, when it came to Dave's more extreme fetishes for torture, I used to let Carol skip out and I would continue on my own.

I had Dave strapped to a crucifix style piece of apparatus which made him look a bit like Leonardo's Vitruvian man. Between his legs a piece of wood could be brought into place on a hinge so that the scrotum and foreskin of the penis were available to the dominatrix. On the side was a sort of draw/closet which housed my needles, knives, electricity box, rubber tubing, hammer, an assortment of tacks and nails, plastic gloves, bags, rope etc. etc.

Once the customer was in position and his genitals stitched, stuck or nailed onto the top plate the main body of the instrument can be bent backwards in increments so that the skin can be stretched gradually, causing more pain and discomfort. As the brain starts to accept the pain the body gets pulled backwards to ramp up the degrees of torture and customers who desire to be placed on this instrument usually book an hour and a half or two hours. I had just racked backwards again when Dave suddenly went limp and his eyes rolled back in his head. I shouted to Carol and the urgency in my voice sent her flying in through the dungeon door. She didn't hesitate as we both set about removing ties and straps, pulling out nails and finally, jointly lifting him off so we could get him on the floor.

"What happened?" she asked as she unfolded a thermal blanket and placed it halfway over his body.

"I haven't the faintest idea, Hand me that mirror please. "She knew what I wanted it for and we both became still and silent as she placed it over his nose and mouth. She shook her head and tried for a pulse in his neck. Looking at me intently she shook again, "what do we do now?"

I bent to place my ear in his chest and said, "Do not mention chain-saws"

She looked a little hurt and said, "I wouldn't use it in here" and I saw her eyes follow the path out of the door towards the bathroom.

"He's not breathing, call an ambulance" and I started giving him CPR. Her hesitation as she glanced around the room was miniscule and she was up and off towards the phone. We didn't ordinarily have cordless phones in those days, so she had to shout the questions from the operator to me and pass on my responses. I heard her shout "hold on!" and she had obviously put the receiver down and came and knelt next to Dave on the other side to me.

"I've done this before. My turn" she smiled, "fucking knackering this is, get a glass of water, open the flat door and take five,"

It was knackering and I was so grateful for a brief respite. I downed a glass of water, opened the door and went running up the stairs to look for the cavalry. Nothing, so I returned to the flat and went to take over from Carol. As I dropped to my knees she asked, "Where's my fucking water?"

"I thought you meant it for me?" I spluttered. She rolled her eyes,

"you're a cunt" she blurted, just as the paramedics walked into the dungeon.

Immediately they took over the situation and took out various bits and bobs to do with making someone better, and I had to wonder what was going through their minds as they looked around at the scenery. I gave them all the information asked for and then stepped aside as they placed Dave onto a stretcher and took him upstairs. I was hoping that when I had gone out looking for the Ambulance nobody in the street had seen me, but at that moment I was more worried about our friend than somebody clocking me in my thigh lengths, chain belt, a leather skirt. Just before the ambulance left another paramedic had turned up on a motorbike, had a quick conversation with the other two and then watched them leave using their blues and twos, before turning towards us at the bottom of the steps. He came into the flat and we showed him into the lounge. After several questions which he was visibly surprised that I was able to answer, such as his full name, address, name of his wife and children, he then carefully asked 'what' was going on when he had collapsed. I'm not stupid and I obviously minimised the extent of Dave's fetishes, but I did mention about the strange moments he had, had when with us and that because of those incidents I had the name of his Doctor. After a few more questions he got up to leave and Carol moved like a shooting star to block his exit and smiled sweetly up at him.

"Could you do us both a huge favour?" she purred. "Under the circumstances we can't very well enquire after him at the hospital. We're not related". She said.

He smiled, "As soon I find out, if you give me your number, I'll let you know. He is very poorly, but you saved his life. No doubt".

She handed him our card and quite coquettishly lowered her eyes to the floor and almost whispered her thanks to him for his acknowledgement. It was as if an electricity went between them and after a few seconds passed she almost slithered out of his way, slowly raising her head and meeting his eyes with an intensity of a fire. It was one of those moments where it seemed as if time had suddenly stopped and as an observer it played out in front of me in such a way, that I half expected him to scoop her up into his arms and kiss her. Expectation filled the doorway. The moment passed and she moved slowly, like a cat and showed him to the door, while I sort of shuffled along behind. She held it open for him and something unspoken passed between them as he exited. She was just about to close it when he suddenly leant backwards and said,

"Which one called the other a cunt?"

Dave was seriously ill. He had had a massive haemorrhagic stroke and was placed into an induced coma. We knew that he was literally fighting for his life but that the nature of our knowledge prevented us from having anything to do with his recovery. The story we had been told was that as far as his family was concerned, he had been found in his car. Obviously, his clothes, wallet, keys etc. had been handed over to the ambulance people in an innocuous black refuse sack which I assume was just handed over to his wife. I now realised, after looking up the why's and wherefores of a stroke and my guess was that the strange little 'missing's' he had experienced in our company were probably, 'transient ischaemic' attacks, usually known as mini strokes.

The individualism of our chosen profession means that a great many of our relationships are by their very nature transient. Whether we care about an individual isn't really the point. I set out earlier, that for me personally, there is no bridge between my professional and personal lives. Yes, I wore a lot of leather and the way I carried myself may have been a dead giveaway to those in the know, but that was as far as it went. When I had become involved in relationships with men, I would always explain my work in detail, both the sexual side of it and the fetish side. I needed them to understand exactly what I did so that it was never flung in my face or could come a barrier between us. Which is probably why my romantic relationships rarely succeeded. A friend of mine once called me a tragedy magnet and the term has stayed with me. I am not saying that things just 'happen', none of it being my fault! but I do believe that there are traits within my make-up that has caused me to walk headlong into trouble without looking back. A friend of mine once said,

"You know Roma, that when you go see a litter of puppies, from the perspective of choosing a strong, healthy puppy, you need to choose the one that waddles over to you, interacts with you, has bright eyes and is interested in its brothers and sisters as well as the world around it. You look at all of them, play with them I bit and then you see the one cowering in the corner. It has a bit of a snotty nose, gunge in its eyes, moves backwards as you try to pet it and cries, wriggling when you pick it up; and guess what? That's the one you choose!"

I got it. I knew exactly what they meant, but although I have lived my life being independent and supposedly in control, I have never been able to control my heart. It doesn't help that somewhere in my growing up years I learned to believe in this pure, intense love 'that conquers all' (amor vincit omnia, a line from a poem by Virgil which caught the worlds imagination and mine. Amor is Roma spelt backwards). Somewhere there was a love that could never be destroyed or broken. A love that transcends the earthly boundaries of human failures. In my head, choca-block with common sense and the knowledge of human frailty, even my own, I could recognise the nonsense of such an ideal, but in fact, I couldn't let it go?

A year had passed since Dave had had his stroke in my dungeon and thankfully, I can say hand on heart I managed not to kill anybody in the intervening time. It was a warm Sunday afternoon and Carol and I were strolling along the sea front with the dogs off lead talking crap when suddenly we heard somebody call our names. We looked around but could see no one we recognised however our attention was captured by a very beautiful woman who had appeared from inside a café and seemed to be walking towards us. We both stopped and allowed her to approach. There was something tickling my brain cells about her, making me feel like I should recognise her. When she was standing in front of us, she apologised for shouting and smiling introduced herself as Dave's wife. Neither Carol or myself said anything, so she continued.

"I'm sorry", she said looking from one to the other of us. "I thought you knew that I know?". She shook her head and tutted, "He's in the café, please come and join us, you can bring the dogs".

I shook my head, "We would love to, but we've tried before and the owners are really cranky if you even mention the word dog".

She laughed, "I'm the owner. Mr and Mrs Wallis just manage it for us. Come on", and with that she walked back to the café as we put the dogs on leads. Seeing how well Dave looked and his smile made us forget any awkwardness and in turn we hugged him and started bombarding him with questions. Tea and cakes were ordered and we were both thrilled to be able to see Dave with his wife at his side, behaving as if we had met at a tea dance. It was amazing to hear his wife explain that she had always know Dave's predilection but she couldn't hurt him. She loved him too much, so she was happy for him to find it elsewhere and even suggested that we produce a gift voucher that she would gladly purchase for his Birthdays. Not something most of the wives and girlfriends would come to us for, of that I am fairly certain.

Dave had been left unable to speak, walk, or co-ordinate his movements, now with the help of the best therapy he was left with a slight weakness on his right side, he was using a stick, and a slight delay in his speech, but he had just spent the last month in the Bahamas and was looking fit and healthy.

I decided after seeing him and his wife so happy together, that I no longer wanted him as a customer. It was a difficult conversation but I think I finally made him understand why. We used to still see each other and occasionally go around to his house for dinner, but his wife couldn't help herself and kept trying to make us take him back, (I really did understand. She believed that whatever went on in the dungeon, we were 'safe'). For her we had saved his life and she trusted us. Like all good things though, as they say, finally we saw less and less of him and his family and eventually everybody's lives moved on.

28. THE END IS NIGH

I said earlier, that as the years wore on Carol's demons had started to stalk her and despite her talking about it and assuring me things were ok, I knew we were coming to the end of our partnership. We still worked together normally and generally let our hair down together normally, (normal for us) but it was like having some horrid type of premonition that when I tried to bring out into the open, was simply foiled. I had always understood that there would be a time limit to the life we were leading at the time, but Carol resented anyone trying to tell her what was best for her. She had to make her decisions herself, regardless of whether she recognised that somebody was right about where she should be heading. She was one of the stubbornest people I have ever met, but that was her, and in my own way I loved her anyway.

We used to buy drugs regularly, mostly E's or cocaine as well as buying grass which I will happily admit to smoking every day. Dope wasn't something to be used until the day ended. Something we smoked together in the evening or occasionally early evening on the weekend. Actually, sometimes we did smoke in the afternoon on the weekend, but we never opened our eyes and lit up a joint.

As things started to deteriorate between us, we started going out separately and she made friends with a young girl who didn't seem to have any ties to anyone or anything. I would be wrong to call her a prostitute, in my eyes, done correctly it's a profession, but she didn't mind who she slept with as long as it gave her a roof over her head, drugs, alcohol and hopefully some cash.

When Carol started bringing her home, both of them in a horrible state and then so out of it, I couldn't wake them in the morning and I was unable to open the dungeon, I started to get annoyed. Every time I attempted to try to talk with Carol it went one of two ways. She would be surly and basically ignore me until the two of them had washed, dressed and eaten something before fucking off or behave like a simpering child until the same outcome was achieved. I was becoming more and more concerned, not just about myself and my business, but also for Carol herself. I actually initially felt sorry for this girl. She had a sad back story, but like so many, it had started to be used as an excuse for bad behaviour.

I had stayed in on a Friday night and was awoken at about four in the morning by Carol falling through the front door. When I got out of bed and got a dressing gown on, I walked into the hallway to find Carol, face down, the front door wide open and a large puddle of urine spreading out into the hall carpet.

I tried to pick her up but it was impossible, so I manoeuvred her around so that I could close the front door. There was nothing I could do about the carpet until she wasn't laying on it, so I concentrated on trying to wake her up, which honestly rapidly became a reason to batter her!

At first, I had almost gently tapped her cheek and called her name to wake her up, but the longer I sat there the harder the tapping started to become, and it would be fair to say that I had started really slapping her. I knew she wasn't dead because periodically I felt for the pulse in her neck. Slapping wasn't getting me anywhere and the escalation of the slaps in severity was getting slightly out of hand. That, combined with the intermittent shaking I was resorting to, which caused me to bounce her head on and off the carpet, would probably have amounted to an assault. By the time she actually opened her eyes and blearily acknowledged my presence, I was practically beating her up. With a huge effort she raised herself up onto her knees and proceeded to fill my lap with vomit.

I cannot bear being sick.

ANYONE being sick closer than a twenty-five-mile radius to me, will make me start to retch. I was horrified and I tore off my dressing gown and dropped it, vomit side down onto Carol's head as I fled to the bathroom. In the shower I was behaving like a rape victim, scrubbing again and again in fear that a piece of carrot or sweetcorn (whether she had eaten that or not) would miraculously appear somewhere on my person during the day, proving that I had not washed off all of the vomit. When I was finally ready to leave the bathroom, I gingerly opened the door and peered down the hallway, genuinely afraid of what I may see. Nothing, she wasn't there, just a pool of piss and vomit which actually made me want to cry at the thought of having to clean it up. I tiptoed into my bedroom and checking the time, telephoned a 'sub' who I often let do my housework. I briefly explained what was wanted, afraid that if I hadn't checked, the situation could be made worse by him adding to the pile of human waste, and then proceeded to pace up and down my room desperate for the doorbell to ring, but terrified of how to get past, to open the door! After several different plans, I finally grabbed my keys and my cigarettes and chose to me, the most obvious way of resolving the situation, by climbing out of my window and meeting him outside. When he arrived, I almost kissed him, but I was quickly irritated by his protestations of climbing through my window to get back into the house so that he didn't risk spreading 'hurl' throughout the home.

We almost argued because he could see the keys in my hands and being quite a tall man he would have to crumple himself up to gain entry in the way I was suggesting, however I was the Dominatrix and after stopping him mid-sentence with a look only a Mistress can give, he finally sighed and complied with my request in an extremely difficult way, which had him land in a heap taking most of the objects on my dressing table with him!

It seemed to take him forever whilst I smoked cigarette after cigarette, but when he finally tapped on my bedroom door and I looked out into the passage it was as if nothing had ever happened. Obviously in my mind I kept catching a smell of vomit, but I am sure it really was just in my imagination. I didn't see Carol all day and by the time she did suffice I had realised that the week's takings were missing as was fifty E's and a small wrap of cocaine. To say I wasn't happy was an understatement, but I still prepared the Sunday dinner for both of us, usually eaten around sevenish. When Carol walked into the kitchen she had bathed and had done her make-up and hair. She went to the sink and downed two pints of water before opening the fridge and pouring herself a large glass of wine, which I noted she didn't bother to offer me. She was up for a fight and her belligerence poured off her like sweat. I was about to speak when she interrupted me and asked, "Is there enough for Sarah, only she'll be here in a minute?"

I stopped what I was doing and looked at her. She shrugged and went to leave the room but I called her back. I wanted to remain calm but I could feel myself slightly trembling with emotion. I didn't know if it was anger or not but once I started, I had to say what I wanted to say and knew I couldn't stop. I started with the night before and the way she had come home and then disappeared leaving her mess for me to clean up. Her argument was that I hadn't actually cleaned it, I had brought somebody in to clean it and if I paid them, well take it out of her wages?? I ignored the irony and complained that recently she had stopped doing the housework, which seeing as I did all of the shopping, cooking, bookings, banking, bills etc. I didn't think it was too much to ask her to keep the dungeon and the working bathroom clean? she disagreed with me on the basis that I was overly picky, it only really needed doing once a month and that if I asked her to do the shopping she would. I was trying to point out that that wasn't fair when the doorbell rang. Oddly Carol and Sarah stood on the doorstep speaking in whispers and occasionally letting out peals of laughter, until I snapped and walked into the hallway and asked if Sarah were coming in or not?

As Sarah walked past me, she winked at me and with a huge grin asked, "Ok?" as she proceeded into the kitchen, grabbed a glass, opened the fridge and helped herself to my wine.

I exploded.

We were both shouting while Sarah watched in a sort of gleeful, silence like watching a spider creep up on an unsuspecting fly. When I tackled the question of the money, the argument was somehow twisted round so that it appeared that I controlled everything, that she had to ask me for everything and that she was entitled to be able to have money of her own to spend in whatever way she chose. I stupidly argued that she knew where the money was and if she wanted money, she could just take it, which she pointed out was exactly what she had done!

As for the drugs it was a similar argument, but when I pointed out that it was wrong to take everything and leave me with nothing, either money or drugs. She pulled a face and filled up both glasses of wine and shrugged as Sarah chipped in, "The thing is Roma, Carol does most of the work doesn't she and she owns the flat, so really it should be the other way round. You should be the one who does the cleaning and everything and that it should be me asking her for money?"

I felt my jaw drop as I went from looking at Sarah to fixing Carol with a stare that would freeze summer. Carol had obviously been boasting and telling porkies and I was furious with her as well as this stupid little girl she had brought into my home. Before I could respond Carol, who had suddenly turned a brilliant shade of red threw the glass of wine she was holding in my face and bellowed, "Just fuck off!"

With that she stormed out of the kitchen, grabbed a small vanity case which she had obviously packed earlier and her hand bag, which I had failed to notice in the hallway and to my amazement, went to the draw to look for money!

I virtually spat out my next statement to her. "There's nothing fucking left you greedy bitch, you took it all yesterday," Then I turned to Sarah.

"And you? You can fuck off and stay fucked off. This is my flat, my dungeon and my business. This last week she has seen two fucking punters, just regular service, while I've bust my balls and seen 'special clients' for two hours at a time and one all fucking night, while the two of you were out having fun and getting drunk, I was bringing in fifty per cent more money than we usually do. If I said that the money in our pockets was based on the work we do, then recently you would have been forced to go off and sponge off some other stupid cunt!"

She said nothing but quickly picked up her glass and downed it in one. She looked like some sad washed up tranny for one so young and as I looked her up and down, I could feel the sneer planted on my face. When she had finished the wine, she scooted around the other side of the table and almost nervously said, "Waste not want not" as she attempted to grab the bottle and glass and follow Carol. I was faster than I would have believed I could be, but I think the anger was my spur. I stepped in front of this stupid child and she actually froze in front of me as I took both the wine and the glass out of her hands. I leaned forward so that she could feel my breath on her face, though unfortunately that meant I could smell her breath which was rank. The tips of our noses almost touched.

"Backed the wrong horse didn't you, you fuck wit?" I laughed like a vampire in a terrible B movie, and then fixed her with a stare. "Like I said. Fuck off and stay fucked off. No second chances," and I stepped out of her path and let her run to catch up with Carol.

I know I had said that I knew there were things in Carol's life and that at some point she was going to have to face up to and sort out, but I had never anticipated that her demons would come between us and I had hoped that I would be there, holding her hand when she faced up to her reality. All these years later I realise that I actually wasn't helping her to face up to this and if I'm honest I was probably an impediment to her being allowed to make her own decisions. I was as much of a pressure on her, though not obviously, to making her feel pulled in different directions and ultimately stopping her from facing up to what she needed to do. Carol's reaction was to party the night away, sleep all day the next day and ultimately party again and I had become an enabler in that too. I knew she wasn't working because she was too hung-over, but I let it slide and still gave her access to cash to help her be able to go out. At first, I questioned whether I was just jealous that she had found a 'new friend', but it wasn't that and by the time I recognised what was happening, it had happened.

I was determined not to reach out and find her. She was a grown up. She had most of her stuff in her closets at home and she knew where she had been living for the last few years. I hadn't changed the lock, but I confess I was doubly hurt that I had had a two-hour regular and that when I came out of the dungeon, she had obviously entered the flat and taken some of her stuff, without letting me know that she had been there. Oddly she did leave a bag of laundry in the laundry room, which I promptly moved into her bedroom.

Even today I have a whole myriad of emotions about this time in my life which I still don't seem able to place into any sort of order. It really was a time of change but despite my instincts and knowledge of humanity, I didn't see it coming.

I left her to her own devices, but when I realised that my home was being almost regularly entered if I were out or in the dungeon, and that where we had always kept money had been rifled, to no avail I might add, but I hated the thought that someone was coming into my home uninvited. I still do not believe Carol would steal from me, but I guessed her new 'friend' came with her and had a bit of a fishing trip. Sounds ridiculous but when two bottles of wine disappeared, I decided to act. I had new locks placed on all of the windows, three new courses of bricks added to the garden wall, bolts placed on the garden door and the glass panel changed to reinforced glass and a new front door lock which was a mortice lock and a Yale. I alternated from being angry to my heart aching. We had shared so much together, gone through so much, held each other when the pain came and gouged out new lives for ourselves, always with the others blessing. I worked but I missed her and in honesty I missed the laughter. I have only ever had one other friend in my life, who I sadly let slip through my fingers, where there are so many memories of being beside ourselves with laughter. Carol was one in a million and even today I smile when I think of her. In truth I know a little of her life after she left me and it truly isn't a world that I would even want to look at, let alone partake in. If she is happy and the choices, she made give her contentment, then that is all one could ask for, but still…I miss the laughter.

Carol did come home and despite everything that had happened I was deliriously happy that she had returned. We had been talking on the phone and preparing ourselves to strike out on our own when she asked if she could come back for a bit to get some dosh together for her journey back. I accepted gleefully. One of the things, if you remember was my ire at the fact that she wasn't keeping the dungeon clean, and I confess that I was a bit of a nightmare in this aspect of our relationship. She came home on a Sunday morning which ordinarily would be a day of rest, but I had received a request from a regular bondage customer who was happy to pay double for however long I could give him, in view of his wife actually going away for the day. I told him of my plan and he more than readily agreed. He was a customer who was into ropes or straps starting at his ankles and moving up to cover as much of his naked body as possible, as tight as possible with separate ties around his dick. He wasn't into masks or anything, but was happy to be rolled under the bondage bed with a duvet thrown over him to cover him up.

When Carol arrived, we sat and drank tea whilst apologising to each other and once the awkwardness had dissipated out came the champagne. I don't really remember the conversation but I managed to steer it around to her cleaning the dungeon and got up whilst talking so that her natural instinct would be to follow me. I walked into the room and caught her by saying, "It's always been your responsibility Carol, you know that?" And she nodded. With that I whipped off the duvet to expose this figure, wrapped tightly in bondage, beaming like a Cheshire cat and said,

"How long has that been there?"

She was just about to say something when the idiot spontaneously ejaculated and if she hadn't moved as quickly as she did, she would have caught it in the face! We looked at each other and burst out laughing.

I had no expectation of her staying, in fact quite the opposite and we worked hard together to make sure that she returned home with a bit of money for whatever she wanted to do. Most importantly we parted as friends.

Nothing is ever the same when you go through what we went through. There is no going back, you just have to raise your chin and go forwards. That's just how it is.

29. OUT OF THE DARKNESS

My previous husband had died several years before I had moved to Brighton. He had been born with a condition called spina-bifida and was constantly in pain. His IQ was high in the regions of genius but his temperament made it almost impossible for him to use his brain in any constructive way, despite training first as a research chemist and then taking a degree in biomedical sciences. He was affiliated to a University but to this day I cannot really tell you what, if anything he did. I do know that before he passed, he was working on a vaccine for HIV because I had to type all of the papers and conclusions of his research. His theory was that the world of pharmaceuticals was looking in the wrong direction. He believed that for people who already had the disease, drugs to alleviate suffering and prolong life was basically manageable with the drugs already on the shelves, but that the way forward was a vaccine to prevent infection. This was quite some time before the idea of a vaccine was mooted.

He had the most amazing photographic memory, but only seemed to use it as a party trick and constantly railed against the world and everything in it for making him the way he was. Yet again I had chosen the stinky puppy and this one really gave me a run for my money. There really was far too much between us that even now, that I just want to forget about. He consumed my life for thirteen years. I worked tirelessly at my business and was lucky enough to be able to find a Tranny maid, who had been a specialised surgery nurse, who moved in and cared for him whilst I worked. It was all on the same premises, so in many ways one might assume that everything was hunky-dory.

I loved this man with all my heart and nearly destroyed myself and everything I had built up because of my love for him. The day his heart stopped beating, I had truly believed that my own heart would stop too. For me it was a day when I could have run for the hills literally and kept on going until I could go no more and I could sink down into the earth and stay there. My life, as I had known it was over and yet I had been set free to finally live again for myself. So many emotions, so many tears and yet I slept that first night like I had not been able to sleep for years. Quietly and without dreams.

Coming out of that relationship, I thought it had made me harder, more resilient, but like most things I have seen as a sign that it would make me stronger, if anything it just caused scars on my heart that bled with each new battle. It dragged me back into a place which I understood, but still didn't have the means to prevent, regardless of the drugs. It was a problem to do with my own mental make-up, my hereditary, my chains that held me to the earth in a certain manner and that gave me no peace. As the years have gone onwards, I have learned to recognise when it starts and therefore have been able to work out when the medication starts to stop working and that it's time for the professionals to take over. Having learned to understand this part of my make-up has helped me to be a more balanced human being. Not able to prevent a psychotic episode, but able to see it coming just before I trip over it and therefore ask for help. I had moved to Brighton with everything in place to fashion myself a new life. There were no obvious warning signals and nothing out of place. My new life started in a very normal way, although as a sub carried in the specialised crucifix, a neighbour appeared and looked at him and the piece of furniture with an expression of wonder. The sub, noticing her interest gave her a huge smile and said, 'Its Easter next weekend. Bless you for being a Christian', and lowered his eyes humbly as he carried the piece of equipment into the inside of the flat.

I worked and settled into a new Life, like I had so many times before. As always there were moments, ups and downs, needing and not needing, just all the things that make up a normal life, though many would not have used the phrase 'normal'. I had several brief affairs. My eldest sister got married and my family obeyed her wishes and didn't bother to tell me, and I was doing a little bit of other work on the side, training grumpy dogs, to give them a chance of a new family. I actually loved this work. It wasn't paid, I did it for local rescue's and as I became more experienced, I discovered a different way of treating an angry animal. I got bitten, actually I got bitten quite a lot, usually the first time I tried to get a muzzle on. Muzzle training is a must if you are to show a dog a different way of seeing the world and at the same time make them safe to deal with, but trying to get one on a dogs face that requires him to have his mouth closed whilst he's barking, snarling and snapping at you like a crocodile, just isn't easy. In fact, it's bloody dangerous but I have always believed in the 'no bad dogs' adage which I still believe, however I have had to learn that either by their treatment or a glitch at birth there are some, sadly very mentally ill dogs and trying to treat them would be impossible. I used to think that I would never recommend that a dog be put to sleep, but I have had to do that many times and I've had to hold them whilst they gave up their lives to an injection. At least they had someone there to cry for them. Inevitably if you decide to take on the worst of the worst you will encounter dogs that are not viable in society, but when the coin flips and you take a 'nasty' dog and turn it into 'man's best friend' the sense of achievement is phenomenal. I did several different courses on dogs and did a fascinating one on wolves and how the wolf relates to the domestic dog. I learned the body language of the wolf, male and female where the differences are quite marked and I found it easier than some to pick up those unspoken nuances, giving me a step ahead of how to approach an animal that doesn't trust.

I had to be interviewed by the agency that wanted volunteers, initially just as a foster mum and when they came to my home I had to try and disguise the room we were seated in. I had dragged in a table and two comfy chairs, but the dungeon was painted red and black and I had literally just thrown sheets over certain pieces because I had forgotten that they were coming. Luckily, I had a delicious home-made cake (nothing to do with me. The last cakes I made the RSPB gave to their birds of prey as beak rubs!!) and I made a pot of tea. I don't remember how long she stayed, but I remember starting to get worried because I had a client booked in and a lady that looked like every-ones' granny happily munching on cake, sitting on the bondage bed, may well have appealed to someone's inner most fantasy, which I was actually worried about!

I had various dogs come and go in the space of nine months and my 'boss' noticed my abilities. She had sneaked a rogue animal to me a couple of times and had been impressed with the way they turned out. It was whilst visiting a shelter, that my attention was drawn to a large black Greyhound, lying with its head on its paws whilst various dogs around him barked and screamed for attention. He was an ex racer that, like so many other greyhounds, had been given up to the shelter because his running days were over. He had been there two years and when I spoke gently to him and the tip of his broken tail almost wagged, I opened the kennel and went down on my knees beside him and stroked his soft ears. He didn't move, greet me or really acknowledge me until it was time for me to leave and then he gently lifted his head, placed it on my lap and closed his eyes as if he believed that if he just stayed there I would leave quietly and he could pretend I was still there stroking his ears. My heart called out to his and suddenly he raised his head and looked me in the eyes, as if he were afraid that our unspoken moment wasn't true. I ran my hand down the side of his face and I whispered, "I'll be back in a minute". I went to the office, sorted out the little hairy rat thing that I was taking home and told them that I wanted the greyhound to go home with me as well. There were a few irritating moments where the girl behind the desk started going on about Greyhounds and small hairy things, which I simply overrode with my voice, age and an air of authority. I said if she had a problem take it up with my 'handler' and with that I plonked the little hairy thing into a bag which under the circumstances I thought may be safer and proceeded to Max's kennel. He was standing, nose through the bars of the kennel waiting for me, which I knew he would be. On the way home I took a detour and went to London road park, which is probably about five acres. I went down on one knee and looked him in the eye. His whole body shivered with anticipation but he held my gaze and waited. I slowly unclipped the lead, smiled and said, "Go on!" and with a joy that was tangible he hurtled around the space, bouncing, leaping, bounding with sheer excitement. I took the little hairy thing out of the bag and started to walk with it, trusting Max to follow. Suddenly a huge Greyhound that was striped like a tiger with yellow eyes came thundering towards Max and literally jumped over his back and the two of them played chase all around the field. When I reached the exit, Max came trotting up and happily greeted the little hairy thing and just stood for me to put on a lead. I looked around for the big tiger dog but he was nowhere to be seen.

Max settled in as if he had always been there and so loved being loved. The grouchy little hairy thing was much nicer than the person who gave him up had led the kennel to believe, in fact he was quite cute and the only time he ever snapped at me was when I strode down the hall just as he came out of a room and accidentally kicked him the length of the hallway, him landing on his back. He leapt up and flew towards me grabbing the toe of my shoe, shaking and snarling whilst Max and I looked down at him in amazement. Mid shake I said, "sorry. I didn't mean to" and with that he left my toe looked up at me and wagged.

Periodically I would have a 'paying dinner party' in the dungeon. Each guest would wear hand cuffs and would be served by a maid and a young lady dressed as a dominatrix. It was good money and made a change to be honest. It was early evening and I decided to walk Max in the park, with my other two dogs (I wasn't fostering at the time) before people arrived so that they would be more settled. As always Max bounced around and greeted all the other dogs on the park especially a very silly, nine-month-old black Labrador. Like always I stood and chatted with the other dog mums and dads always keeping an eye out for the need to go and pick up a pooh. I was watching the dogs play, running in an ever-widening circle, when suddenly the Labrador decided that rather than just chase, he would cut across the other dogs and head Max off. Max didn't see it coming and as the Labrador reached its target I saw Max hit the stomach of the other dog with his head and with the speed that he had been travelling and the momentum he was thrown wildly up in the air, somersaulting uncontrollably before landing on his back, screaming as he hit the ground. I ran to him but before I could get there, he had staggered back up onto his four paws, looking slightly dazed. I did all the normal spontaneous checks but as he was upright, I felt that he was probably alright. I walked home slowly and could tell something hurt but I just kept soothing him with my voice. When we got home, I made him a bed next to my chair in the dungeon so that I could keep an eye on him and gave him a dose of Metacam. The dinner party was going well, with plenty of stories and laughter but as the evening wore on, I became more worried about Max. He just looked odd to me, as if he were slightly bending his head back over his back and as pudding was served, I left the table and knelt down beside him. I don't know what I touched because it all happened so quickly, I was lifting his lip to study his gums for signs of shock when he suddenly screamed, almost a human sound of agony and accidentally clamped his jaws together with my hand inside his mouth. I actually felt my thumb break, but while everybody panicked and started shouting and despite being in shock, I managed to calm the dinner guests and got one of the blokes to try to open his jaws, but he couldn't. I knew Max was not hanging on to me deliberately, but the amount of blood running down my arm made me realise that I had to urgently get my hand free and discover what the damage was. I showed the man how to poke his fingers into the dog's mouth and carefully open the jaws without getting hurt himself and also allowing me to get my hand out. Once it was free, I went into the bathroom and closed the door. The blood just kept coming so I ended up using a stretchy sports bandage, placing a roll of gauze as a pressure point and then filled it with ice and made a make-shift sling to keep the hand upright. I had to muzzle Max because we needed to get him to a vet and I knew moving him was going to hurt him. I can't really remember how it all went down other than leaning on the Blue Cross night bell with Max awkwardly lying at my feet. Once we got inside despite trying to fob me off with, 'there's no Vet here' I made enough of a noise and Max was by now curled into a very strange shape. When a vet arrived, I explained what had happened earlier and she, with the nurses help x-rayed Max's back. We helped her get Max to a kennel and she immediately set him up a drip for pain relief, before starting to insist that she wanted to see my hand. The wound took eight stitches and my thumb was broken but I refused to leave my dog. The vet explained that the reason his neck and head were being pulled back was because when he had landed on his back, although the bones had stayed intact, the fall had severed his spinal cord. She told me he was inoperable and in a great deal of pain as the sensation travelled towards his brain as the cord died. I crawled into the kennel, took his head in my hands and whispered my goodbyes as the vet gave him the lethal injection and I held him there, making sure that he knew he was loved and that it broke my heart to say goodbye. As his breathing slowed a tear welled up in his right eye and rolled down his face, landing on my hand and as I watched, my own tears running down my face, I watched the life slowly fade from his eyes.

I felt dazed and immeasurably sad. I knew everything would be cleared up at home but in case anyone had stayed to see me, I chose to walk. When I came to a phone box, I telephoned my 'hired helps' and asked that when I returned the flat would be empty. I don't remember consciously heading for the park, but I found myself there amongst the trees, a strange mist rising from the ground, in total silence. When I first heard the sound, a guttural moan rising in intensity, I didn't realise it was coming from me. I sank onto the ground and my body physically shook with each wave of pain that escaped from my throat whilst tears blinded me in their abundance. I was free to give in. Free to express my love for some sad animal who had patiently waited for me for two years and was then cruelly taken from me after only nine months. It seemed to go on and on but as I released my grief, I realised that I was not alone. Standing like a sentinel in the darkness, head bowed but with eyes watching me that almost seemed luminous, was the big 'tiger dog', motionless but with a small puff of breath escaping his nostrils as he breathed. He didn't come towards me and was probably just out of reach but I shared my grief with him, told him how his friend had died and asked him for solace. As I wiped my eyes on my skirt I didn't hear or see him leave, I just looked up and he was gone and I felt as if the whole world had abandoned me in that moment.

I believe my tears weren't just for Max. When my husband died, I never cried. Somewhere in the back of my thoughts I guessed that I had already cried so much during my life with him that it was time to stop, but then I hadn't truly grieved either. When Max left me, it was like a door had sprung open and all the terrible things fell out, surrounding me with hidden hurt. I couldn't move fast enough to close it again so I just stayed there in the moonlight letting the waves of pain assault me like a tsunami. By the time I had finally stopped, the sun was coming up and a few odd humans were appearing heading for work. My legs were stiff and weighed five stone each as I sort of stumbled home and my other dogs were delirious to see me, somehow understanding exactly what had happened.

I wasn't ready to take on another foster dog and when I walked the others, I had to say what had happened again and again and it was difficult. The lady with the Labrador was mortified that her dog had caused Max's death but it was an accident and for me there was no blame to be attached to anyone or thing. I left it for about three months before I contacted the rescue and when I did, I told them I was done. My 'handler' tried desperately to persuade me to stay but I said my heart wasn't in it, however as time passed, I was less sure that I had done the right thing. When she phoned me about a dog, she told me that unless I could do something with the beast, she had in mind he would be PTS. She asked to meet me in the park because she said she was unsure what he was like with other dogs however he had since the call, he had tried to eat her and it was obvious that she had misgivings about her decision to give him a chance.

As I approached the dog standing next to her was the big, tiger coloured dog with the yellow eyes. I went down on my knees and put my face inches away from his nose, which almost caused the woman holding him to faint but I was looking into his eyes, learning how to talk to him without words. Seconds later I was holding his lead and saying goodbye to her as I found a bench to sit on so the others could have a run.

He never resisted especially when I turned his head so that he could look at me. Slowly I removed his lead and waited to see if he would shoot off never to be seen again, but instead he just stood looking at me and I could feel his questions even though I had no means yet of being able to decipher them. After a few seconds a beautiful black Saluki came bouncing over and as if a magic button had been pressed, they both acknowledged each other with a play bow. The game was fast and furious as the two dogs were well matched and it was good to see them play even if a little bit of fear lurked at the back of my mind because of the way Max had died. The evening was getting darker and colder and the mist was settling like a shroud so that the dogs could only be seen when they rushed past a few feet away. Finally, Bruno bounced out of the mist and stood before me bringing his pal with him. Out of the mist a woman's voice shouted, "Max" and the Saluki dipped his head as a gesture of goodbye and bounced off somewhere where his mum had called him from. I stood wondering if there was some connection that I wasn't understanding with Bruno being the key. He trotted home like a dream on the lead and was gentle and considerate of the smaller dogs. When I fed him, he was polite and did not attempt to snaffle the other dog's food and allowed me to remove his dish half way through his meal without argument. The evening was calm and as I watched television, he laid beside me and allowed me to play with his ear. When it was time to retire, I let the dogs out into the back garden, turned out the lights and headed for bed putting on the bedroom tele. Bruno was lying cross ways across the bed and as I attempted to pull down the duvet so I could get into bed he snarled and snapped, catching his target, me, with a healthy bite across the same thumb which had been broken by Max. After finally stopping the bleeding and placing a bandage around my hand I removed Bruno from the bed, gently but firmly. We had both set our stalls out and it would be a battle of will against love and I was determined that I was going to be the one that won.

30. NEVER UNDERESTIMATE OUR PUBLIC SERVICES

I was working with a very experienced girl called Sonia on a week day but business had been slow and by late afternoon we were both a bit bored. The telephone rang and she booked in a customer and said, "I'll take this one if you like?" which was not unusual but there was something that tickled my senses. Something was wrong but it was nothing obvious. I watched and waited. When the doorbell went, she practically ran me over, assuring me she would get it and to just stay there. 'It wasn't necessary for me to get up, just read a book or something!'?

Now I knew something wasn't quite right because she just didn't normally behave like that. She wasn't lazy but she equally wasn't someone to push herself forward. When we worked together the money was split straight down the middle, although she also paid me a peppercorn rent for the use of the facilities.

As she opened the front door, I popped out into the hall to try and get a glimpse of the punter but he was so wrapped in coats, scarves and hats that I thought she was letting in the Elephant man? Almost like a scene from a farce she protectively placed an arm around his shoulders and propelled him into the Bathroom. She could see the look on my face and decided she had better explain.

The bloke was apparently her boyfriend of five years and periodically he would visit her at work and pay for a session to spice up their sex lives. She hadn't realised that he was off that afternoon as he did shift work and normally, she would have checked with me beforehand, but she had sort of been taken by surprise and was now coming clean with me. She handed over the money and I realised it was doubled so I asked if he wanted both of us and she burst out laughing.

"No, no, he's terrified of you!" she laughed. "that's why he came in, in disguise"

I was confused. "I don't get it. I don't know him, I've never met him, so a disguise is a bit over the top isn't it?"

She shrugged and smiled but I still felt that something wasn't right, however each to their own and when she explained that part of the thrill for him was to have to pay properly and that she wouldn't want her half, I decided to just let it be. I trusted her around my equipment and knew she would clean up after herself so checking the time I went through to the kitchen and found an open bottle of champagne. I diverted the telephone and just before going into the lounge I lightly tapped on the dungeon door about to say that I wouldn't be booking anyone else for the rest of the day, when the door whisked open as if she was expecting me to be looking through the keyhole I was slightly taken aback. I stumbled on my words apologising for disturbing her and said that I just wanted her to know that there would be no more bookings and she could 'play' as long as she liked. She thanked me and closed the door before I could say another word.

Before I move on I would just like to inform you that even if I had ever been tempted to peer through the keyhole, (Which I promise I cannot think of a reason why that would be the case) The rules of the dungeon was that the door was locked whilst a session took place between Dominatrix and customer even if the second were wanted at a pre-arranged point during a session, the door would have to be unlocked by the working Mistress. When the dungeon was busy the key was in the lock, which meant there was no way to see into the room.

I turned on the television which was more habit than actually watching anything and settled myself, boots off, on the couch with dogs, going through and sorting my accounts. I cannot actually tell you the time when the bang went off, but it was very loud and made me jump which caused the dogs to all start barking, throwing themselves at the door. I wandered out towards the front and looked out to see if there was anything visible which could have made such an enormous bang, but I couldn't see anything and there appeared to be no obvious curfuffle in the street, so I walked back through the flat to the garden door and went and stood in the garden with the dogs just breathing in the fresh air. I returned to the flat when my glass was empty and I was just closing the fridge when I heard Sonia calling me. Confused I walked to the dungeon door and ranked the handle but the door was definitely still locked however my action had obviously conferred to those inside, that I was there.

Sonia's voice was sounding rather strained and slightly upset, so I leaned into the door and said, "is everything ok?"

"No" her voice came back loud and clear. "I'm sorry but I can't get to the door and I need you in here..."

I took a step back and stared at the door in confusion as if by looking at it I would be able to grasp what was wrong. I realised that something definitely wasn't right but decided that nobody was in actual danger. I tried again.

"Sonia just open the door?"

"Roma I can't. Sorry but can you get something to push the key out of the lock and then use your spare?"

I immediately saw the problem. There was no spare key and I started to explain the uniqueness of the double cuffs and why nobody was supposed to use them, but before I had finished Sonia called out again asking me please to refrain from the history lesson and just find a way of getting them out!

I knew that the first hurdle would be pushing out the key in such a way that it didn't bounce away from behind the lock, making it impossible to use something under the gap to pull the key backwards under the door. I explained the situation to Sonia and heard an audible sound of panic, but I assured her that I would do my best. The first hurdle of poking the key out of the lock went relatively well, however my fear was realised when I laid down on the carpet and could see the key, from under the door, quite a distance away. I told her what I was doing and hoped that somehow, she was going to say that it was alright, however there was nothing coming from the other side of the door to make me feel that this was going to happen. I made a wire grab of sorts from metal hangers and seemed to spend a year trying to get it to move the key closer to me under the door. When I finally managed to get it into my sweaty little paws, I laid on the carpet almost in tears as the tension left me. I got up and put the key in the lock and turned it wondering what I was going to find on the other side of the door.

The scene that greeted me initially had me wondering what the fuss was all about, but I recognised her boyfriend immediately as our local beat constable who was a regular, which obviously she was unaware of. The two of them were both wearing my set of double hand cuffs which attached them both to a huge iron wall ring which I had found in situ when I was designing my dungeon. The cuffs were of a design from the fourteenth century so the key was specially made at the same time as the cuffs. The boyfriend was naked but for a rather nasty Ann Sommers Basque with suspenders. The stockings were pulling the Basque downwards so that it looked as if it were going to cut his dick off and along with the ridiculous blonde wig, make-up and super high stiletto's he was wearing long black, rubber gloves and of all things, seemed to have a tail pinned to the back of the Basque? I decided to pretend that I had never seen the man before and concentrated on Sonia's explanation as to the whereabouts of the key to the cuffs. Apparently she had put the key in her mouth and was teasing her boyfriend with it on her tongue when that terrible bang had gone off, a sound that to her sounded a bit like an explosion and as it happened it made her jump, so much so that she had accidentally swallowed the key.

Both of them were standing when the 'game' had started and by now they were both wilting noticeably, but there was little I could do other than try to place something under each of them to help with the rules of gravity. It was stupid of me but without thinking I said, "well you can't stay here till it passes through and when it does, I'm not looking for it!"

If Sonia had had a hand free, I think by the look on her face that she would have clocked me a shot. I shut up trying to think if I could get a slave or maid who could come around and destroy the cuffs to set them free, but I confess I was actually unwilling to just destroy something that was unique, especially as I had told everyone who I worked with, NOT to use them. Unlike in Manchester, where I had access to a Blacksmith, in

Brighton there just wasn't one around the corner. We argued backwards and forwards until I finally said that I would leave them in situ and I would go away and find somebody to give me 'advice'?

After chewing everything over and becoming irritated with Sonia's pitiful begging, I decided to walk around to the fire station, taking Bruno with me and just ring the bell. This bell ringing business had always amused me. I had visions of one of the big hotels going up in smoke and somebody standing patiently waiting for somebody to answer the doorbell so that they could be informed that it was happening? Hilarious in my mind's eye, but obviously not so funny if you were on the sixth floor of said hotel?

As I explained the problem, it was decided that a couple of them would grab some tools and come back with me, but suddenly a sort of well-intentioned argument arose between them as to who would come back with me. All of them wanted to accompany me, but it meant leaving the fire station completely unmanned. Ultimately it was decided between them that it was highly unlikely that a fire would break out in the next hour and I walked back to the flat like a mother duck with fourteen firemen in various stages of uniform, laughing and giggling like a crowd of school girls trotting along behind me. At no point had I realised that the firemen, like myself, were bound to know Charlie as our local beat police officer. When we entered the flat there was a lot of jostling and elbow digging as the men surged into dungeon and sort of fanned out so everybody could get a decent view.

Both Sonia and Charlie looked mortified at the amount of nudging and giggling going on and then a big Australian guy who had noticed a pair of bloomers on a chair, picked them up and went to hand them to Charlie saying, "Nice to see ya me old mukker but I'm seeing just a bit too much of you if you don't mind my saying?" and he winked at his sniggering audience.

"Cover yerself up mate...oops sorry, ya can't can yas?" and he started losing it almost to the point of hysteria. They were all laughing their heads off as I struggled to get Charlie into the bloomers and when enough was enough, I called them to order and two of them started examining the cuffs and discussing the possibilities. Gradually they all wandered away back to the fire station but I was damn sure Charlies first job when he next tasted freedom was to run to the Police station and request a transfer!

It was decided that ultimately the cuffs were best being cut through without touching the lock, which was where all the decorative art work had been chiselled in. Repairing the cuffs if they were careful to choose the right place would be relatively easy and then when the key reappeared, the lock could be opened normally.

I never worked with Sonia again, which is no surprise and I never did get back my key?

As a little postscript, about two months after this happened the doorbell rang one evening and standing there in his civvies was the Australian Fireman. Surprised, I wondered what on earth he could have wanted, so I invited him in and showed him into the lounge where he proceeded to flourish a chilled bottle of Bollinger and said, "Hope you don't mind? I took the liberty…" but I think in that moment his courage melted and his voice just trailed off.

It was actually a very pleasant evening, all the obvious questions about my work was covered and I learnt quite a bit about his early life living in the outback. What was strange was that as he was leaving, he asked me where he could get a pair of bloomers like the ones, he had seen the day they rescued Charlie from the handcuffs. Slightly taken aback because he offered no explanation, I found him the catalogue which he took down the name and number of, as well as the model number and sizes of the bloomers but he was quite insistent that he did not want the catalogue, despite my offering it to him. With that he briefly brushed my lips with his and left. I never saw him

again, not even when I passed the Fire Station. Strange

31. LET THEM BEAT CAKE

I was at a private party in one of London's most up market clubs, when I spied a woman who I couldn't stand. In all honesty I didn't know her and I have no idea where this utter contempt came from, but I hated her! Strong words to use about a virtual stranger, but I just did. I hated the way she looked, the way she moved around, nose in the air, her stupid simpering voice which had more in common with Shirley Temple than any Dominatrix, and she almost always wore PVC! Utterly contemptable (Dominatrix snobbery raising its ugly head). The other thing that galled me was that wherever she went she had this huge following of idiots who wanted to look the part but if you went near them with a crop, would faint. On this evening she must have had at least ten of these numbskulls in her wake, sneering at the other submissive's there with an air of superiority, which I could not in my wildest dreams comprehend.

Cathy and I were sitting in one of the alcoves whilst I was having my bare feet licked and Cathy was using someone as a footstool. As Miss PVC sauntered past us, I heard Cathy mutter, "I don't know why, but I hate that fucking woman,"

I nodded my head in recognition and said, "So do I", and with that Cathy's footstool rose his head and said, "so do I", which made my foot fetishist pause for a second and say, "Yeah, I don't like her either".

As we were all in agreement the conversation stalled and we all went back to our silent thoughts until Miss PVC spied us and with a smile that revealed two gold front teeth started moving towards us.

"Oh shit," Cathy whispered. "She's heading this way" and an audible sigh trickled through the booth. We all tried to look elsewhere in the hopes she would sense our obvious withdrawal, but luck wasn't on our side and once she pushed her piggy Little visage into our space, we knew we were going to have to interact

"Roma, Cathy, how are my girls?" she squealed and bent over to lean her elbows on our table. "Excuse me Cynthia" said Cathy, showing a side of herself that I knew all too well; as did her footstool from the visible cringe that rippled through his body.

"Could you possibly remove your elbows only it makes me feel nervous that you might knock my drink over and get it all over your PVC".

The rest of us looked like we were eating as we contorted our faces to hide our smiles. Cynthia stared at Cathy with a look of confusion and then her hideous smile spread across her stupid face and a very fabricated laugh followed. She stood and waived a hand in Cathy's direction.

"No worries. At least it can be washed" she said, and with that she turned and would have left in a flourish but for the fact that all of her followers had seated themselves around her feet and moving away from our table became more of an obstacle course than a dramatic flounce.

I looked at Cathy and smiled, "prick" she muttered.

As the evening wore on, we circled the club a bit, watching various mistresses and masters show off their talents. We had decided that we weren't going to work this particular evening unless the spirit moved us and it was quite entertaining to watch the relationships between the various clientele. I've always been a people watcher which means I often spot something that is about to happen. I nudged Cathy and gave a slight nod towards a large party seated at a long table. The crowd were obviously there for a Birthday or something and were all dressed as if they were going to the Rocky Horror Show. Not real participants in the scene, but harmless enough. Cathy grabbed a couple more drinks as a waiter wafted past and settled against a pillar with a glasses rail so she had a good view. The first person we watched was a young woman who had obviously had rather too much to drink. She was seated about halfway along the table with people either side of her, obviously engaged in conversations with other people. Her head appeared to be attached to her body by a spring for a neck because it rolled and bobbed around while she desperately tried to keep both of her eyes looking in the same direction. At times her head would bounce backwards almost resting the back of her skull on her back, only to be lunged forward with such ferocity that the odds were that at some point she was bound to head butt the table. We watched fascinated and then suddenly she was so still we both glanced at each other in surprise. After what was probably only seconds but seemed like forever, in the same upright position she gradually slid downwards like a ship cut from its moorings, disappearing under the tablecloth, never to be seen again! We were just about to share the vision with each other when a waiter arrived at the head of the table with a huge birthday cake covered in a zillion candles. The birthday girl stood up and was obviously about to speak when the waiter shifted slightly and she did what for many young girls is a bit like a conversation spacer, and flicked her hair, right into the path of the cake. I have to assume that she had used a great deal of hairspray as her head instantly turned into a fireball with flames threatening to reach the ceiling. In the ensuing panic the waiter virtually threw the cake at Cynthia and it hit her with such force that it virtually separated and splattered her from head to toe. One of the guests had grabbed a large jug of water and had plonked the lot over this poor young woman saving her from any actual burns but leaving her dripping wet with what looked like a fried Brillo pad on her head and smoke rising from what may have been her ears.

We were finished. Unfortunately, the laughter between Cathy and I had us bent double. With tears streaming down our cheeks. After several attempts at controlling ourselves we finally managed to move off to another area but as we were leaving, we spotted Cynthia using heaps of kitchen roll in a vain attempt to remove cake. As we passed, Cathy leaned into her and said

"No worries. It can be washed!"

Which set us off again!

I also remember another incident involving Cynthia which was no less embarrassing than the previous, not for me of course. It was obviously at another function somewhere because I never socialised with her in a personal capacity because I didn't like her. There was nothing very exciting happening but I was there in the capacity as Mistress of ceremonies, which meant a couple of demonstrations, but it wasn't hard core and very easy for me. It also meant that the various Masters and Mistresses had to come and ask me or the Master to use the centre stage, as a matter of manners. I had just sat down after the last caning exhibition and accepted a drink when the queen of PVC, Cynthia, came (swaying slightly) into view. I was working with a Master called Steve who must have caught the look on my face and out of the corner of his mouth asked, "is this a no no?"

I hadn't realised that he had followed the direction I had been looking in and turned to him to ask what he meant, but before I could question him, he half whispered, "the woman in the red and black PVC?"

"You mean Cynthia" I stated flatly. "well if she asks to go on 'centre' be warned they'll be so many hangers on going on there with her, she'll get lost in the crowd".

He laughed and waited to see if she would approach when a couple of others politely asked to use the stage before her. She was obviously a bit pissed and thought about arguing that her status should mean she should go on first, but something in Steve's deliciously handsome face made her decide to keep quiet and just stand there like a giggly schoolgirl. Now there is a rule about certain practices within the 'scene' which are not strictly allowed unless the organisers are given prior notice or areas are set up to accommodate them. It's to do with hygiene really though no-one seems to care in the 'fucking pit', but you only go there to take part in some way, not to 'party'.

Cynthia had continued whilst waiting, to down several more pints of 'snakebite' and out of the corner of my eye I could see her start to sway slightly, not to the music. Finally, Steve graciously walked her onto the floor, but she half stumbled and his grip prevented her from losing her balance, so when he let her go, I was interested to see how she would cope. As predicted suddenly there were hordes of men flooding into the arena, two of which grabbed an arm each to keep her steady. Steve stood up and started directing men to wait in the audience clearing the area, but even as one left another would try to sneak back. Giving up, Steve gave the usual commencement statement and sat back with an air of amused anticipation.

Cynthia's opening piece was with a small riding crop and a cane which she brandished with dangerous abandon. The two fellows holding her, passed worried expressions between themselves when not ducking and out manoeuvring the cane. At one point she swished the cane so hard she accidentally let it go and it disappeared into the crowd causing a disembodied voice to yell, "OW"!

Various shuffling between her minions seemed to signal her finale as she downed her pint, handed the glass to one of them and with a flourish attempted to rip off her own skirt, which didn't happen? Within seconds she was covered in people trying to assist and after much fiddling about they, had her facing the audience wearing a sort of

Basque that stopped at the waist with a small peplum. She had bare legs squeezed a little too tightly into rubber stockings and rather old-fashioned ankle boots; but it wasn't what she was wearing that had us all staring with open mouths but rather it was what she wasn't wearing. In the gap between the Basque and her thighs was such a long, bushy minge that she could've put rollers in it.

What occurred next had to be seen to be believed, as she took the empty pint glass from one of her helpers, raised one of her legs by placing a foot on a slaves back and then proceeded to piss in the pint glass. The problem was obvious before it actually occurred because she had not taken into account the volume of liquid she had consumed. Once she started it was a flow that a donkey would have been proud of and she didn't stand a chance of stopping it. As her followers watched the yellow liquid fill the glass in seconds, they started trying to get between her legs to drink it, but the force was so heavy that it was much more like water boarding than the usual agreement between a Mistress and a slave. Trying to take a drink from a water cannon was another scenario that popped into my head but the actuality was indescribable. As more and more of them struggled to get under her she was physically lifted into the air ending up on her back and spraying the audience like a fireman.

The crowd started pushing and shoving to get away from the stream but were getting tangled up in the melee of subs that were pushing and shoving in the other direction, trying to get in on the action.

Wonderful memories!!

32. THE END?

When I retired there was no incident that changed my perceptions about the work I did, I just met somebody who promised me that I would never have to work again and that he would look after me until I died. We got on and had known each other as friends initially, which was possibly why we are still together.

I had been working alone or training young mistresses after Carol left, but I was still stupidly vulnerable to 'wanting to be in love' so I packed up my emotions, rolled them into a bundle and put them somewhere where they wouldn't cause any damage. It worked. As the years have rolled on, I have learned that the passion and the lust are such transient expressions of commitment that they inevitably wither and that love can grow steadily over years becoming far stronger than one could imagine and these last years of my life have actually been some of the happiest.

We didn't get married but we have lived I suppose as man and wife and we have shared together our style of mishaps, which sometimes on a boozy night we have conjured up again and laughed as much as we did the first time. We're both a bit telepathic and very often we share a moment that anybody else in the vicinity wouldn't get.

After living for a few years by the sea we decided that we would preferably live in Somerset, a place we both liked and had holidayed at with our dogs, even after we could no longer get tickets for Glastonbury

Living in the countryside is a joy that we have both embraced. The house he purchased for us was in a horrible state when we first bought it that the first time, we viewed it was a beautiful day with a warm sun, which as we entered the property made the smell even more vehement and it hit us like a wall! Without a doubt the general smell of cigarettes and dogs piss burnt your eyes and Neill just started to retch which wasn't helped by my elbow stabbing him in his ribcage. It was a sad story which had left the woman unable to cope with a house that had a footprint over a hundred years old. She had lost the will to try and had a succession of dogs that she couldn't be bothered to house train. The run up to the move was one of the most distressing and anxious times in both of our lives, as having accepted an offer, when it came to completion, she kept saying she wasn't ready to leave. On the day we moved she still hadn't left and I had to help pack her stuff as quickly as possible to get her out, so we could get in. As luck would have it, we had been here less than a week when Neill was made redundant. When he couldn't sleep with worry, I would find him staring out over the beautiful Somerset Moors and he'd smile and reassure me, no regrets.

I have virtually nothing that I feel remorse for in my life, mainly because I think it's a total waste of time. At the time of writing this I suffer from an illness which is terminal. I'm not afraid or worried about it and I think that it happens to all of us and is possibly the gateway to another adventure?

I don't mind but it's maybe come just a little sooner than I would have hoped. I think that because so far, I'd cheated the prognosis and wasn't at a stage expected some years ago, I forgot that at some point it was going catch up with me, and it has. Like I said, I am not afraid and my only worry is that I may die from suffocation or worse lose my marbles before I die from suffocation? Either way the choice will not be mine and unlike most people, if we do meet those we have loved on the other side, I'm hoping to meet dogs, a sheep and a very special little cow.

When we were making this a home, I probably used at least a gallon of Jeyes fluid, two gallons of bleach and another gallon of assorted cleaners. After spending hours on hands and knees literally scrubbing, I would then drag anyone, like the postman, delivery bloke, whoever into the house and ask them to tell me if they could smell piss?

Invariably they would shake their head and look uncomfortable until I pushed it and then, looking apologetic they would nod their head and agree that it DID undeniably still smell of piss!

Neill just doesn't have the stomach for it, so when it came to removing the layered carpets in the lounge I volunteered and went at it with industrial scissors, a knife and rubber gloves. There were so many on top of each other that I had to peel off layers at a time and when I got to the last as I tugged and dragged them to the window, they still left wet drag marks of dog urine, possibly twenty-year-old dog urine, on the floorboards beneath. I had to do it in sections and chuck the pieces out onto the lawn where Neill, wearing face mask and gloves would take them to the skip, but it was a long, tedious and smelly job which I hope I would never have to do again.

As we went from room to room, making it relatively comfortable, we both realised that this was one of those never-ending labours of love, where as one bit is fixed, strong winds come and blow more bits off!!

Somerset is a different world running at a different time and it takes quite a while before one gets used to, "I'll be there in a minute" which actually doesn't inform you which minute? It could mean a minute in an hours-time, a days-time or possibly even a weeks-time???

Be careful who you are rude about because there is a strong likelihood that they have at least fifty relatives in your immediate area and potentially even more as far as the coast in Cornwall.

If you weren't born there, and your ancestors weren't born there, then you aren't from there and 'locals' come from the same gene pool and how many of your immediate family live in the same area. YOU will NEVER be local. If you settle into country life for over twenty years, some may start to acknowledge you with a nod or even mumble a greeting, but never forget your place.

A few years ago, Neill bought a small field opposite the house and since living here we have had chickens, Goats, Sheep and cattle and despite various problems, we have enjoyed our decision and loved our lives here. When sadness takes you, standing anywhere around our house you are looking at the most beautiful landscapes and the potential to watch deer, hares, foxes etc.

Since arriving I've been a midwife to sheep and actually brought a lamb into the world which wouldn't be here if it wasn't for the internet and my intervention.

It is good for the soul and a place to heel if need be.

Like so many others I've managed to get various health problems which sadly, as we get older have the ability to leave something nasty in its wake. Despite swallowing enough tablets to mean that shares in a pharmaceutical company would be an excellent investment, I still have things wrong with me that apparently they can't do anything for, such as a degenerative condition to my spine caused by a cyst that appeared out of nowhere and apparently was so rare that many Doctors have never seen one. Well just stay with me because three years later

I developed another one, so if you missed it there was a second opportunity. Same place, just as big and unfortunately the damage from the two has meant lasting complications. I have COPD and Bronchiectasis and suffer from osteoarthritis in various joints, and I'm actually probably at a stage along with the house, very soon I imagine bits will just start dropping off me?

Just recently a young man was trying to chat me up whilst I waited for Neill in a bar and offered me a dirty weekend in Cornwall. Immediately in my minds' eye I caught a picture of me with no make-up, no teeth in, stretch bandages around various joints and baggy skin which looks like it belonged to somebody a size larger, with an oxygen cylinder on a wheely carrier thingie beside me and I thought, you've no idea what you have just asked Mister, and being a kind human being, I refused.

Getting old wasn't something I had ever really encouraged. My lifestyle over the years with the drugs, drink and partying all night meant I was more disposed to it all ending around the age of thirty-five, before the ravages of enjoying myself left its mark. Obviously not to be, but a tad disappointing from the perspective of having to look into a mirror and witness the degeneration as each year whizzes up to the next and instead of improvement you have to stand straighter so that you get a view of your whole face, including the jowls!

So my life is coming to an end, hopefully not tomorrow, but I haven't included huge parts of my life, my travelling, some of the people I have known, running a breed specific dog rescue for thirteen years, the slow awful loss of my mother and various things that have happened to me and the people who played a part in those things. The last part of this book is just my other 'writings' where I suppose my darker self gets an airing. Don't be too hard on me, if you get bored, just stop reading?

ANNECDOTES

INVITATION TO A PARTY

There have been some wonderful moments too, like when Neill was talking to a group, having been invited to an elderly gentleman's Birthday party. Somebody said, "You know he'll be eighty, don't you?"

And John said, "will he b'buggered?"

To which Neill quipped, "No I don't think so, just a Birthday cake like anybody else!"

ERRRMMM SORRY

There is a certain uniform that virtually all farmers wear when going 'out'. Check shirt, Barbour quilted waistcoat, jeans or chino's, Barbour or Dunlop wellies and very often a tweed cloth cap and Neill has adopted this way of dressing because other than the cap and boots, he dressed that way anyway.

Well, we were in a farm feed shop getting chicken pellets or something and this was my first outing after a dose of said Noro Virus. We were in different parts of the shop when my stomach gave one of those awful lurches that spells trouble. I instantly looked for Neill and spotted him at the end of an aisle. I quickly approached him and touching his arm said reasonably quietly,

"My bottom is about to explode"

It wasn't Neill and the bloke staring at me had a look of complete horror on his face as he kept looking at my hand gently touching his arm and back to my face again. I tried to smile but it probably looked more like a grimace, and tentatively moved my hand to my pocket and said,

"Erm, sorry, you probably didn't want to know that did you? Terribly sorry", and with that I shot off to find Neill.

HALELUYAH

We rarely go out but this was one of those odd occasions where on the spur of the moment we decided to go out for a curry. Where we live there is no such thing as a take-away Indian or Chinese unless you want to travel a fair distance so we decided to eat in. The restaurant we chose was only moderately busy with only one other couple sitting in our side of the restaurant about five tables down. The toilets were behind me at the far wall and honestly I can't tell you if they arrived after us or before, but when the lady rose to go to the toilet her dramatic hauling herself out of her chair and then dragging herself along, grabbing chairs, tables and at one point I thought me, had to be seen to be believed. I couldn't help wondering with all the puffing and ooh-ars why she didn't have a stick or zimmer with her, and it was just a passing thought so I got on with my meal. I guessed Neill had clocked her but he didn't comment even when she made this arduous journey several times and during the time, they had been there I had noticed another bottle of wine being consumed, which I vaguely counted as three. Oddly it was the gentleman who was starting to flag and as she hauled herself past us again, he waited to attract the attention of the waiter, which made him face in a direction towards the front of the restaurant. While he was looking away the lady left the ladies room and walked smartly to her chair in a few short strides and sat down.

Neill never even looked up but I heard him say "It's a miracle!"

KISSAGRAMS

I was working as a kissogram just to earn some extra pocket money and though when I first started out, I was really nervous, by the time this story happened, I was an old hand. Kissogram have probably died out now because they were really very tame and as the years roll onwards people want different things. In my day a booking was made by a spouse, friends, work mates, anyone really. They gave you some details about the target and you turned up dressed as a policewoman, a pregnant bride, Salvation army girl, traffic warden, you get the drift? So, you would turn up start off with a ruse to contact the mark, strip down to a Basque, stockings and suspenders, read the poem that you made up using the person's details, supposedly kiss the target, (something I point blank refused to do but by keeping the rhyme funny, always got away with it) and then you would pick up your clothes, run for the door, jump into your waiting driver's car and scoot off to the next one. The money was all cash and they could book an ordinary Kissogram or a topless Kissogram, which meant just folding down the cups of the Basque. Now people paid thirty pounds for a straight Gram but forty-five pounds for topless and to me, who sunbathed on nudist beaches, it was a no-brainer and there was a strictly no-touching policy.

An example. I arrive dressed as a policewoman, find the mark and politely inform him that there is a warrant out for him and he needs to accompany me to the station, quickly handcuffing his hands behind his back. Then I would strip as I said something like:

"Well I'm sorry to muck up your birthday by taking you off to jail

It's your girlfriend Sarah's way to say that your behaviour's beyond the pail

You must give up your beer swilling Sundays, only turning up when there's food

I think we would all agree here that that practice is ever-so rude

So, you've one last chance to redeem yourself, say sorry and don't pull a frown

Cos if you don't promise here to change your ways, I'll pull your trousers down!!"

Police women were very popular and I had my uniform made for me so that it was easy to remove but really looked the part and my handcuffs? Need I say more? This particular evening a topless Gram was booked in a pub and as I went into my routine my driver was gesticulating at me, with exaggerated mouthing, which I had No idea of its meaning? Suddenly he hit his forehead with an upward sweep of his hand, rolled his eyes and went back out to the car?

I did my job, grabbed my clothes and went out into the street to find the car having popped my tits away…except I hadn't. When I had looked down, I had seen my right breast nestled happily in its cup and assumed that I had put them both away. As I jumped into the car, I turned to my driver and said, "What the fuck was that all about?" Except it wasn't my driver and following his eye-line, my left boob was still out in the open. I quickly tucked it away, and said "Ooops…sorry" as I scrambled back out of the vehicle, spotted my driver, dived into his passenger seat and asked the same question.

"You did the whole job with only one tit out!"

"Did I?"

"Yes. So urry-up cos the bastards might want half their money back" and with that he put his foot down and we sped off.

I also did a job at a house in the seafront which was set back into a rock cave at the base of the cliff. I had never seen anything so strange and it was as if hundreds of people were crushed into this tiny space, to the extent that I had to do the Kissogram outside, leaning in the window?

Well again it was decided that I would be a policewoman and there was nothing in his details that led me to believe there would be any sort of problem. The first thing was that as I started to approach a woman made a bee line for me, grabbing my arm and turning me away from getting near the house, leaning right into me and whispering, "I just need to know that your tidy?"

I must have looked as confused as I felt because she looked around to make sure nobody else was watching, and started pointing towards the floor, mouthing, "Down there?" I started looking around near my feet and she almost had apoplexy. "No" she stage whispered, "not the fucking floor, between your legs?"

I was so taken aback I didn't know what to say. She gave a theatrical roll of her eyes and said, "Pull your skirt up. No one can see you, I need to av a look" and without taking a breath she bobbed down and pushed her head up under my skirt. As I pulled away her face reappeared all smiles. "Lovely and tidy" she said. "No offence but I wasn't avin some bird with hair all hanging out her gusset for my boy. Ee's special" she stepped back and as she did so she nodded and winked, "I've put a bit extra in there for ya. It's been a long time since I ad my boy. Very nice. Very tidy" she smiled and then stood back obviously urging me to start.

As I said this was the strangest house with part of it cordoned off as if for cliff falls and the other half pushed back into a really dingy little room where a bloke was sitting with a paper hat on his head and a huge German Shepherd curled around his feet and chair. There was no chance of me getting through the crush of people into the room, so I managed to get close enough to lean through the window, when all hell broke loose! All I heard was the bloke shout, "Raspberry Kill" which sent the dog flying at the window as the chap somehow managed to get through the hoard of people and the last I saw of him he was legging it, paper hat miraculously still attached, at great speed off down the sea front!

Later I learned that he had absconded from prison and had been 'on the run' for the last nine months. His mother thought he would love the joke and apparently took on 'Raspberry' after he left so suddenly. Shame, I would have liked him to know that I was, "Tidy".

In the same garb I was booked to turn up as a policewoman on a busy building site. The lad was only in his teens and the older blokes hired me for his birthday to play the 'joke' on site so that they could all join in. When I first arrived two or three blokes quickly hid me from his view, as they tried to get everyone together for the Kissogram. As always, the best laid plans of mice and men notwithstanding, when I was finally pushed out into the open, the lad clocked me and ran straight for the toilets. I tried to intercept him but he was a lot faster than I was and wasn't wearing high heels. As I got to the door the mark had dived into a cubicle and so the other blokes pushed me forwards as they all crammed into the toilet block. My nose decided that I should get this done as quickly as possible. Building site toilets are seriously frightening and I was having misgivings about taking on the job in the first place as everyone roared and started stamping their boots on the floor. Suddenly the sound of the lock on the door caused silence amongst the audience and I decided to launch straight in on the job without worrying about undressing just so that I could say I had fulfilled my part of the booking. As the door slowly opened, we were all faced with a young lad whose face was cherry red his breathing almost a pant. When he put his hand up to stop me, I just stopped and as he surveyed the faces of his work mates and started to tremble, I had a bad feeling. Suddenly he just exploded

"You're cunts. You fucking stupid cunts. A fucking Policewoman? A policewoman? Are you so fucking stupid or just in the business of sharing a fucking brain cell?". He took a breath as I looked at the stunned faces of his work colleagues. "What were you thinking?" he stammered. "I just flushed over a hundred E's, over a fucking ounce of green and all my speed and tabs! Do you know what this has fucking cost me? You fucking cunts" and he shook his head sadly looking at the floor and plonked his bum down on the toilet seat his head in his hands. I didn't wait. I'd been paid so I just pushed my way out and went and found my driver. When I opened the envelope, it was obvious that there had been a whip round because it contained a hundred and sixty quid. Did I feel guilty?... Well maybe just a little.

GRRRRRRR

When we were running the rescue Neill had to go, on the way home from work, to pick up a dog from Battersea Dogs Home. We had been told that she could be a bit grumpy, but Neill assured me on the phone that she was small and he saw kindness in her eyes... So that was alright. When he arrived home, he came and got me and we both walked to the back of the fan whilst he extolled her virtues as a quiet, good dog. With that he swung open the doors and she flew at the cage door spitting and growling, hanging from the wire like one of those window Garfields! Neill took one look and just shut the doors again, looked at me and shrugged? We did actually get a muzzle on her and into the house, but only after Neill had pushed the steel toe of his boot towards her and whilst she desperately tried to savage it, I snuck up behind her with a muzzle and waited until she had to let go to draw breath and get a better hold, like lightening I squashed her jaws together and secured the muzzle. Having spent the night with us although she took to our dogs, if we went near her, she showed her teeth. One of the ways I have found to get through to grumpy dogs is to muzzle them and then just keep cuddling them, talking softly and fussing them. We had to go out for something and I suggested we take her with us and I would sit with my arm around her to get her used to us. Everything went swimmingly until we had to actually leave her in the van whilst we entered a shop. When we returned there was no sign of her, when suddenly her head popped up on the drivers. side…minus the muzzle! A very similar operation took place to the one the first time round but I promise you she became the dog that Neill had seen with kindness in her eyes. It Just took a bit of a detour to get there.

PARTY

Every year we hold a party in the field opposite our house with music, the teepee for chilling, strobe lighting dancing in the trees, loads of home cooked food, an old bath filled with ice filled with beer, cider and bottles of wine and a huge bonfire lit after we are sure there's nothing living in it. We provide our caravan for first dibs and tents and in the house we can accommodate (providing people don't mind sharing) several people as we have two double beds in our annex, another in our porch and three large leather couches in our lounge with loads of floor space to encourage people to stay rather than drive and as most of the few friends we have live a way away, we encourage the slogan stop where you drop!

Something us locals understand is that every field in this part of the world is surrounded by a deep ditch filled with water and a disgusting black slime at the bottom that actually works like quicksand and really stinks, so when we hold a party, we rope off the sides of the ditch with fluorescent tape, except when it comes to the road. Now I wasn't there to witness this I was doing food etc. but enough people did, for me to enjoy the tale second hand. Despite being the Countryside, we actually live next to a fast road so when a couple of our guests arrived on our drive Neill spotted them and left the party to collect them. After greetings he shepherded them across the road and shining a torch was leading them into the field when a car whizzed past and he heard a plop. One of the women he was escorting had sidestepped when she heard the car and had fallen backwards into the ditch so that all Neill could see was her legs sticking up wards. On investigation he found her at the bottom of the ditch, upside down, desperately trying to keep her head out of the water and making a sort of mewing sound afraid that if she bellowed, she would get a mouthful of stagnant water. Being a hero, he went down the bank to rescue her and discovered that despite his six foot plus height the water was above his chest and despite himself he did her yelling for her. Thankfully enough bodies heard him to help him lift her out of the ditch and then help him out as well, but I truly wish I had been there to witness the sight of Jo, upside down and Neill walking bravely down the bank and discovering that he kept going deeper and deeper in his bid to rescue her!

SHOES

We had gone out shopping for nothing in particular but Neill was looking at shoes and having seen a pair he liked we went into the shop. Now he is normally a UK size ten but like all of us, as more things come into our shops from Asia the Continent and other far-away places the sizing can be a bit iffy. We entered the shop and after a reasonably long wait a young girl with a fairly disinterested expression asked if she could help us. Neill explained the shoe and the size and asked to try them on, which left us sitting for what seemed an age until she returned with a shoe and handed it to Neill. He tried it on and after a few seconds nodded and asked to try the other one which sent our more than disinterested helper off to get the other shoe. When she returned, she handed Neill the box and was staring out at the street outside, when Neill opened the box and removed the shoe, it was the same design, but it was tiny and it was obviously a child's size ten, despite our laughter the assistant just stared at us. Neill held the shoes up together, sole to sole to show the huge disparity between them. But the girl still just stared. Finally, Neill pushed the two shoes upwards still soles squashed together so that she had to be able to see them both and said, "they're not a pair?"

She looked hard at him, looked at the box and nodded at him before saying, "Yes they are. They're both size ten. Look!" showing him the end of the box where it shows the size. When that didn't seem to satisfy, she said, "If you don't believe me", Sighing and rolling her eyes,

"Look at the bottom of both shoes and you'll see the size on the sole. They are a size ten!"

Neill looked from her to me and by now I was starting to snigger. He inhaled a long breath, turned to her and said, "Look, I don't doubt that they both say size ten, but look at them. One is obviously an adult size ten and the other a child's size ten?"

She looked at the two shoes and then for a few seconds stared hard at the end of the shoe box before turning her attention to Neill again.

"Well it says size ten on the box, what am I supposed to do? I don't see why you're making a fuss it's obvious they're a size ten!"

Neill almost quivered. "But they are not a pair, whether they say ten or not!"

More rolling of the eyes and with real irritation in her voice she said, "Do you want to try them both on or not?"

Neill shook his head dropped the shoes on the floor and stood up. "C'mon" he said and we started to leave.

Just as we reached the door, I heard the shoe assistant say, "Moron!"

Luckily, he didn't hear it.

DIY

I am a person who really doesn't like strangers in my space. I'm quite tactile with people who I know and like, in fact I'm a bit of a 'hugger' but if I don't know you, neither of us gets too close. Neill and I were in a well-known DIY store and after pottering around we joined the queue to pay for whatever it was Neill was buying. After only seconds this bloke came and stood behind me far too close for my comfort. I tried moving forward a little but it only made him shuffle forwards behind me making him even closer. Neill could see that I wasn't happy and tried to use his body to shelter me, but I told him loud enough for the man to hear that I really, really didn't like people who wanted to get up close and personal when It wasn't appropriate. I thought it was rude and that the person doing it should stop and if they didn't...Neill tried to quieten me, not because he was irritated by me, but because he understood how I feel about things like that. I could feel myself getting stressed and as I cleared my throat I accidentally let out a very loud, staccato fart. Suddenly we were all alone in the queue and Neill turned to me and said,

"Well, that did it!".

FISH

Without boring you with too much detail, when we first moved here, we ended up having to clear the property next door and one of the things that needed clearing was a huge stone pond with Koi Carp. Both of us are aware of the value of these fish but we just wanted to get rid of them, so we just put out a local ad. Several people came being a nuisance because they only wanted this one or only the big ones' blah, blah. So, when a chap turned up all full of smiles and politeness after, chatting for a bit and me making a cup of tea, it was decided that he would take the lot for £100 which he was ecstatic about. In fact, we were very, very generous because there were two ghost carp that were probably worth more than that each. We organised a day when he would come and help us drain the pond and collect the fish and he arrived promptly with his son. Now obviously, as I have sheep, dogs, chickens and a much more rural lifestyle, I do not put make-up on daily anymore and I tend to wear old clothes or just very cheap ones, so that they can keep being washed, (cheap things always fade out on the line in the sunshine), or that can simply be binned. I never really thought about it, I just like being practical. As the action started, catching fish, collecting precious plants (apparently he had some really rare water Lillie's which to buy would have cost an arm and a leg) and drain the pond, I ran round grabbing tubs, insulated boxes, plant carriers, nets and such like, as well as making conversation and making tea.

The son had been in the army but one night on leave he was terribly badly beaten by a gang of yobs and would have died had it not been for the paramedics first on the scene. The recovery was so long and with doctors unable to give a clear picture of what lay ahead he was invalided out of the Army and once all of his faculties returned, he trained to be a Paramedic himself.

As they day wore on and more and more expensive fish kept being captured and I think that the son had started to feel guilty about what his dad was paying us, on the basis that he thought we were just ignorant as to what everything was worth, which was probably true. Either way for reasons best known to himself he asked Neill and I to please come to his wedding reception which was about a month away. Now I hate things like this because I don't know anyone, in this instance not even the bride and Neill and I always end up on the periphery of whatever is going on, keeping an eye on our watches to see when it would be polite enough to leave. Well Neill thought we really should make the effort, so off we go suited and booted and absolutely nobody acknowledged us, or even asked if we were gate crashers or even seemed to care. After what felt like forever we were just starting to nudge towards the exit, when Mr 'Just-Married' comes over and desperately attempts to make conversation with

Neill and it is obvious he can't remember who we are, So Neill gives him a clue and asks after the fish?

With a huge sigh of relief as his brain acknowledges who we are, he obviously felt he has done his duty by engaging in less than five minute's conversation, and finishes his sentence and goes to walk away. Almost as if he suddenly remembered that I was standing next to Neill he turns to me, looks me up and down, gives me a thumbs up says "Good effort" ?

We left.

MINE'S A PINT

Neill had to work away for the Saturday and because it was so far away, he booked a hotel on one of these late room websites and managed to book at a really up market hotel. He booked a double and as they accepted dogs the whole family went. This place had a spar, clay pigeon shooting, swimming pool, a golf course, three restaurants and their own pub set on the border of their land with lots of country walks to get there.

We had had dinner (which incidentally was so expensive it completely over-shadowed the cost of the room) and decided we would walk one of the paths that allowed off lead and head for the pub. Now we had four Shar pei and one Douge-de-Bordeaux so when we reached the pub I went in alone and asked if it were alright to bring the dogs in, but just as I said this, I realised that it wasn't just full of people, but loads of cats? The landlady wasn't fazed and said as long as we could hang onto them initially, once the cats saw the dogs they'd disappear. I hoped she was right, told Neill what she had said and so in we ploughed. Hanging on was absolutely necessary because as the punters saw us enter, they picked up their glasses because cats were flying in all directions. Across the bar, up the curtains, scooting across the floor, landing on punters backs to be used as a stepping stones. Charlie, one of our Shar Pei's was definitely up for a piece of cat and was bouncing and bounding as the cats whipped past and then...nothing. No cats. Punters went back to their drinks and conversations. Neill started to gather up leads for me to hold whilst he got us a drink at which point having enjoyed the whole debacle, Charlie calming a little from all the excitement, shook his head vigorously sending a huge dollop of gob up into the air, across the heads of some people and landed with a plop in this man's pint just as he took a huge swig of his beer. The man he was speaking to, seeing it land and get swallowed let his jaw drop to his chest, as did several others who had seen it and ourselves. Smacking his lips having downed most of his pint the man said to his friend, "Another pint?" to which his friend just nodded slowly. We had a quick drink and left.

FART STORY

We were going to a house to pick up a plastic chicken house and when we arrived were greeted by a very nice chap and a nice little dog. He invited us in through to the back garden where the chickens had been kept and his wife stopped me from following by saying, "oh let the men sort that out. Cup of tea?".

I declined but found it awkward to push past her through the kitchen so hovered where I was. She was very friendly and introduced me to their bald cat who was very laid back, but she kept getting into my personal space until I was virtually cornered between two units. I was trying to be nice but as she chatted on, I could feel a fart brewing. Desperately looking for a way out, despite myself it forced its way out between clenched buttocks and my relief that it had been silent was soon withdrawn when the most awful smell surrounded me. I had no choice and put a hand up to stop her advancing any further and said,

"I'm ever so sorry but I just farted and it smells dreadful. If we were anywhere else, I may have tried to blame someone else, but I can't because there's just you and me here so I felt that the smell was so awful I should fess up and apologise"

She stared at me literally with her mouth open which made me nearly making a joke about chewing on it, but her expression stopped me and gratefully Neill appeared carrying an awkwardly bulky chicken house, so I made my escape.

IN MEMORIAL

For those who were loved and lost

And for those who were never found

For those tiny lights that were never born

And for those who we left behind

For those who were never missed

And for those who would walk alone

For those who passed after one short breath

And for those who were just unknown

For those who were washed with many tears

And those who were taken with strife

I allow my senses to reach to them all

And acknowledge there once was a life.

All life should have at least a second where somebody, or something, remembers it existed. As you read these words, bow your head and give a moment of your time to the fallen and know that when you have gone, someone else takes your place.

THE LOSS OVER AND OVER AND OVER AND OVER AND...

There is a moment during every day or night that in my mind or in my heart, your memory comes back to touch me.

I never know which time or place the realisation that I still miss you, gently strokes me into some awareness of the gap

That hole inside my life, my heart, my everything that makes up who I am and how I function, who I'm meant to be

A sudden shiver, a coldness that seeps through consciousness to make me feel the lack.

I stop and check myself because I know that I must cease the silent tears from running down my face.

I hide from seeing eyes and battle with my will to gain control and start to reapply the face that others see

I wonder if somewhere in another time, in another world or maybe just another space

You freeze and try to find the crack that is letting in a blast of emptiness where once you just felt me

In these moments do we find our limbs behaving like we had no willingness to stop us reaching out

Is there suddenly a moment where we close our eyes as flesh touches flesh and suddenly our wholeness can entwine

Just a fleeting touch suspended in a moment from those years when we loved and saw no reason to explore or doubt

A sensory photograph wriggling free to hold us to each other from another place and time

They tell us that the time comes inevitably, where the cold seeps in and you can never feel the warmth of it again

That we move on and over time the love that burned so brightly loses all its' power and becomes a feeble breath

That the images, once certain lose their colour and at last we feel that we are able to release the pain

As if the whole of you was lost to me, because my brain can simply turn you out as when I felt your death

But there are still those memories we deny and still the instinct that I'm certain everyday there IS that second where we touch

The sweetness which was you, floods through me like a broken dam, all-consuming and I feel that you're still there

A split second, so strong that no matter where I am, when it reaches me, it feels too much

And infiltrates and holds my soul aloft, regardless of my grief and I am forced to face that I still care

There is a moment during every day or night that in my mind or in my heart, you still come to touch me

I know that at a time or place the realisation that I ache to hold you, gently strokes me into some awareness of what's past.

That gaping wound that makes me who I am and how I function, never letting me be free

A sudden shiver, a coldness makes me realise that the die is cast.

THE DEAD

There by the hanging tree I see them tread their nightly walk

Would that I walk with them for that final time and hope to chance I rest

The battered and the bloody wend their silent path towards another dawn

No recognition of the others as they each walk from a different time

No sound but some move lips as if they try to talk

Some left alone whilst another had the time to ask that they confess

Some are lights in others eyes but they were never born

Some were innocent and others paid the price of crime

There in the shadows of the wall I see them wander in and out of life

Some seem unaware that they have passed whilst others know their lot

Some enter then as quickly they disappear again from view

Each unaware of those around them living and reliving the moment that they passed

Were these the ones that never had a husband or a wife

Were these those taken when it wasn't time to stop

Were these the ones in life that others never noticed, those we never knew

Are these the ones that lived a lifetime in a moment and had moved too fast,

Then as the dawn begins, they start to shimmer in the light,

Some like a dust cloud quickly fragment and dissipate as part of the morning air,

Others seem to desperately cling to human form and won't let go,

Each with their own mission and their own repeated way to tread,

Fading quickly as the sun creeps up and birds begin their flight,

A hint that some were nightly living and remembering some dark despair,

Why are these chosen whilst others close their eyes and do not know

Who is it chooses when the dead are dead?

SHORT STORY: THE PEOPLE
19th February 1992

He watched the stranger hiding in the shadows while he idly scratched his ear, His one beady black eye penetrated the darkness as he peered between the steel bars. Sniffing the air, he shifted to acquire the full feel of the intruder's scent and frowned. He could not completely recognise the smell, but he knew it was female. It hovered against the skirting before scuttling across the floor towards the rack where his cage rested. He could hear the sound of her having a scratch and the twitching of her whiskers as she searched the unfamiliar room for food.

He waited, hardly breathing and pushed himself forward against the bars to get a better view.

He felt the vibration as she crawled up onto his level and held his breath. She scrambled up onto his shelf and catching a whiff of him, froze!

Half-hidden behind the feed trap, she cocked her head on to one side and her whiskers clattered together as she tried to get the measure of him. He let out a deep chuckle and winked his eye at her. She took a tentative step forward and raised a paw, squeaking a greeting.

As her curiosity got the better of her, she whispered, "what are you?"

He moved lazily and raised an eyebrow, "I could ask you the same question. Come closer that I may look at you" he said. His voice was deep and languid. She took a small step closer and used her sonar to check that it was safe to continue. A frown crossed her pretty features and she shuffled towards him.

"What holds you?" she asked curiously. He tilted his head to one side. She had stepped into the pool of light and he admired her streamlined figure and the sheen on her coat.

"So, you are a rat", he said quietly, almost to himself. A low grumbling laugh escaped between his sharp teeth and he pressed closer to the bars. Ignoring him she sniffed and pawed at the cage that held him. Sitting back on her haunches, she daintily smoothed her ears while she examined him.

"Are you a rat too?" she asked politely. He laughed again, only this time much louder. A wicked grin distorted his features and he placed a gnarled paw in the gap between the bars. "Do I look like a rat?" he asked. She studied him again and sniffed the air around him.

"Yes" she said finally, "but you don't completely smell like one!"

He shifted his bulk and leaned backwards, so that she could get a better look at him and took a deep draught of her scent. "I could say the same about you" he said with a shrug, "What wing are you from?"

She leaned sideways and scratched her side vigorously. She looked confused.

"Pardon?" she said finally.

He winked his eye at her and chuckled. "Someone's in for the high jump," he laughed. "Technician leave your cage open then, did he?"

She took another step forward and twitched her nose. A small frown creased the silky fur between her eyes. She looked uncomfortable, "I'm from outside", she said.

The big rat stopped speaking and stared, trying to grasp the truthfulness of her words.

She smoothed her whiskers, trying to guess what his body language told her.

Finally, he closed his one eye and chuckled, "A joke, right?"

She shook her head and felt aggrieved that he would question her. She interrupted his laughter.

"No! I came in through the air vent. It's raining outside so I thought I'd take a chance and come in here to see if there was anything to eat?" She twitched her whiskers and leaned forward trying peer into his cage. "Have you got any food in there?" she asked coquettishly, her nose already telling her that there was something available.

The big male shifted his position and scratched his head with his back paw, emitting a little groan as he did so. Leaning sideways, he picked up a pellet and pushed it through the bars towards her. She sniffed at it suspiciously and then looked up at him.

"Is it edible?" she asked.

He nodded. "Processed" he explained. He watched as she picked it up in her front paws and nibbled a little piece off the end. She sat back on her haunches and chewed the small piece she had bitten off and looked at him.

"What's it like?" The big male asked.

She shrugged, "I've tasted better!"

He let out a low chuckle. "No. I mean the outside?"

She looked at him steadily and stopped chewing. "Have you never been?" she asked sincerely.

He shook his head and lowered his chin, making it difficult for her to read his expression. Placing the pellet to one side she shuffled closer to the cage and wrapped her tail around her haunches. "At the moment it's raining and when it's wet it's harder to smell the food. There's..." she stopped in her tracks hesitating a moment she asked, "Do you know what I mean. Do you know what rain is?"

He shrugged and kept his face in the shadows. "I've heard it...but that's all"

She thought for a second and tried to explain. "Rain is water that drops from the sky and it tastes..." She shrugged, "Well it tastes of the Sea and the Wind and the Fire. Of the grasslands and all the animals and of the human and their food. It cleanses the ground and the air and it is sweet with the juice of the flowers and the clouds".

She smiled with rapture. "It's wonderful," she said.

His voice was quiet. "I can't imagine it", he said honestly.

She thought for a moment. "I can get you some!" she said eagerly. He shifted again in the shadows and as he turned his head his one eye glinted in the moonlight.

"You're laughing at me," he said.

"No..!" she protested. "There's a gap there by the window. I could get a drop on the end of my nose and bring it to you?"

"Why?", he asked warily.

She shrugged again, "Well you gave me a processed. Shall I?"

The big rat was loathed to send her away afraid that she may not return, but his craving for the thing she had described plagued him. He nodded his huge head and hoped she would return. She scuttled off and he felt the vibration again as she deftly descended the shelving. He heard the patter of her paws across the laboratory floor and strained to hear her catch the raindrop. After what seemed to him an eternity, he finally felt the weight of her light body slowly creeping up the shelving and she reappeared. Balanced on the end of her nose was a blob of shimmering light. She shuffled to the edge of the cage and tipped up her head for him to reach, He leaned forward and sniffed at it.

"Take it!" she said impatiently, "or it will dry".

He pushed his nose through the bars above her and lapped at the glimmering drop of water. The taste of it exploded on his tongue and in his throat with sensations he could never have dreamed of. It was all that she had implied and more.

It was the taste of freedom.

He closed his eye and wallowed in the mixture of flavours and she watched him. After a while she tentatively spoke.

"What holds you?" she asked more softly than before.

Opening his eye, he studied her pert features and smiled but the expression showed no humour.

"People" he said with bitterness.

Her head tilted to one side, "But we are the People?" she said questioning his statement.

"No", he said shaking his head, "We are rats" he explained.

"But that's what the Human calls us?" she insisted. We call ourselves the People. No human is a person? Unlike them when our colonies become too large, our bodies prevent us from having 'kits' Human cannot do this?

He listened to all of the questions in her voice.

"He kills when he has no reason to, we do not kill for pleasure. It takes the land of the animals for itself; we live beside other creatures. It makes poison to destroy us but ultimately poisons himself and the sea and the air which we all must breathe; we do not make poison. It generates filth and then accuses us of living in squalor". Her voice was strong and passionate.

"It thinks it is superior because it speaks in strange tongues, but one human can not necessarily speak to another. We speak with our brains and all animals; all species can communicate with each other. We live side by side, but it makes war with other human and it starves its children," She shrugged, "How can you call them people?"

The big rat laughed but there was no humour in the sound. "We use human words in this place. Here we are just rats," He looked away, at a time long ago that only he could visualise and whispered, "I had forgotten that we used to be called the people."

He closed his eye and a shudder rippled through his bulk. Resting his head on his chest he emitted a pain fuelled sigh.

"Are these bars?" she asked. He opened his one eye and nodded slowly.

"Are they steel?" she asked and saw him nod again. She brightened, "We can chew through steel. Shall I try?"

The big rat tipped his head. "Can we?" he asked.

She nodded enthusiastically. "We are the only animals which can!" she said proudly.

The big rat looked far into the distance. "Maybe that is why he hates us so much?".

She poked her nose through the bars and sniffed at him. "Is it the human that makes you smell so strange?"

He looked at her kindly and nodded. She pushed her nose farther into the cage and raised a paw to touch the bars." How long have they held you here?" she asked sadly.

He shook his head. "I can't remember. It was all so long ago."

She twitched her whiskers.

"How did you lose your eye?" She asked and started to groom her ears.

"The people needed it" he said flatly.

She stopped washing and stared at him. "You mean the human? Why, they have their own eyes?"

He chuckled his deep throaty laugh and the yellow of his huge teeth flashed at her.

"I know", he grinned. "I never have worked out what they want them for. First, they fill them full of liquid that really stings and they keep doing this until it goes blind. Then they take it for themselves. I don't think they realise it can't see any-more. They can't do because they always need more…. they just keep doing it." His laugh had subsided and he scratched the end of his nose with a long misshapen claw.

She looked confused. "Don't they learn?" she asked.

He thought for a moment, then shook his head. "No. I don't think so."

She turned and looked around the laboratory. Thin shafts of light were appearing in the night sky.

"I could chew through these bars, you know," she said. "Would you like to come with me?"

The big rat smiled and tried to turn onto his side but winced in pain. He shook his head slowly, "It would do no good. I cannot follow you," he said sadly.

"Are you afraid?" she asked twitching her whiskers. He laughed long and loud and his whole body shook with the effort. Finally, he controlled his mirth and studied the little female staring up at him. He knew that she could not understand.

Grinning, he leaned his nose closer to the bars and whispered. "Stand on your hind legs and look into the cage".

She hesitated for just a second and then did as he asked. Wires and tubes led from the flesh of the big rat and snaked into a black plastic box. The box had dials and switches and a needle that wrote strange squiggles onto continuous paper. His fur had been shaved and big metal clips held his flesh together. Blood had oozed onto the tape that held a needle in his rump, and a thin tube wound its way out of the cage and out of sight. Dried blood covered the newspaper lining his cage.

She gasped in horror and looked deeply into his remaining eye.

"What did you do?" she asked.

The big rat chuckled. "Be born a rat in a human's world, I guess."

She crouched down and pushed her furry nose through the bars as far as she could reach. Closing her eyes, she breathed her scent onto him and whispered, "Is there anything I can do?"

He smiled. "Nothing. You should leave now, before it gets light."

She opened her eyes and they were misty in the growing dawn.

"I can never come back here. Not now. You do understand, don't you?"

He nodded. "just think of me when you taste raindrops," he said.

Stretching just a little more their noses touched and he brought a gnarled paw down to rest on her own delicate paw squeezed between the bars. They stayed together motionless until the birds started to sing. Silently she eased herself away from the cage. When she reached the edge of the shelf, she turned to look back at him over her shoulder.

"When I taste raindrops then," she whispered and disappeared over the edge.

WHO?

Is that the man who claims that he's our lord who walked to Calvary, a cross upon his shoulders, that I see?

Or Is that the person who took the blame, a different man supplanted so that most of us believed that were set free

Can I detect a stench that where the blame lies, it festers and is sour and it makes the air around it stink?

A rottenness built from never owning up to what was done, a lie that causes life to close a door

Without the understanding of the cause. It is not what seems to be, but what another handed onwards long before

I realise sadly it is not what some religion holds before us as a man who carried a cross to save us from ourselves

It is the item that a person gives you without acknowledgement of where in this they place themselves

Simply put, it is easier to ignore the steps one takes along a road that paves the way for shame

And by handing on the outcome, with a silent smile, you hand the weapon onwards and of course, the blame.

WRITTEN FOR NEILL 12/01/2016

I have a life now that I dreamed, I'd never have

A place I call my home that has given me a place to end my life

All the dreams I ever had has brought me to this place

My isolation satisfies the part of me that needs to be alone

A place in which whatever happened made me always feel safe

Throughout my life my friends have always left

To be precise, like baggage as I moved, I made no effort to stay close

My only ties were that that happened through my birth

And when my parents died it was just another chapter that had closed

Another memory to gently put away and concentrate on now, my time on earth

So many times, I gave my heart believing I was loved

My sad romantic dream was something I had read about in books

I gave my heart, with hindsight, to a few that as it played did not deserve

I flew on wings of rapture my eyes blinded by my love as bright as sun

And I burned and stood in ashes knowing that I should have had a glimmer of reserve

The tempest that was passion has become a gentle breeze

The whisper in the leaves no longer have me straining for the words

The cloak I wear inside my head is lighter no longer sodden by so many tears

The warmth around my shoulders is the heat that is left when the fire starts to die

And I am comforted as I start to face the autumns of my years

We all have had to learn that nothing tends to end as it began

The tendrils of the moment touches places that were intimate between

Another person, another feeling, another chance at finding what we seek

Too soon the passion that once bound us starts to wane

The bed where once we joined becomes an ending that seemed bleak

No shame, for when a flower blooms it withers in its time

Perhaps sometimes we yearn to feel that touch again; an ageless need

The body cries for something it has lost but that is all

We have to tame ourselves and understand that wanting more is greed

You have given me a future that slides gently to my death

No matter what the cause, I leave this time shadowed by a sense of calm

My surroundings now allay the doubt and I can see it through

I've made a peace with life and look across the field that I can call my home

And though it's never said it came from being with and loving you

AN EXPLANATION

This next section may seem a little unusual but I thought I might encourage you to do the same. So many funerals that I have attended are either painful, boring, difficult or far too long. I have written my Eulogy and have sent it to the person who I have asked to read it. It saves people from getting upset and hopefully opens the doors to a memorable piss up. Now this may seem like I've drifted off, but bear with me please.

When I moved to the countryside, I decided to take up taxidermy, an art which I have always admired. Maybe it's because I am an undertaker's daughter that I find taxidermy a celebration of the beauty that the animal owned in life and I have always seen it as a compliment to the animal. I have read books, used the internet, studied anatomy and I'm still absolutely awful at it. It's partly to do with my hands no longer wanting to work and the pain in them and for some reason I just can't get it right. I'm good at skinning and 'curing' and stabilising the skin so that it is supple and will be around long after I'm gone. In view of this I have made for my friends a genuine mole fridge magnet. I expect it to hold pride of place on their fridge until my death and then I have asked that everyone brings their mole to my funeral. I have managed to obtain a 'golden mole' to sit on my coffin until I go through the curtains towards the flames. I just think it will be funny for everyone to have their moles with them. Hopefully there will be some innovative ways of showing their moles? A magnet on the other side of their lapel? I just want people to think about how they bring and show their own little moles as a tribute to me, my life and my sense of humour.

MY EULOGY

I decided I would write my own eulogy and the person who I have asked to read it at my funeral, is happy to do so. I only bring you into this so that you maybe understand me a little better, or not. I hope I made you laugh and that you have enjoyed everything I have written. Live life properly, love, laugh and only ever hurt somebody if they are paying

Even now when I have gone, I still insist on having the last word. Thank you those who have come to say a last goodbye. In a fashion my life was quite nomadic and I never regretted moving on to other places, other skies and another life. It is a part of the hearts discovery and I have been blessed to love and be loved, not always for the time

I may have wanted, but then we have no real concept of time…especially now….

I put Neill through so many hoops emotionally that I truly hope he forgives me. If he had not met me his life, no doubt, would have been easier, but without me he equally would have never had the laughs, the weird experiences, the ghosts and the joys of communicating with animals. Even keeping for a short time and loving, wild things like foxes in Eastbourne, Crows in the South West and then there was the Shar pei that he could never have known that I had only ever dreamed of ever owning. I take complete responsibility for bringing the little fat faced Pucheen into our lives, even though he so desperately wanted a puppy. And then there was me…and wherever we went or put down roots he looked after me. He gave me so much. So many beautiful things.

I suffered my whole life with manic depression, which was a burden for me and anyone who got close to me. I'm sorry that I was such a pain. That I put you through ambulances and all-sorts. Please…. any of you here now, understand that I was just wired wrongly. Despite my misery at times, you all made me smile, laugh and at times lose it completely in a good way. Thank you for befriending me. For those that did, thank you for loving me, and thank you for allowing me to love you too.

MY GOODBYE

I lived for decades knowing that the black dog circled me and called my name

Showing me the way to follow without pain or fear

I feel him in my shadow now, no need to push for me to join him in his play

I feel my time is leaving

He has no need to hunt me down

I've always known that there would be a final day

Despite the quietest steps I hear the padding in his wake

It is not frightening or deceiving

I have not the strength or will to go to ground

He warns that what is left I have to take

That years, like spring is nearly over and my time has come to smile and quit the game

The young woman in my heart is just a memory of what once was and not the thing that I am now

It feels real to you only because the kernel still remains inside you

Like an actor you have played the roles, felt the lights donned the make-up or the mask

You learned your lines and ad-libbed when the need arose

Soon you must call the dog and play your final role with gusto

You will always be the one who chooses when to go and how the part is played

Your final curtain call will show the doubters you were true

You never wavered in your conviction that you would never abdicate the task

The patron in the corner waits patiently a space around him because he smells of death

It seems to me that as I speak the words, he tries to catch my breath

And I will know he stands beside me when I take my final bow

Old friends I have never met, yet years rolled by I sensed them in the wings, then I'd forget

Some go onwards never having shaken your hand or stopped to fuss your dog

My fractured mind had more than once propelled me forwards in the hope that I'd find peace

Those like me have felt your fingers brush my cheek

But then gently push me back, refusing to collect me out of time

Despite your dog keep calling, you would never let me have that quick release

And you came to watch me cry and laugh and tremble as I trod the boards of life's great stage

All the moments in my life were cut from cardboard and were painted every week

I played with passion and allowed myself to rage

To laugh, shed tears, to speak

But now the time has come to bring the curtain down and leave this stage without a spoken word and no regret.

GOODBYE

Printed in Great Britain
by Amazon